SERENADE FOR NADIA

ALSO BY ZÜLFÜ LIVANELI

Bliss

SERENADE

for

NADIA

ZÜLFÜ LIVANELI

*Translated from the Turkish
by Brendan Freely*

OTHER PRESS / NEW YORK

Production editor: Yvonne E. Cárdenas
Text designer: Jennifer Daddio / Bookmark Design & Media Inc.
This book was set in Goudy Old Style and Serlio by
Alpha Design & Composition of Pittsfield, NH.

1 3 5 7 9 10 8 6 4 2

Library of Congress Cataloging-in-Publication Data

Names: Livaneli, Zülfü, 1946- author. | Freely, Brendan 1959- translator.
Title: Serenade for Nadia : a novel / Zülfü Livaneli ; Brendan Freely [translator].
Other titles: Serenad. English
Description: New York : Other Press, 2020.
Identifiers: LCCN 2019024800 (print) | LCCN 2019024801 (ebook) |
ISBN 9781635420166 (paperback) | ISBN 9781635420173 (ebook)
Subjects: LCSH: World War, 1939-1945—Turkey—Fiction. | World War,
1939-1945—Personal narratives—Fiction. | Holocaust, Jewish (1939-1945—
Fiction. | Historical fiction gsafd | GSAFD: War stories | Jewish fiction
Classification: LCC PL248.L58 S4713 2020 (print) | LCC PL248.L58 (ebook) |
DDC 894/.3533—dc23
LC record available at https://lccn.loc.gov/2019024800
LC ebook record available at https://lccn.loc.gov/2019024801

SERENADE FOR NADIA

CHAPTER 1

I'm settled in a roomy seat on the Frankfurt-Boston flight, sipping white port and listening to the sweet hum of the jet engines. I have no fear whatsoever of flying, I forget that I'm suspended in a metal tube at an altitude of over 26,000 feet, and all I care about is the quality of the wine and the food and the comfort of my seat.

The cabin was darkened as soon as the meal trays were collected. Some passengers have put on sleep masks and nodded off; others have put on headphones and are watching movies on their personal screens. Someone watching a comedy laughs out loud, unaware of the noise he's making. The elderly man in front of me can't settle down, and his legs keep twitching.

The German flight attendants have finished collecting the dinner trays and are closing the blinds so the light won't disturb the passengers when dawn breaks.

If you don't want to be woken for breakfast, you're supposed to put a sign on your headrest. But I, for one, have no intention of sleeping.

I'm writing this on my laptop, and will continue writing until we land in Boston. I have to finish writing my story before I arrive.

I'm not sure why, it's just something I feel I have to do. The story has to end, I have to finish this task, and I can't leave anything out. All the old grudges, all the suffering, all the terrible things we've done to each other have to be laid out in the open. We can never move forward unless we see ourselves for what we are, until we accept that we still live with the vestiges of our most primitive reptilian ancestors. There's a crocodile lurking within all of us, just below the placid surface of our civility, ready to lunge at the first hint of threat, or opportunity. Perhaps, too, I just need some sort of catharsis. I won't be able to move on until I've told the whole story.

I started my journey this morning in Istanbul, and had to change planes at Frankfurt, that labyrinthine city of an airport where no one lives and people only pass through. I waited in the long, slow line for non-EU citizens, and when my turn finally came I handed my passport, embossed with the star and crescent, to the stone-faced immigration officer. He typed all of my personal information onto his computer.

Name: Maya
Surname: Duran
Sex: Female
Date of birth: 21 Jan 65

He's probably done the math and knows I'm thirty-six.

Fortunately our religion isn't listed on our passports, but I was sure this German immigration officer assumed I was Muslim because I had a Turkish passport. What else could I possibly be? Yet I also harbored three other women within me. I wasn't just Maya; I was also Ayşe, Nadia, and Mari.

I would enter America with these four identities. And as soon as I was through customs, I would take a taxi straight to Mass General Hospital.

No one there would ask about my religion. And if they did, I had an answer ready. I was Muslim, Jewish, and Catholic. In other words, I was a human being.

All the flight attendants are tall, blond, and pretty, and their uniforms fit them perfectly. I've never seen a people who can both wear clothes the way the Germans do and go through an entire day without getting a single crease or wrinkle. No matter how carefully and elegantly I dress, I'm always disheveled and crumpled by the time I finish work, but that never seems to happen to Germans. Perhaps it's the way they're built, or perhaps it's just a matter of posture and comportment.

Over the years I've entertained a lot of foreign guests at Istanbul University, and I've come to certain conclusions about people from various cultures. It may not be politically correct to generalize like this, but I'm seldom wrong.

One of the sleek flight attendants takes my empty port glass and asks in English whether I would like another.

"Yes, please. Thank you." I've been fond of white port ever since my friend Filiz brought me back a bottle when she went to a medical conference in Portugal. Though I don't come across it very often . . .

In fact I really don't drink much. It was Ahmet who introduced me to wine. I didn't like the taste at all, but I didn't say so because I was in love with him. I suppose I got used to it over time. Oh, those first years! Ahmet seemed so different then, before the monster in him woke, when I still believed he was the kind of man I'd dreamed of, strong, but in touch with his feminine side.

If I'm jumping from one subject to another it's not because of the port but because I'm in such turmoil.

Ahmet was tall and had brown hair, and I suppose you could say he was handsome. His eyes were a bit small and a bit too close together, but that isn't as much of a defect in a man as it would be in a woman. We're no longer married; we divorced eight years ago.

I had a lover (I suppose I should say boyfriend, no one says lover anymore), but I've left him behind with the rest of my memories of Istanbul. Maya has to be free; she can't be constrained by any tie, by any relationship.

The flight attendant glides silently down the aisle with my port. I take a sip and close my eyes. Then I take off my high heels and put on those thick socks they give out. What a relief it is to free my feet. I know they'll swell on this long flight, and I'll have trouble putting my shoes back on, but it's worth it.

The story I have to tell, or at least my part of the story, began three months ago, in February. February is the most miserable time of year in Istanbul. Cruel, cold winds blow in off the Black Sea, bringing rains that last for weeks. The days are short, you seldom see the sun, and spring seems impossibly distant. Occasionally the rain turns to snow, but never enough to cover the city in white. It just turns to slush, and then to ice. There's mud everywhere, you can't walk down the street without being splashed by passing cars....

Anyway, it was a truly nasty day. I'd just dashed from the rector's office to his official car, when I stepped into a puddle, possibly ruining a new pair of shoes. My phone rang just as I was settling into the back seat. It was Tarık.

Without thinking, or even asking why he'd called, I started complaining. About my job; all the paperwork I was drowning in; how I'd had to spend my morning talking to reporters and trying to put a good spin on some bad press; how the rector kept pestering me to write a speech for him; and how, on top of everything, I had to go out to the airport, in this weather, in the middle of rush hour, to pick up some foreign professor.

Even as I spoke, I realized I shouldn't be talking to him this way. It was still a fairly new relationship, but we'd already developed "problems" and "patterns." One of them was exactly this. He felt I had a tendency to launch into long litanies of complaint. He couldn't get a word in edgewise. And so forth. This had already led to several arguments. But this time he didn't seem annoyed. In fact it seemed as if he wasn't really listening, and I guessed that he was following the stock market on the internet as he spoke to me. That was all he really cared about. Money. Not just having money and making money, but following it, keeping track of where and how it was flowing. He could talk about the markets for hours, and while I admired his dedication, which bordered on passion, I didn't know or care that much about it. After a while it was as if he was speaking a foreign language and I couldn't follow anything he was saying.

I kept complaining anyway, wondering at the same time how I was going to turn the conversation around and end it on a pleasant note.

"Is there anything else you want to whine about?"

I made a face at the phone.

"That's it. I'm done complaining. But you might be supportive instead of making snide remarks."

Of course I hadn't told him everything. I didn't want to tell him about the stomach cramps I'd had for three days, or about how I'd had to rush to the pharmacy on my way to work because I'd left my tampons at home. That would probably be too much information for him.

"Who is it?"

"Who is what?"

"The foreign professor? The one you're going to meet at the airport."

"Maximilian Wagner, apparently he's at Harvard, his name sounds German but he's American."

"Why on earth is he coming here? Some kind of conference?"

"To tell the truth, I have no idea. I didn't have time to read up on him."

"OK, then. Good luck. See you later."

"Why did you call me?"

"I just wanted to know if we could get together later."

Then he hung up. They're all the same. I wish I could meet a man who heard what I mean rather than what I say. Who'd understand that when I complain about the weather I'm not really talking about the weather. That when I complain about my job I mean that I need a man to comfort and support me. Do I have to come out and say that I'm fed up with my life? Why couldn't he realize that I only talked about the rain because I couldn't say I wished he were with me? If I have to ask him to hug me it defeats the purpose. It all seems so hopeless sometimes.

By now, the driver, Süleyman, had brought the rector's black car onto the highway. The highway was completely jammed; traffic wasn't moving at all. But fortunately the car had official plates so we could use the emergency lane. I get so tired of living in such a crowded city—the seething masses of people everywhere—and having to sit in traffic for hours any time you go anywhere. People glanced at us with envy as we sped past, and I could see that some of them wanted to follow our example but didn't dare risk the fine. Somehow I resented them, resented their presumptuousness, even though we were doing exactly what they wanted to do. But I wasn't here because I wanted to be, and besides, I couldn't survive in a city like this unless I had a few privileges.

"Why are you laughing, ma'am?"

Was the driver watching me? Keep your eyes on the road!

"Nothing, I was thinking about something and..."

I wasn't aware that I'd laughed, and realized I'd been laughing at myself, at my own self-righteousness.

"How much longer?"

"About twenty minutes," he said. "But if we weren't using the emergency lane we wouldn't get there before midnight."

Two traffic policemen watched us approach, wondering whether they should salute us or stop us and give us a ticket. As soon as they saw the official plates they realized we were members of the elite, and saluted us. What a wonderful country we live in! How easy everything is. As long as you have official plates, that is.

I glanced at the information I'd been given about the man I was meeting. Law professor, German, single. Were there any single professors anymore?

Then I saw his birth date. 19 August 1914. He was 87. It must have been difficult for him to travel so far at his age. His wife had probably died, or they'd divorced. Though divorce wasn't nearly as common in his time. Marriage was permanent, not temporary as it is now.

So it looked as if I was going to spend the next three days taking care of a frail old man. Maximilian Wagner was the last thing I needed right now. Why did he have to pick February of all times to come to Istanbul?

I could already imagine the first thing he would say.

"I didn't think Istanbul would be so cold. I packed for a desert climate."

I could also imagine the rest of the things he would ask and say. Sometimes I was amazed by how ignorant these professors could be. They might at least spend half an hour on the internet before visiting a country. But no, they thought they were coming to Arabia, and expected to see camels in the streets and people living in tents. Some were even surprised at being met by a woman, and a woman who didn't have her head covered at that. I would smile, and be patient, and explain that Turkey was a modern, secular country; that women had been granted the right to vote earlier here than in many countries in Europe; that no one had worn a fez for more than seventy years; that polygamy had been abolished; and that we, too, froze in winter. Yet even as I looked down on them for their ignorance I would realize that some ingrained sense of patriotism or pride kept me from telling them another side of the story: that this was still a society in which many found violence against women acceptable, and that in some regions, family councils condemned young girls to death and men still practiced polygamy.

Even though I complained about it, entertaining these foreign academics was actually the best part of my job. At least it got me out of the office when I took them to the Blue Mosque, and to the Grand Bazaar to shop for carpets and leather jackets. There were worse things I could have to do. So I made the best of it, answered inane questions, pretended not to understand when elderly professors made passes at me, and put up with overly friendly hugs and kisses and speeches about Turkish hospitality when I saw them off at the airport.

In a sense it was a break from the desperate struggle to survive as a single mother whose deadbeat ex-husband didn't pay the alimony and child support he was supposed to.

You rush out of the house at the shriek of dawn, get into a crowded bus, go to your miserable office, and drag yourself home in the evening to feed a son who thinks his purpose in life is to play computer games. Day after day, with no end in sight, no appreciation, no hope, just doing your best to get by.

By Friday you're completely worn out. You want to see a couple of friends, relax, and have some fun, so you head to one of the huge shopping malls, the temples of our consumer society.

You feel a bit better, a bit lighter, after watching some romantic comedy, and you go somewhere for a glass of wine to hold on to that feeling for as long as you can. Most of the tables are occupied by groups of young women, and you wonder how and when the sexes became so separated. After they've finished telling each other about the virtues of being alone and independent, the women always start talking about men. Then the gloom returns as it hits home: the reality of being a modern, educated woman in a conservative, male-dominated society, in a place where a woman without a man is seen as someone to be pitied or taken advantage of.

I'm always proud to tell our foreign guests that in Turkey there is a greater percentage of women in positions of power than in most developed countries and a larger percentage of women who graduate from universities and occupy senior positions in academia and in the business world. Women in Turkey are much more strongly represented in the sciences than are women in Europe or America, and nearly forty percent of Turkish senior executives are women. Women have equality under the law, and receive equal pay for equal work. Yet thirty percent of the women in this country are still illiterate, fewer than nine percent are members of parliament, and forty percent of the men believe it is justifiable to murder a female relative to protect the family's honor.

If you have the good fortune to come from the right class, to come from a family that believes in equal education and opportunity for women, you can go as far as you want in just about any field except politics, though if you're ruthless enough you can become prime minister. There's no glass ceiling, and there are no institutional barriers. Yet if you belong to that small class of educated, professional women, you have to walk a fine line. You have to remember that in spite of your status you're living in a society that still harbors very backwards, even medieval attitudes toward women. You always have to be careful to behave and dress like a "respectable" woman. If anything at all that you do causes you to be perceived as a "loose" woman, you're despised, and you deserve any harassment or worse that you suffer. You always have to erect a barrier against the men you encounter in the course of your daily life, particularly men of lower socioeconomic status, who are more likely to have sexist attitudes. At work you have to take an almost feudal tone with drivers and janitors and so forth, because they still have a feudal worldview, and this is all they understand. In their world the only way not to be oppressed is to be an oppressor. They're oppressed at work, so they go home and oppress their wives and children. They'll accept your authority because they have to, but they'll undermine it at every opportunity, even if only passively.

And if, naturally, you want male companionship and partnership, you have a very small pool to choose from. That is, educated, professional men who are neither fundamentalists nor alcoholics, who have read a few books and who bathe regularly. And most of these men have their own problems. They've either been spoiled rotten by their mothers or browbeaten by their fathers. They're tied up in such a thick web of family expectations, obligations, and prohibitions that they can barely breathe.

You feel so depressed after thinking about all this that you're tempted to have another glass of wine. But you don't, because if the taxi driver smells alcohol on your breath he might feel this gives him license to make a pass at you.

The elderly man in front of me has fully reclined his seat, but his leg still keeps twitching and he can't get comfortable. A young couple across the aisle from me have also reclined their seats and have covered themselves with a blanket, as if they're in bed at home.

We arrived at the airport, and again because of our official plates we could pull right up to the door, though in fact our grand official car was an ancient Mercedes that was in the shop more often than it was on the road. I checked the arrivals board and saw that I was just in time, the Frankfurt plane had already landed. I held up a card with his name on it and watched people coming out, Turks from Germany, some of them being greeted excitedly by groups of relatives; bewildered tourists; businessmen who looked as if they spent most of their lives in airports and airplanes. Then I saw someone who stood out from the others, a tall, strikingly handsome man with bright blue eyes, wearing a long black coat and a brimmed hat. He was carrying a small suitcase in one hand and a violin case in the other. He paused, looked around, and as soon as he saw my card he strode up to me, put down his bag, and introduced himself. I realized that for the first time in my life a man was doffing his hat to me, and I almost expected him to kiss my hand, though he didn't.

"Welcome, professor," I said. "My name is Maya Duran. Our car is waiting right outside."

Just then Süleyman appeared as if from nowhere, greeted the professor with one of the few phrases of broken English he knew, and took his suitcase. The professor insisted on carrying his violin himself.

I noticed that as soon as we were outside the professor put his hat on and tied his gray cashmere scarf around his neck. "I don't get ill very easily," he said smiling, "but Istanbul is quite cold at this time of the year."

"You came prepared," I said. "For some reason a lot of people think it never gets cold here."

He laughed.

"But I know Istanbul. I know what the winters here are like."

Now, as I write this in my comfortable seat on the plane, I recall how sadly he smiled as he said this.

When Süleyman opened the door of the black Mercedes, the professor said, "Oh, an old car for an old man!"

We laughed together. I'm not a particularly warm or outgoing person. In fact many people find me cold, but for some reason I felt I'd clicked with this man right away. There was something about his demeanor, about the way he looked around at the vast new concrete city that spread as far as one could see on both sides of the highway—an air that was at the same time dignified and deeply wounded. He was, I realized, quite different from any of the other professors I'd shown around Istanbul.

"When were you in Istanbul?" I asked.

"From 1939 to 1942."

"Well, the city has gone through tremendous changes since then."

"Yes, this was all open countryside then. The airport wasn't much more than a shed, and they had to chase the sheep off the runway every time a plane came in, which wasn't much more than twice a week or so. The road was barely wide enough for two cars to pass each other. Not that there were many cars. Or people. The population of the city wasn't much over half a million then, but it must be more than ten times that now."

"Some people say it's over eighteen million. Have you been back at all since 1942?"

"No, no I haven't. It's been…well, it's been fifty-nine years. Time begins to slip past so quickly. Where will I be staying, by the way?

"The Pera Palas."

"I'm happy to hear that. That's where I stayed when I first came to Istanbul, and later on I often met my colleagues at the bar there. I'm glad it's still there. I heard that a lot of the old buildings were torn down. I heard that the Park Hotel is gone, and the Tokatlıyan, though you probably don't even remember those."

"No, I've heard of them, but they're before my time. The Tokatlıyan building is still there, but it hasn't been a hotel for a long time."

"Ah, the Tokatlıyan was one of my favorite places to have coffee. Though we all decided to stop going there after…well, that's a long story I'd rather not get into now."

He fell silent, and to keep the conversation going I asked, "Where did you live?"

"In Beyazıt. I rented a house there to be near the university."

"Do you know Turkish?"

He smiled and replied in Turkish: "A little." Then he added, "Very little."

After a brief silence, he continued in English: "By the time I left I could speak fairly well, but I haven't spoken or even heard it since, so I hardly remember anything."

"I'm sure it will start coming back. Though you'll find that even the language itself has changed quite a bit since then. To my son, the Turkish my grandparents spoke would sound almost like Shakespearean English would to a young English person. Well, maybe that's an exaggeration, but it has changed considerably."

He nodded, and fell silent, and this time I decided not to try to keep the conversation going. A car had broken down in the emergency lane, and it took some time to maneuver around it. I gazed out the window at the sea of cars around me; the highway and the surrounding streets; the vast, ugly slums of hastily constructed buildings shrouded by a haze of coal smoke; the lashing, windswept rain. How was I going to get home after I dropped the professor off? It was impossible to get a taxi in weather like this, and the bus would take hours.

Kerem would already be home from school. Was there anything in the house for him to eat? Not that he would care; he wouldn't eat at all if I didn't make him. All he wanted to do was sit in front of his computer, and he might not even realize I wasn't home. I worried that he didn't seem to have any friends, that he lived such an isolated life. When I was his age I had lots of friends in my neighborhood, and we used to play on the street for hours, but I don't think Kerem knows the name of even one child in our building. How and when did our society change so profoundly? It used to be that community was an essential part of our life. A city neighborhood was like a village, almost like a large family. Everyone knew every-one, people looked out for each other, and they helped each other out. But now we've become isolated from each other, and even the man at the corner grocery store treats you like a stranger.

How would Süleyman react if I asked him to drive me home? He was the kind of person who would never do any-one a favor out of kindness, he'd always think about what he could get in return. He was also the kind of cunning, calculating person I wouldn't want to feel indebted to.

As I was thinking, I became aware that there was a car behind us in the emergency lane. A white Renault with ordinary plates, and for whatever reason the police were not stopping it.

"Is the traffic this bad in Boston, professor?"

He came out of his reverie and said, "Well, it can be quite bad there, too, perhaps not on the same scale. It's a smaller city, but some of my colleagues complain about being stuck in traffic for hours. Fortunately I live in Cam-bridge, quite close to the university, so I can walk to work."

"I suppose unmanageable traffic is a reality of our age. If you live in a city it's something you just can't escape."

"Yes, sometimes I wonder how we let this happen, and where it's going to go. People keep buying cars, and one day there just won't be room for all of them."

"Where are you from, by the way?"

He seemed uncomfortable with this question, and I was sorry I'd asked.

"It's just that you don't strike me as American."

"Well, I am an American citizen, but I'm originally from Germany, from Bavaria, but I haven't been back since I left in 1939. Nor have I ever felt any desire to go back."

The way he said this made it clear that he didn't want to talk about it, so I let it go. We'd left the highway and were making our way toward the district of Beyoğlu, and I noticed that the white Renault was still behind us.

Soon, we were making our way down a narrow street lined with nineteenth-century buildings, and I could see that the professor had cheered up a bit. This, at last, was an Istanbul he could recognize. As we pulled up in front of the Pera Palas Hotel, he turned and gave me a warm smile.

While we dashed through the rain to the lobby, Süleyman gave the professor's luggage to the bellboy. Again, the professor insisted on carrying his violin himself.

When I glanced back at Süleyman, I saw that the white Renault that had been following us had pulled over just down the street. Meanwhile Wagner stood looking around the lobby, taking it in, his eyes misty. This was the oldest continually operating luxury hotel in Istanbul, completed in 1895 for passengers arriving on the Orient Express.

"Have a seat while I get you checked in," I said, and sat him down in an elegant antique armchair.

"May I have your passport please? In the meantime would you like a coffee or a glass of something to drink?"

"When you're done would you join me in a whisky?"

"Certainly," I said, even though I was worried about getting home to Kerem.

Mustafa at the reception desk called out, "So you've got another guest have you?"

"Yes," I said, "What can I do, it's my job. He's a tired, elderly man. Please give him a quiet room..."

"Of course."

"Thank you."

As I went over to Wagner I asked the waiter for a double whisky and some white port.

"Please bring some ice and water with the whisky as well. And some nuts."

However, when I reached Wagner I saw that he'd fallen asleep in the chair. He was breathing deeply and regularly with his head leaning against the corner of the armchair. There was an innocent expression on his face.

It was just as well, because I wanted to get home as soon as I could. I canceled the order and asked the waiters to leave the guest in peace.

"When he wakes up you can escort him to his room."

Then I wrote a short note on the stylish Pera Palas stationary.

Professor Wagner, you were sleeping so soundly I didn't want to disturb you. I'll pick you up at eleven tomorrow morning.

As I left the hotel and walked over to Süleyman I made an effort to be cheerful. And before I spoke, I even fleetingly touched his arm.

"We're running late today," I said.

I leaned in closer to him. "Kerem's waiting for his dinner. Would it be too much trouble for you to take me home?"

I suddenly felt embarrassed by my choice of words, and how they could be interpreted. Now, as I write this, I wonder if I was being deliberately coy to get what I wanted from him.

Süleyman thought for a moment, as if he were considering what might be in it for him, and then said, "Sure, hop in."

As I got in, I noticed that the white Renault was still there. There were three men in the car, and the man at the wheel was smoking. I got the distinct impression that all three of them were watching me.

Süleyman tried to start the car, but the engine wouldn't turn over. It wheezed a bit, shuddered, then stopped. He kept trying, turning the key and pumping the gas pedal. For a moment it seemed as if it was just about to start, but then it shuddered again, and after that it didn't respond at all. Süleyman threw his hands in the air and turned to face me.

"I'm sorry, ma'am, the engine's flooded."

I got out of the car and was suddenly at a loss for what to do. All the taxis passing by were full, there were none at the taxi rank outside the hotel, and I was getting wet, so I dashed back into the hotel.

The professor was still sound asleep. I touched his arm gently and called softly: "Professor...professor!"

He opened his eyes slowly and looked around with a bewildered expression, as if he didn't know quite where he was.

"I'm sorry," he murmured. "I fell asleep."

"There's nothing to be sorry for. You just got off a fourteen-hour flight, and it takes a while to adjust to the time change."

I waited a few moments for him to pull himself together, and then said, "Your room is ready. Come, let me take you up."

I helped him up from the armchair, led him to the wonderful old elevator, and brought him up to the third floor. When the bellboy opened the door with a large metal key, a musty smell wafted out, the musty smell of years of history. A smell that evoked visions of all the people who had stayed here: kings, princes, presidents and ambassadors, spies and entertainers. Kim Philby and Mata Hari, Josephine Baker and Louis Armstrong. Agatha Christie, who once mysteriously vanished for eleven days, was said to have hidden a clue to the secret behind her disappearance in room 411. She used the hotel as a setting in her detective novel *Murder on the Orient Express*, which was later made into a film. Eric Ambler also used the Pera Palas as a setting for his thriller *The Mask of Demetrios*, as did Graham Greene in *Stamboul Train*, Ian Fleming in *From Russia with Love*, and Alfred Hitchcock in his film *The Lady Vanishes*. Atatürk stayed at the Royal Suite, Room 101, when he came to Istanbul, and the suite was now preserved as a museum. King Zog of Albania also stayed in 101 after his country was invaded by Italy in 1941. Other heads of state who stayed here include Shah Riza Pahlevi of Iran, King Edward VIII of Great Britain, King Ferdinand of Bulgaria, King Karol of Romania, King Peter of Serbia, President Giscard d'Estaing of France, President Tito of Yugoslavia, President Fahri Korutürk of Turkey, and President Adnan Menderes of Turkey.

The bellboy put down the suitcase, and the professor laid his violin carefully on top of the antique mahogany chest of drawers. I helped him off with his coat and said, "I have to leave now, professor. You're scheduled to have lunch with the rector tomorrow, I'll pick you up at eleven."

"I thought we were going to have a drink together. Perhaps I could also invite you to dinner…"

"I would love to, but I have to get home to my son."

The Mercedes was still outside the door.

Süleyman grinned broadly and said, "I finally got it running. Come, let me drive you home."

As we moved off through the rain, I couldn't help but look back to see if the white Renault was still there. It was gone, and I felt a sense of relief. But as we drove up Tarlabaşı Boulevard, I kept glancing back to check, even though I had no reason to think that the men in that white car posed any threat to me.

By the time we got to my street I was almost dozing off, so I pulled myself together and got out my keys.

When we pulled up in front of my building I thanked Süleyman and dragged myself to the door, not even caring about the rain. Then I glanced up, and saw that the windows of my apartment were dark. For a moment I felt a stab of alarm. It was after nine, but Kerem wouldn't have gone to bed yet. Had he not come home, had something happened? But of course he was probably, as usual, hunched over his computer in the dark.

I went into the building and started up the stairs. As I climbed I could hear televisions blaring from behind several of the doors. I could smell that someone was cooking fish, and that someone else was making some kind of stew. I unlocked my door, turned on the living room lights, threw my coat and my bag on the sofa, and went straight to Kerem's room. And of course there he was, just visible in the pale glow of the computer screen.

I greeted him as warmly and cheerfully as I could, and went and kissed him on the forehead, but he just shrugged me off and mumbled something and wouldn't even look at me. So I went to the kitchen, heated up the pizza left over from last night and brought it to him. He didn't look at me, didn't say thank you, but just reached for the pizza without taking his eyes off the screen. So I went and took a long, hot shower; made myself a cheese sandwich; sat on the couch in my bathrobe; and turned on the television, surfing through the channels but not finding anything that caught my interest. There was nothing on but dreary talk shows, inane game shows, and ponderously slow-moving soap operas.

After a while I decided to give up. I called to Kerem that it was time for him to go to bed, knowing that he wouldn't pay any attention to me, and then went to bed myself. I often spent an hour or so just lying in the dark, thinking, before going to sleep. I would daydream; imagine different, better lives; imagine that I was someone other than who I was—all the people I might and could have been.

That night, though, the escape and freedom the day-dreams offered didn't come, and I found myself worrying about Kerem, and what I was going to do with him. Was I a bad mother? Had I made him like this? Or was it just a phase he would grow out of? I wondered if I should try to find one of those programs that would shut off his computer automatically. It couldn't be good for him to spend this much time in virtual worlds. He didn't speak to me at all anymore. He didn't speak to anyone. The only relationships he had were with people he never saw, people he met online. Was he afraid to live a real life, to interact with real people?

Once when he was out with his father I turned on his computer and looked at the history of the sites he'd visited. I just wanted to know what it was that absorbed him so much, what interested him. To catch a glimpse of the world in which he spent so much of his life. And

I was horrified to discover that a large part of this world consisted of pornography. I was also very concerned to think that this was what he was learning about life and human relationships. Concerned that this would warp him somehow, make him incapable of having a real, warm, intimate relationship. That this was what was making him so cold and distant, so self-absorbed, and, perhaps, cruel.

When I tried to talk to Ahmet about it he just laughed and told me not to worry, that "boys will be boys." All Ahmet cared about was his new girlfriend. He didn't want to be bothered with the son he'd practically abandoned.

I must have fallen asleep, because the next thing I knew it was almost morning. And the first thing that came to my mind was the white Renault. What was that about? What, if anything, did it mean? I couldn't keep from getting out of bed and going to the window. The street was completely deserted, but there was a white Renault parked just across from my door. I couldn't see if there was anyone in the car, couldn't even be sure that it was the same car, but I felt deeply unsettled.

Then, suddenly, the alarm clock was ringing, and with a sense of dread I realized that once again it was time for my hellish morning routine. It was bad enough to have to rush to get myself ready, but most of the time I had to struggle with Kerem too, to try to force him to get out of bed, eat some breakfast, and be on his way to school before I left. I knew that if I left before him he wouldn't go to school at all, that he'd just spend all day on the computer. Sometimes he refused to get out of bed, and once I got so exasperated that I called his father. But of course Ahmet just said he was late for a meeting and didn't have time to deal with it.

That morning was a little better. Not easy, but at least I was able to get him out of bed and out the door in time for me to catch a bus that would get me to work less than half an hour late.

As I made my way down the hall to my office, I saw Süleyman waiting at the door.

"Good morning, ma'am. Do you have a moment? There's something I'd like to talk to you about."

"OK, but I don't have much time, I have a meeting with the rector in a few minutes."

"Well, that's just it, I mean, you see the rector every day. The thing is, my cousin Hüseyin, he's been out of work for a while. I was wondering if you could talk to the rector about him, maybe talk him into giving him a job as a janitor or something. Anything."

"I'm sorry, but first of all the rector doesn't hire janitors, you'd have to go to the head of the maintenance department, and even if he did, I'm not really in a position to ask him that kind of favor."

He gave me an angry look, and I realized I'd handled the situation badly, and perhaps even made an enemy of him. I should at least have said I would help. I could even have had a word with the head of maintenance. It wouldn't have cost me anything and I might have made an ally, or at least got a ride home whenever I needed one.

"What time do we need to leave to get to the hotel by eleven?"

"If we leave at ten fifteen we'll have plenty of time."

His tone was politely neutral, but I could tell he was angry. He left, and I started gathering together the files, papers, and memos I had to bring to the rector for our daily public relations meeting. Among the memos was one about a talk that Professor Wagner would be giving that afternoon.

I look up when the flight attendant asks in a whisper if there's anything else I would like. I was so absorbed I didn't even notice her take the glass from my tray table. I consider having another drink, but decide against it. She smiles and tells me not to hesitate to ask if I want anything. I think it's time to take a short break, take a little walk up and down the aisle, go to the toilet, and maybe have a glass of water.

CHAPTER 2

When we pulled up in front of the hotel I instinctively looked around for the white Renault. It wasn't there, but somehow I didn't feel reassured.

I went to the front desk and asked for the professor. The young receptionist looked at the key rack behind him.

"His key is here. I'm not sure, but I think he may have gone out," he said.

It was five to eleven. I waited in the lobby, thinking he must have got up early and gone for a walk. Nearby, an elderly American couple were looking at a map, planning their day's sightseeing. A few minutes later the professor strode in, looking refreshed and alert. He was wearing a gray flannel jacket under his black coat and had put on a pale blue tie. Again he greeted me by doffing his hat.

I smiled and was surprised to realize that I was actually happy to see him.

"Have I kept you waiting?" he asked. He sounded much more cheerful than he had the last time I saw him.

"No, professor, I just got here. It isn't even eleven yet."

"I was just taking a stroll around the neighborhood."

"I'm sure you found that things have changed a great deal."

"Ah yes, of course. So many of the places I knew are gone now, though I'm sure you don't remember any of them."

"Probably not, but it's changed even in my time. It's a shame, really."

"A shame? I don't see it that way. I expected things to have changed. Places change. In a sense, to exist is to change, and places that don't change become sad and stagnant. I also remember that in my time I used to hear people talk about the good old days, and I'm sure that when they were young they heard the same thing. I'm sure there'll be a time when people feel nostalgic about the way it is today."

"Yes, I suppose so, I hadn't thought about it that way."

He gave Süleyman a small tip as he got into the car, and Süleyman was genuinely pleased, both by the money and the gesture.

It had stopped raining an hour or so earlier, and as we crossed the Galata Bridge there were shafts of sunlight piercing the clouds, illuminating the domes and minarets of the mosques and reflected here and there on the water. The professor peered out the window at the skyline of the old city, with flocks of seagulls spiraling slowly above it, the Golden Horn and the Galata Tower, ferry boats and motor launches coming and going, the crowds surging across the bridge, and the people fishing over the railing. I crossed this bridge several times a week but had long since stopped admiring the view. It had become ordinary for me, something I hardly noticed, but the professor's enchantment was so palpable, so infectious, that I looked at the scene with new eyes and felt its magic again.

"Ah yes," he said, "This is it, this is the Istanbul I remember. I used to love to come here. There was a coffee house on the lower level, I used to spend hours there, just gazing out across the water and taking it all in. It's changed of course, but in some essential way it's the same. The bridge itself, though, it's not the same bridge."

"No, this one was built in the 1980s, I think."

"Ah, and there's the Süleymaniye Mosque. That was another of my favorite places. I used to go sit in the courtyard, there was such a sense of peace and tranquility there. Yes, this is still such a beautiful, bewitching city."

"The ugliest beautiful city in the world," I said, and he laughed.

It struck me that even though the Süleymaniye Mosque was only a short walk from the university, it would never occur to me to seek peace and tranquility there. I only ever went when I was showing people around, and although I'd memorized everything there was to know about it, it was not in any way a part of my life. Everyone always assumed I was Muslim; it said so on my identity card, and if I was asked I usually said I was.

But I didn't really know anything about the religion; I derived no strength or guidance or hope from it, none of the things faith is supposed to give you. In fact I'd never actually prayed in a mosque, I'd only ever been to mosques for funerals.

My parents were just old enough to have been part of the generation who wholeheartedly embraced the Republic, and who devoted their lives to building a new and modern nation. Before she married, my mother was one of the young teachers who went to remote villages to teach not just the children but also many of the adults how to read and write. She also organized the villagers to build a sewage system and taught them hygiene and basic facts about health and nutrition. Would I have had the courage to do that? She was barely eighteen when she went off to this village all by herself. At the time it was the thing to do, it was what all her friends were doing, it was what had to be done.

During his student years my father dedicated himself to helping establish People's Houses, cultural centers that offered adult education and a wide variety of cultural and artistic activities. He saw himself almost as a missionary, and believed that the people's freedom could only be achieved through their education and the broadening of their cultural horizons. He also saw the People's Houses as a way to break the power of the mosque. It gave the people someplace besides the mosque where they could gather, an alternative center of the community.

They took their strength from an ideal, and an essential part of this ideal involved rejecting what was seen as backwards and feudal. They believed in "revolutionary ethics" and "secular morality." They wanted to be free of the "tyranny of tradition" and believed in the establishment of a "perfect democracy." And in a sense they were at war, because there were constant rebellions by those who wanted to restore the Caliphate or by feudal tribal leaders who felt their power and way of life threatened.

I don't think either of my parents was against religion as such. They saw it as a private matter, a matter of conscience, and believed that religious authorities had no business dictating public policy. Yet somehow being Muslim remained part of their cultural identity. The republican elite was made up almost entirely of people who considered themselves Muslim. Why did this regime, which proclaimed itself to be egalitarian and secular, insist that our religion be listed on our identity cards? If your identity card listed you as Christian, you were regarded as a potential enemy, assigned to construction brigades during your military service, and subject to the ruinous "wealth tax."

"But all of this," I said, "The Golden Horn and the mosques and all that. This is what tourists come to see, but it has nothing to do with the city I live in. That city has no magic, no beauty, nothing at all to recommend it. It's just a machine that grinds people up."

"You forget that I wasn't a tourist when I was here. I lived here and worked here."

"Yes. I'm sure the city was much nicer then, though."

"Every age had its own problems, and I appreciate the many difficulties you must face. But the war years were very hard. I sincerely hope that you never have to live through a war."

As we were approaching Beyazit Square, he asked if he could get out and walk the rest of the way, so I sent Süleyman on ahead and joined him. He stood for a while on the edge of the square, just looking around and taking it in, and then we started strolling slowly toward the university's monumental front gate.

"So many memories are flooding back to me. It's almost overwhelming."

We passed through the gate and crossed the large yard through the crowds of boisterous students.

"Why are there policemen at the entrance?" he asked.

"They're protecting the university from the students."

He smiled, and I continued, "A lot of the female students come from conservative religious backgrounds, but they're not allowed to wear the traditional head covering inside the university. The police are here to make sure they don't."

"So what do these girls do?"

"They either take off their headscarves and wear hats or wigs, or refuse to enter and end up dropping out."

"This wasn't a problem in my time. None of the girls wanted to wear headscarves. Indeed, they found it very liberating not to have to cover their heads."

"Yes, well, things have changed. Maybe we're going backwards."

The rector was waiting for us at the entrance to the building, and addressed the professor warmly in German.

I left them and headed back to my office. On the way I checked my phone and saw that I'd missed two calls from Tarık. I hesitated for a moment, realizing that I didn't really want to talk to him, and then called him back anyway.

"What's your visiting professor like?"

"He's actually quite nice, I like him. He's very handsome and gallant and charming, and he has such a broad perspective on things."

"Should I be jealous?"

"Don't be silly. He's eighty-seven."

"Listen, I was wondering if we could get together this evening."

"I don't think so. I don't think I'm going to be able to get away at all while this professor is here."

"Well, give me a call if you can escape. There's something I want to talk to you about. I might have some good news."

Once again, I thought about whether it was time to end this relationship. It was clear that it wasn't going anywhere, and I had to admit to myself that I didn't really even like him. But it was nice to have someone, and I didn't want to be alone again. It was difficult to make the decision to take such a drastic step. I told myself that I'd put a lot of effort into the relationship, that even though he could be annoying he was a decent man at heart, that things could work out. But I knew deep down that he just wasn't right for me, and that I probably wasn't right for him either.

Just then the rector's assistant popped her head in the door and told me we were leaving for lunch. A group of us filed out of the building. The rector and Wagner and another professor got into the black car, and I got into another car with a couple of other faculty members.

Lunch was at the Konyalı Restaurant in the gardens of Topkapı Palace, at a long table looking out over Seraglio Point, with a view of the mouth of the Bosporus, and the islands and the Asian shore. There was a fairly large group, and I sat as far as I could from Wagner and the rector. They were talking in German, so I wouldn't be able to take part in the conversation anyway.

Unfortunately, Professor Erdoğan seized the chance to sit next to me. Erdoğan had somehow deluded himself into thinking that he was a ladies' man, and also had the notion that all divorced women were available and just waiting to fall into his arms. He started flirting with me right away, with his usual lack of sophistication and tact. Fortunately, the first course arrived, and I was able to give my attention to my food. He kept at me, though, and it took all my strength to keep from snapping at him and putting him in his place. I already had something of a reputation for being a bitch, and I didn't want to make life at work any more difficult than it was. I felt a deep sense of relief when the meal came to an end and coffee was served. I hadn't been able to enjoy my food, but the coffee seemed like the best I'd ever had.

When we got back to the university we went straight to a large lecture hall that was already full of students and faculty. The rector went up to the rostrum and gave Wagner a glowing introduction, and then invited Professor Hakkı, who'd been Wagner's student, to say a few words. Hakkı spoke at rather too much length about the work Wagner had done, how he had helped lay the foundations for modern university education in Turkey and about the rigorous standards he had established at the law school. Then, finally, Wagner himself was invited to speak.

He strode confidently up to the rostrum, and then, with a warm smile, looked around at the audience. Right away, he had everyone under his spell, and the hall fell completely silent.

I can't, of course, remember his entire speech. I can only paraphrase what he said. At first he addressed the crowd in Turkish, glancing at his notes. His sentences were well phrased and grammatical, though he stumbled over his words a bit and occasionally had some trouble with pronunciation. He also used some words that were no longer in general use, for instance he used the word *talebe* rather than *öğrenci* for "student." He spoke of what an honor it was to be invited back to the university after fifty-nine years, what fond memories he had of the place and how happy it made him to see his former student and to know that the people he had taught had made such a great contribution to the nation. The audience was touched, and broke into applause.

He continued in English, praising the early leaders of the Republic for their courage and vision in establishing modern standards in university education. He also praised the Turkish colleagues whose hard work against great odds had inspired him. Then he continued with a few anecdotes about what the city and the university were like when he was here. They were mostly amusing anecdotes, and he got a few laughs from the audience, but of what he said at this point only one phrase remains with me.

"Fyodor Dostoyevsky says that one can only reach maturity through suffering. In this sense Istanbul is very important to me; it was here that I reached maturity."

Then he went on to talk about the state of the world today, and the idea being put forth by many about a clash of civilizations between East and West, or more specifically between the Islamic world and the Christian world. He talked about the tensions from which civilization had emerged, the tensions between the need for cohesion and the need for exchange. From the beginning, man as a social animal has had a need for identity as a member of a group, and a principal means for group identity is exclusion of others. We compete with other groups for resources, and we strengthen our identity by dehumanizing our competitors. Yet at the same time, all civilization and progress grows from the exchange of ideas and goods. He continued with a list of historical examples, reaching the conclusion that the idea of a clash of civilizations was based on the false view that there were or had ever been different civilizations. There were different cultures, but in fact only one civilization, and that the greatest threat to civilization was cultural prejudice and hatred. The irony of our time was that the more knowledge we gained and the more our technology advanced, the greater the scale of our barbarity toward one another became.

My summary doesn't do the professor's talk justice. He spoke with great eloquence, passion, and clarity. Indeed, I felt a sense of pride that this man, my guest, for whom I had somehow developed a sense of ownership (though I hardly knew him, I'd only met him yesterday, and couldn't presume to call him a friend), was making such an impression. I glanced around to see how people were responding to him, and got a sudden shock. The three men I'd seen in the white Renault were at the back of the hall, and the man who'd been behind the wheel was taking notes.

I'd wondered several times who these men might be. The fact that they took no pains to conceal that they were following Wagner had led me to think that they might be some sort of security detail, though I couldn't imagine why Wagner might need protection, unless an extremist group of some kind had made a threat against him for something he'd said or written. Yet from the first time I'd noticed them, my sense was that they weren't there to protect but rather to intimidate. Now, their presence in the lecture hall, and the fact that one of them was taking notes, left me in no doubt that they were secret police of some kind.

As we drove back to the hotel in silence, I found myself wondering who Professor Wagner was, and why the government might see him as a threat. Why would they be worried about someone who hadn't been here for almost sixty years? Meanwhile, Wagner himself had closed his eyes and seemed exhausted.

When we left him at the hotel, I said, "You seem tired, professor, you should get some rest."

He nodded in agreement. "Yes, but there's something I'd like to ask of you."

"Yes, what can I do?"

"I won't be offended if you refuse, but...Would you have dinner with me this evening, Maya?"

I was surprised, both by the invitation and because he'd addressed me by name for the first time.

"I don't know...My son's at home..."

"Don't worry about it. And thank you very much for everything."

After doffing his hat with a slight bow, he turned and started walking toward the hotel. Just as he was going through the door, I called out, "Professor!"

"Yes?" he answered softly.

"What time shall we eat?"

He thought for a moment and asked, "Is eight all right?"

"Fine. Would you like to eat at the hotel or somewhere else?"

"If you don't mind, let's eat here."

As I got into the Mercedes I glanced around instinctively for the Renault, but it wasn't there. As we moved off, I suddenly felt very tired. But my day wasn't close to being over yet. I still had a lot of work to get done, and then there was the hellish commute home. Then on top of that, I had to come back to the hotel. As I was thinking these things and feeling sorry for myself, I looked up and happened to see Süleyman's face in the mirror. For the first time, I thought about how difficult his life must be. Spending his life in traffic, dealing with privileged, entitled people. He made even less money than I did, he lived in worse conditions, and he had a young child to support.

"I've been thinking," I said, "I've had some dealings with the head of maintenance, I could go talk to him and see if there's anywhere he could place your cousin. You have a good record, and if you're willing to vouch for him..."

He looked at me in the mirror. It took a moment for it to sink in, and then he smiled broadly.

"Bless you, ma'am. He has three children and he's been out of work for a while. And I can certainly vouch for him. I know he'll work hard."

"OK, I'll have a word with him as soon as I get a chance."

Then, as we turned onto Tarlabaşı Boulevard, I said, "Listen, Süleyman, I have to do some work with the professor this evening, I'd appreciate it if you could drive me home."

"No problem, ma'am," he said happily. "It would be my pleasure."

I got out at the corner, went to the kebab shop, and ordered a large portion of Kerem's favorite kebab. Then I went to the grocery store and bought some fruit and some chocolate ice cream. Just having this little bit of extra time for myself was such a joy, I felt like a child skipping school.

When I got home I was surprised to find that Kerem was asleep. All those sleepless nights must have caught up to him. I stood for a while and watched him sleep, and felt a strong wave of tenderness. Then I reached out and stroked his head. This was something he would never allow me to do when he was awake. What was happening to him was breaking my heart, but there was nothing I could do. I'd taken him to three different doctors, but to no avail. He just kept drifting farther and farther away from me.

I put away the food and took a shower, and then, wrapped in my bathrobe, went back to Kerem's room. I noticed a light blinking on his computer and, assuming he'd left it on, went to turn it off. I touched a key and the screen lit up, and what I saw took the heart right out of me. There on the screen, in block capitals, the same phrase was written over and over again.

I DON'T WANT TO LIVE ANYMORE
I DON'T WANT TO LIVE ANYMORE
I DON'T WANT TO LIVE ANYMORE
I DON'T WANT TO LIVE ANYMORE
I DON'T WANT TO LIVE ANYMORE
I DON'T WANT TO LIVE ANYMORE

"Are you messing around with my computer?"

I was too startled by his voice to respond right away, and I guiltily moved my hand away from the computer.

"No," I said, "you left it on and I was just going to turn it off."

Kerem reached for the mouse. "I'll turn it off," he murmured.

With quick, practiced movements, he clicked a few times. He also clicked "no" on the box asking whether he wanted the document saved or not. I couldn't keep myself from putting my arms around him. He tried to push me away, but I wouldn't let him

"You know that I love you, don't you? That I love you with all my heart."

He didn't answer.

"I'd do anything in the world to make you happy."

"Leave me alone."

"I'm not going to leave you alone. I need you."

What did I mean when I said I needed him? What was I saying to the boy?

Words I hadn't even formed in my mind began to tumble out of my mouth.

"I'm in trouble. I need you."

He stopped pushing me and asked quietly, "What's happened?"

"They're following me."

"Who?"

"I don't know who they are. Three men in a white Renault!"

"Why?"

"I don't know that either. There's this American professor, I think it has to do him. I'm scared."

I saw that even though I hadn't intended to, I'd aroused his interest.

"I have to meet this American professor for dinner this evening. Make sure the door is locked and don't open it for anyone. Take a look out the window every once in a while and check if there's a white Renault outside."

Kerem nodded and sat up.

"They might try to get into the house when I'm gone, but I have every confidence that you'll be able to scare them off."

He took something from the drawer of his bedside table.

"What's that?" I asked.

"Brass knuckles."

When he realized I didn't understand, he explained: "If you hit someone with this, it'll break their chin. Their chin will shatter!"

I felt alarmed. What was this thing doing in my son's drawer?

"Why did you buy this?"

"To deal with the bullies at school."

He spoke so earnestly that I felt a pang in my heart. The make-believe about the dangerous men in the white Renault had engaged him and brought him out of his depression, but the brass knuckles were a reality. He was being bullied and felt powerless and frustrated. No wonder he wanted to live in a fantasy world.

"I've just thought of something else!"

I went to my bedroom, took out the can of mace I kept in my bag, and brought it to him.

"If they do come, spray this in their eyes!"

This cheered him up even more. "Can I keep this?"

I knew he wanted to take it to school.

"You know it's not allowed, don't you?"

"What isn't?"

"You're not allowed to take this to school."

"Don't worry, I won't show it to anyone."

"All right."

I leaned over and kissed him on the cheek, and this time he didn't push me away. Then I went and heated his kebab in the microwave and set the table. When the smell of the kebab began to fill the kitchen I felt a sense of joy. Something so normal, so ordinary, as putting hot food on the table for my son almost brought tears to my eyes. When it was ready I only had to call him once and he came to the kitchen right away.

"You have to finish it all," I said. "We're getting ready for war, and you have to keep up your strength."

While he was eating I went to my bedroom and got out my black dress. It was a bit low-cut, but if I wore my necklace...

The necklace? Yes, but I hadn't worn it for years...

It was in the safe in the closet. Why had I thought of the necklace now? It didn't matter, I just felt like wearing it. I opened the safe and slowly took the necklace out of the maroon velvet pouch. The diamonds and rubies seemed to glow, and when I put the necklace on and looked in the mirror, I felt alive. Then I put on my makeup and stepped back and looked at myself again.

I need to get up and walk around a little. You're supposed to do this on long flights to avoid deep vein thrombosis. And I don't want to fall asleep either. I have to keep writing until we land in Boston.

CHAPTER 3

The grand Louis XVI dining room was almost empty, and the professor and I sat at a small table near the back. He was very polite and correct and a bit distant, and pretended not to notice how dressed-up I was, which made me feel a little embarrassed. After we'd taken our seats there was an awkward silence, and I struggled to find something to talk about.

"You mentioned that you used to meet your friends at the bar here."

"Yes, mostly Germans like myself."

"Was there a German community here then?"

"Well, you could say that there were two German communities. One was made up of Jewish and anti-Nazi refugees, and the other of Germans who supported or actively worked for the Nazis. I preferred to associate with the anti-Nazi group who gathered here. The others used to meet at the Teutonia Club just below Tünel Square.

Goebbels himself visited the Teutonia once, and they made a big fuss over him."

"I imagine there was considerable tension between the two groups."

"That would be an understatement. It was a very tense time here. The world was at war, and even though Turkey was neutral, the war was being played out here too. Almost every community was split. The pro-Nazi Germans were much more powerful and influential than we were, and we always felt under pressure from them. For instance we used to meet at the Tokatlıyan Hotel as well, but we stopped going there when the Austrian manager began flying the Nazi flag outside the front entrance."

"It's hard for me to imagine a Nazi flag flying on Istıklal Avenue."

"That wasn't the only place. You could see quite a few Nazi flags in Istanbul then. The Nazis had some influential Turkish supporters as well."

"What kind of pressure did they put on you?"

"Well, for one, there were quite a few Gestapo agents operating fairly openly. They knew who was actively anti-fascist, and they watched them and did what they could to intimidate them. We heard that once they even threatened a Turkish cinema owner who was showing anti-fascist films."

"But how could they get away with that?"

The professor shrugged and threw up his hands.

"As I said, they had a lot of influence. The Turkish government was terrified the German army might invade. But they were also terrified that the Russians might invade, and they wanted to have German support in case they did."

"We learned a little about that time in school, but not much. It sounds like the Nazis were practically running Istanbul."

"Well, hardly. The British, Americans, and Russians had agents here, too, and they were doing everything they could to influence the Turkish government and people. I knew that a number of my German friends were communists, and I was almost certain that a few of them were working for the Russians. I didn't know any of the British or American agents, but we all knew that they were here and what they were up to."

"What were they up to?"

"Well, to tell the truth I don't know all of it, probably not even half of it. But everyone knew that they were giving logistical support to the partisans in Greece. Then there was the chromium. Turkey was exporting chromium to Germany. They did their best to find out which trains were carrying chromium so the partisans could blow them up when they passed through Greece. I only found out later about what was happening in Ankara. The famous Cicero affair and all that."

"The Cicero affair?"

"You don't know about the Cicero affair? They made a movie about it, with James Mason. I think it was called *Five Fingers*."

"James Mason?"

"Sorry. When you get old, time just slips away. I still think of it as a recent movie, but I realize it must have come out long before you were born. It must have been the early fifties."

"So what was the Cicero affair?"

"Cicero was the code name for Elyesa Bazna, an Albanian from Kosovo who worked as a valet for the British ambassador Sir Hughe Knatchbull-Hugessen in Ankara. The ambassador was in the habit of bringing secret documents home, and Cicero managed to break into the safe and begin photographing them. Some sources claim that he was working with someone else who helped him locate and photograph the documents, but if this is true, this person was never identified. Anyway, Bazna approached an attaché at the German embassy, a man named Ludwig Moyzisch, and in 1943 he became a paid German agent code named Cicero.

"It's believed that the initial information he gave the Germans concerned plans for air raids on the Romanian oil fields, in which case he was responsible for the deaths of hundreds of British Royal Air Force crews. The RAF went to great lengths to keep the Germans from even guessing when and where air raids in the Balkans would take place, but on several occasions the Germans seemed to know exactly when and where they would strike, and they lost a lot of planes.

"There's been some suggestion, though, that Cicero was actually a double agent. That is, he was working for the British from the beginning, and they passed accurate information through him to increase his credibility with the Germans. Or else the British found out about what he was doing and either turned him or fed him false information without his knowledge. If they did find out what Cicero was up to, it was probably through their own spy in the German embassy, a clerk, and also the daughter of the German consul, named Nele Kapp, who was a secret anti-Nazi. Anyway, if Cicero was a double agent he was very likely used in Operation Double Cross, which was a very elaborate trick to get the Germans to believe the Allied invasion would be through the Balkans rather than Normandy."

"What happened to Cicero in the end?"

"Well, the Germans gave him £300,000, but when he tried to use the money to start a business after the war it turned out to be counterfeit. He was so indignant about this that he actually tried to sue the West German government, but of course he didn't get anywhere. He spent the rest of his life here in Istanbul, giving singing lessons and selling secondhand books. In fact he had his book stall very near here, in the courtyard of the Narmanlı Han on Istıklal Avenue, near Tünel Square."

"Oh yes, I know the building. That's quite a story."

"As I said, I didn't know any of this at the time. But it does illustrate what the atmosphere was like here. Everyone was suspicious of everyone, you never knew when to believe whether people were actually who and what they said they were. The person you were having a drink with could be a spy, or a double or even a triple agent."

"So, where did you fit into all of this? You said you didn't support the Nazis, which must make you either Jewish or an anti-Nazi activist."

"Neither. I'm not Jewish, and at the time I'd never been actively political. That is, I'd never been part of any anti-Nazi movement. Which is not to my credit. I should have been."

"So what brought you to Istanbul?"

"That's a long story that I'd rather not get into now."

"Actually, what I'm really curious about is what brings you back to Istanbul after all this time."

For a brief moment he seemed to tense. Then he smiled and said, "That necklace is very beautiful. In fact it's quite remarkable, and it also looks quite old. It must have a story attached to it, and I'd love to hear it."

It was my turn to smile.

"You're not the only one who has secrets. All I'll say is that it once belonged to my grandmother."

He raised his glass and said, "Well, let's drink to our secrets then."

"So, what are you planning to do for the next two days? I usually take people on sightseeing tours, and shopping at the Grand Bazaar, but that doesn't strike me as your kind of thing."

"I'd like to just wander around a bit on my own tomorrow. But if you don't mind there's something important I need your help with the following day, the twenty-fourth."

"Of course, what is it?"

"Could you pick me up early in the morning with the car?"

"How early?"

"Would four o'clock be possible?"

I was taken aback, but did my best not to show it. Where could he possibly want to go at four in the morning?

"OK, where are we going?"

"I'd rather tell you then."

I was somewhat alarmed, and in the taxi home I began to feel increasingly uneasy. And when I got home I found Kerem waiting by the door with his brass knuckles and the can of mace, still caught up in the excitement of the game, telling me that he'd seen two white Renaults but that no one had tried to get into the house. He was wearing the knuckle-dusters and the can of mace was on his desk. I was a bit concerned that he might be taking this too seriously, but at least he wasn't slumped in front of his computer. Indeed, he seemed cheerful and relaxed. And when I reached out to stroke his head he didn't push my hand away. I got another surprise when I told him it was time for bed and he didn't object.

Then I watered the pine sapling, one of the three I'd brought back from the Kafkasör highlands, the only one that had survived. This one had almost died as well; they hadn't liked the climate in my living room at all. But I'd done everything I could to keep it alive, and finally it had begun to grow. Now, when I sat and looked at it, it brought me some of the peace and happiness I'd felt in those snowy mountains.

CHAPTER 4

The next day was rainy and windy and even colder. The traffic was worse than ever—somehow people seem to forget how to drive when it rains—and I got soaked just walking through the campus. And even though I was wearing a wool sweater and a heavy coat, and had a purple pashmina wrapped around my neck, the cold wind seemed to cut right through me. I was late for work, and had barely hung up my coat when the rector's secretary called and said the rector wanted to see me immediately.

As soon as I walked into his office I got a shock. There, sitting comfortably and drinking tea, were the three men I'd seen in the white Renault, and again in the lecture hall.

"What's the matter, Maya? You've gone pale. Please sit down."

I sat down in the only free chair, which I realized had been moved so that I would have to face the men. The older man, the one who'd been at the wheel and who'd taken notes, and who seemed to be in charge, gave me a look that was almost a sneer. The other two just stared at me with blank expressions. I tried to pull myself together, and looked back at them with as much confidence as I could. I noticed that today the men were all wearing jackets and ties.

The rector broke the silence, "These gentlemen are security agents, they have something they'd like to talk to you about."

I didn't know what to say. Then the rector got to his feet, and so did the men, so I stood as well.

"I have some business to attend to, but you can have your talk here."

After he left, the older man leaned toward me. He was in his late forties and had the kind of thin mustache that right-wing militants used to have.

"How are you, Mrs. Duran?"

The question seemed out of place, but I answered.

"I'm fine, thank you."

"As the rector said, we're security agents."

"Yes?"

"The thing is, there's something important we'd like your help with."

"Me?"

"Yes, you."

"What?"

He paused, and again he almost sneered.

"Are you a patriotic Turk, Mrs. Duran?"

"I don't understand."

"Are you willing to serve your country?"

"In what way?"

"Just answer the question."

"I just don't understand why you're questioning my patriotism."

He paused a moment and looked at the others.

"Why does this question bother you?"

"It doesn't bother me. I'm just not sure what you mean by patriotism."

"What if I were to ask you about your family history? Your grandmother, for instance."

I saw where he was going with this.

"I'm a Turkish citizen."

This time he actually sneered, and so did the others.

"We need to be sure you're loyal to your country."

"Of course I am. What is it you want me to do?"

"You've been assigned to escort Professor Wagner during his stay here."

"Yes."

"Well, we want you to report to us on everything Wagner does and says."

"Does he pose some kind of threat to the country?"

"We just need you to tell us everything he does. Who he meets, whom he calls, what he talks about."

"You mean you want me to spy on him."

"We just need to be informed about his activities."

"How will I report to you?"

"We'll take care of that. Just remember that this is an opportunity to prove your patriotism, to prove that you're not..."

He left the implied threat hanging in the air, and without another word the three of them got up and walked out.

I didn't know what to think. I didn't know any more about these men than I had before. They said they were security agents, but from which agency? Nor did I have any idea of what they were after. It made me feel very uneasy, indeed almost violated, that they knew everything about me, even more than most of my friends knew. It made me even more uneasy to realize that these were the kind of people who could make someone disappear without a trace. Then there was Professor Wagner himself. I still couldn't imagine him being any kind of threat to the nation, but why was he always so evasive?

I went back to my office and stared out the window for a while. The trees were bending in the wind and rain slanted across the yard, and every once in a while people with umbrellas dashed from one building to another. I had work to do, I didn't have much time to get things ready for my daily public relations meeting, but I just couldn't get started. Why hadn't Professor Wagner wanted to see me today? What was he doing? Who was he seeing?

I called the hotel and asked to be put through to the professor, but then I hung up as soon as he answered. I had a sudden urge to get out of the office. Then it occurred to me that, in fact, I could. I could just say I spent the day showing Professor Wagner around. It might seem strange that I hadn't taken Süleyman and the car, but if anyone asked I could say we took a walking tour of his old neighborhood.

So without giving it any more thought I put on my coat and slipped away. As I crossed Beyazit Square the rain was beginning to turn to snow and the wind seemed to cut right through to my bones. I got into a taxi and went straight home. Then once I got there I turned on the heat, took a hot shower, and went to bed.

It was after three when I woke up, and I felt groggy and disoriented. I had a quick coffee, then went straight to Kerem's school to pick him up. I waited outside his classroom, and when the bell rang I watched the children pour out, all laughing and talking and joking with each other, full of life and exuberance. Then I saw Kerem. He was the last one out of the classroom and he was alone, walking slowly with his hands in his pockets, looking at the floor. He was very surprised to see me. In fact he seemed alarmed.

"Did the school call you in?" he asked.

"No, I just decided to come pick you up."

"Why?"

"I felt like it. I thought we might do something together."

"Like what?"

"I thought we might get something to eat, talk a little, maybe go to the movies."

He made a face.

"I'm not really in the mood. I'd rather go home."

He meant that he'd rather be in front of his computer.

"I thought you were going to help me. I got a visit from those men in the white Renault today."

"Really?"

"Yes."

"How could I possibly help?"

"For one thing you could do some research on the internet."

"OK, then let's go straight home."

"No, we have to talk first."

We went to one of the more upscale restaurants in the shopping mall. I had soup followed by lamb chops, with a glass of red wine. Kerem had what he always had wherever we went. Hamburger, fries, and cola. Though it cost twice as much here as it did in the fast-food places.

As we ate I was happy to see that he'd forgotten his misery for a moment and actually seemed to be enjoying himself. I felt a wave of tenderness, and couldn't help reaching out to stroke his head. Which was a mistake. He pushed my hand away and looked around in embarrassment.

"All right, all right," I said. "I'm sorry."

Then I told him I wanted him to find out everything he could about Maximilian Wagner and Istanbul

University during World War II. And anything else he could find out about Istanbul in those years, and particularly about the Germans who were here then.

"Is this real or are you putting me on?" he asked.

"I swear, it's real."

His eyes lit up, and he took a notebook out of his bag to write down what I'd asked him to look up.

"You've got my grandmother's eyes," I said.

"So what?"

"I'll tell you about her one day. She was quite an extraordinary woman."

He shrugged his shoulders.

I let him chose the movie, and afterwards, when we got home, he ran straight to his computer.

"I have to leave very early tomorrow morning. Can you get yourself off to school?"

"Yes."

"Let me know if you see anything unusual."

"Does your leaving early have to do with that German man?"

"Yes."

"Where are you going?"

"To tell the truth I don't know. He didn't tell me."

"Are you scared?"

I wasn't, but I said I was.

He turned his attention to his computer. I said good night, and he mumbled in response. I set my alarm for three and went to bed.

CHAPTER 5

I dreamt that I was with my grandmother. We were walking through a barren, desolate landscape toward a ruined church on top of a hill. The church was very old, yet somehow I remembered how it had been. All that remained were parts of the walls, standing amid piles of tumbled stones. Yet I could vaguely envision it filled with worshipers. My grandmother took me by the hand and led me toward the crypt. She brushed away cobwebs, and then, as we began descending into the darkness, I woke with a start. The digital clock on the bedside table showed 2:35.

The dream had been so real, it was as if I'd actually been with her, and as I lay under the covers in the darkness I began to think about her and remember her. I remembered how she used to rouse me in the morning by stroking my hair, and how the first thing I saw when I woke would be her smiling face and her dark, animated eyes. I felt a deep longing for her, a deep sadness that she was gone.

Her husband had been a mailman who'd left her widowed at a young age with three children, the middle of whom was my father. I grew up in an apartment in Üsküdar with my parents, my brother Necdet, who was eight years my senior, and my grandmother. My father was a bank clerk and my mother was a teacher, and my grandmother took care of us while they were at work. She always had bread and butter waiting for us when we got home from school.

On Sundays my brother and I would be sent to the bakery with a tray of food to be baked in the oven. I used to love watching the baker slide the tray in over the hot coals on a long wooden paddle. Then we would go outside and play in the street until it was ready. Almost all the other children in the neighborhood would be sent to the bakery like this as well, and we had enormous fun. Then, when it was time, we would go back in with our number. By then the bakery would be filled with the mingled smells from our trays mixed with the smell of freshly baked bread. We would carry the hot tray with cloths and towels and, maddened by hunger, would rush to get home as quickly as we could.

I looked at the clock. It was almost three and time to get up and start getting ready. But I was so comfortable in the warmth of my bed and my memories, and the darkness of the night seemed so cold and uninviting.

Where was this strange man going to take me at four in the morning? What was he up to? What had my

grandmother wanted to show me in the crypt of that ruined church?

I remembered one of the last things my grandmother
said to me before she died. She told me that I would encounter people who wanted to harm me as well as people
who wanted to help me, that I shouldn't allow my view
of the world to be colored by either, and that I should be
wary of both.

I was studying literature at the university at the time,
and my brother had just graduated from the military
academy and become an officer. One night I heard my
grandmother making strange sounds, and I went to see
what was wrong. She couldn't breathe, she was wheez-
ing and in pain, and she squeezed my hand so hard she
almost cut off the circulation. We called the doctor who
lived downstairs. He gave her something to calm her
down, and told us we had to bring her to the hospital first
thing in the morning.

In the morning my grandmother was breathing regularly but she was pale and weak. My brother and I got
her ready and helped her to the door, but at the door she
stopped and looked slowly around the apartment, taking
it in, as if she knew she would never see it again.

We were able to get her into a military hospital because my brother was an officer. They put her in a small
room and for the next several hours performed a series
of tests. Then my brother and my parents left, and I sat

holding her hand and watching the serum drip into the tube that ran to her arm.

In the evening a senior doctor came, a very stern and serious military doctor. He spoke gently to my grandmother, though. He told her that they were close to arriving at a diagnosis and deciding on a course of treatment, but first he needed some family medical history. Had any one in her family suffered from heart disease? Particularly her parents. Had either of her parents ever had a heart attack?

My grandmother didn't answer, but looked away, at the ceiling. The doctor assumed she hadn't heard, and repeated his questions. Then, when she still didn't answer he assumed she hadn't understood, and rephrased his question.

"How did your parents die? What was the cause of death?"

She looked at me and tears started rolling from her eyes.

There was a long silence, after which the doctor repeated his question, this time a little more loudly, and with a little less patience.

My grandmother looked at him for a moment, and then said, "They didn't die a natural death!"

Her tone was so bitter and anguished that both the doctor and I were taken aback.

"What do you mean?" the doctor asked.

"I mean that they didn't live long enough to have heart problems. They were killed. The cause of death was man's inhumanity to man."

The doctor didn't know how to respond to this. He opened his mouth to say something, then changed his mind, turning to me instead, and telling me that they would start her on medication and see how she responded.

After he left I sat on her bed and put my arms around her. She'd begun to sob bitterly and I did my best to comfort her. She kept crying for a long time, and all I could do was just hold her. After a while her sobbing started to diminish, and then finally she was still. As the room began to grow dark, she pulled away from me and looked at me.

"There's something I need to tell you, something I've never told anyone."

I didn't say anything, but just held her hand and waited, and watched the sky outside change slowly from dark blue to black. Then slowly, almost in a whisper, she began telling her story.

At first I didn't quite understand. It seemed as if she were telling me random memories from her childhood in a town in the east of Turkey. She and her two brothers, and a large stone house with a large walled garden. She told me the first thing she remembered was playing in the garden with her brothers. She must still have been very young then. It was a warm day, and greenish light was filtering through the leaves of the fruit trees.

She remembered looking up and noticing how the leaves moved in the breeze, and how they seemed to sparkle in the sunlight. Then she saw her mother watching her from a window. Her mother smiled, and she was conscious at that moment of being very happy.

When her world ended, she was just old enough to understand that there were two kinds of people in the village. The people like her family, who went to the church on the hill, and the people who went to the mosque near the main square. She also knew that while everyone spoke Turkish in public, her family and the others who went to the church spoke a different language among themselves.

"Then one day soldiers came and began taking people out of their houses and gathering them in the main square. They were only taking the people who went to the church. The soldiers had begun moving down our street. My father had already been taken, the soldiers had found him in his shop. My mother brought us out into the garden. She was in tears, but we didn't understand why, we didn't really understand what was going on. She said we had to hurry, and brought us out the back door of the garden to a neighbor's house. It was much smaller than our house, and it belonged to a family that went to the mosque. There were tears running down my mother's face as she hugged each of us tightly and kissed us. Then she rushed out of the house and back into our garden without saying another word. We never saw her or my father again.

"My real name is Mari, but ever since that day I've been called Semahat. The woman of the house, I'll always remember her as Aunt Semra, did her best to comfort us and make us feel at home, but we cried all the time. Our parents were gone and we didn't know why. We weren't allowed to go back to our house or our garden. We weren't allowed to go to school, or to church. In fact we weren't allowed to go outside at all, not even to play in the street with the other children.

"I don't know how long we stayed there. It seemed like a very long time, but it probably wasn't more than a few months. Then one day some men came to the house, there was a soldier with them, and they put us into the back of a truck with a few other children from our community. Some of them were my cousins. They brought us to a city, to a building where there were hundreds of children like us from other towns and villages. A few days later I was sent with a small group of children to an orphanage here in Istanbul."

She stopped, and for what seemed like a very long time we sat in silence in the darkness. I felt as if the ground had fallen away from beneath me. My grandmother was Armenian. I'd never had any idea. In fact the thought had never occurred to me. I'd always loved her so much, and I felt a sense of shame for not having known about what happened to her as a child. For not having the slightest clue about the pain she'd lived with all her life. Finally, I broke the silence.

"What happened to your brothers?"

"I have no idea. I never saw or heard of them again. I tried to find out once, but I couldn't get anywhere."

"Do you know what happened to your parents?"

"Years later I went back to our town to see Aunt Semra. She was still living in the same house, alone, her husband had died and her children had long since moved to Istanbul. Our house was no longer there. Someone had built a large, ugly apartment there. It broke my heart to see that, but it would have been even more painful if the house was still there, if other people were living in it.

"Aunt Semra didn't want to tell me what she knew. I had to push her, and it was only on the second day that she finally told me. After they'd rounded everyone up they marched them out of town. When they got to the bridge down the road there was a large group of men waiting. They raped the girls and the women, stole whatever valuables people had been able to take with them, and then slaughtered everyone and threw their bodies into the river."

She began to weep again, and as I held her hand I gave in to the emotions swirling within me and began to weep as well.

Hours later, after a nurse had come to check her vital signs and give her medication—I think they gave her a sedative, too, because she was much calmer and a bit drowsy—she began to talk again. She told me that before she'd been at the orphanage for very long she was adopted by a Turkish family and raised as a Muslim.

"They were very kind, loving people. They gave me a home and treated me as their own. I know that they loved me, that they saw me as their own daughter. But I sensed that there was an unspoken condition. That I accept being raised as a Muslim. I don't want you to think that this was forced on me, because it wasn't. I accepted this at first, as a child, simply because I sincerely wanted to make them happy. When I was older I saw it as a way to fit in, to hide my true identity. I never lost the fear that it would be dangerous for me if people knew who I really was.

"My husband, the grandfather you never knew, he was the only person who knew and accepted who I was. When we were alone he called me Mari. He was a forward-thinking man. He believed in the Republic, in democracy and equality, and he thought that the practice of religion was backwards. He told me that I didn't need to be afraid, that he would protect me. But I continued to pray five times a day and to fast during Ramadan. I never forgot that I was a Christian, yet somehow being a practicing Muslim had become part of who I was too. I also didn't believe that anyone could protect me, and I didn't want to put him in danger either."

We talked through most of the night. Or rather she did. I mostly listened. She told me what she remembered about her mother and father, and her brothers, and the world that was taken from her. Her father's shop, celebrating Easter at the church, and afterwards at a long table in the garden with all their relatives.

Toward morning, she sat up and took my hand and said, "There's something I want you to have. It's a necklace that belonged to my mother, and before that to her mother and her mother's mother. It's been in our family for generations. Aunt Semra kept it for me, God bless her. She said she'd always known I'd come back one day. She told me that even during times of desperate poverty she'd never even considered selling it, because passing it on to me was the only way she could repay my mother for all the kindness she'd shown her. I believe that it's rightfully yours now, and that it will connect you to the people you never knew you belonged to. It's in a locked box on the shelf in my closet. You'll find the key taped to the bottom of my bed."

This was the last thing she said to me. Soon afterwards she fell asleep. I sat and watched her for a long time, but I must have dozed off because the next thing I knew the sun was streaming through the window. The moment I looked at her I knew she was gone. She looked so peaceful, and I knew that she was finally free from the pain she'd lived with all her life. I said a prayer for her. Not a Muslim prayer or a Christian prayer, but a prayer from the heart.

The following day, her funeral was held at the local mosque, the mosque she'd gone to every Friday for so many years. She was buried in the cemetery as a pious Muslim, and I was the only one present who knew who she really was.

Later that day I opened the box and found the necklace, the most beautiful, most precious thing I've ever owned, and that I only wear on what I feel are very special occasions. Also in the box were her birth certificate and a small crucifix she must have worn as a child.

She made me promise never to tell a soul, and I didn't tell anyone except my brother. I felt he had the right to know. I also felt he would want to know, but I was wrong. At first he refused to believe me. Then, after I showed him her birth certificate his face went white and he muttered something about our blood being tainted. This made me furious, and I started shouting at him. He started shouting back, saying that the Armenians had always wanted to destroy Turkey, they'd sided with the Russians during World War I, they'd spread lies about genocide to defame Turkey, organized terrorists to kill Turkish diplomats, and so on. This made me even more furious, and we had the fiercest, bitterest argument I've ever had with anyone.

I could see that he was truly shaken, both by what I'd told him and by my reaction to what he'd said. In the end, he took back his words, but begged me never to tell anyone else. If it got out that he was half Armenian, his career in the military would be finished. He'd never be promoted; he'd spend the rest of his career in a back office in some remote province.

We didn't see each other again except at unavoidable family gatherings, where we were always polite and friendly but never close. The last time I'd seen him, when we went to visit our parents at the house they'd retired to on the Aegean coast, he acted as if our falling out had never occurred, as if he'd forgotten all about it, and perhaps he had.

But those men in the rector's office yesterday.... There were others who knew our secret, and this worried me. If they knew about me they knew about Necdet as well. But his career hadn't been blocked; on the contrary, he'd risen quite rapidly. He was a full colonel now, and had an important position in military intelligence.

I was startled by the alarm. It was three o'clock. I got out of bed and dressed quickly. Kerem had fallen asleep in front of his computer, and was sleeping so soundly that he didn't wake up when I put him to bed. I couldn't resist the temptation to kiss him on the forehead, something I could never do when he was awake. Then, as I was turning off his computer, I saw that he'd already started looking up the things I'd asked him to research. One of the articles caught my attention. I wanted to start reading it, but I didn't have time.

I put on my warmest coat, tied a green scarf around my neck, closed the door quietly behind me, and walked down the silent, empty hallway. It was so cold outside that my chest tightened instantly. The rain had stopped sometime during the night, but the sky was still overcast and I was sure it was going to snow.

The black Mercedes was waiting under the streetlight. I was grateful that Süleyman was on time, that he hadn't made me wait in the cold, but as soon as I got in the car, I was assaulted by a thick cloud of cigarette smoke.

"What the hell is this! It stinks. Why couldn't you get out of the car to smoke?"

Süleyman muttered, "It's very cold."

"You could at least have opened the window," I said as I opened my window.

Süleyman put the car into gear and drove off aggressively, and much too fast. I realized that I'd hurt his feelings, and that I shouldn't have spoken to him that way. But the way he was driving was childish and dangerous and I didn't like it.

"Slow down!" I said sharply. "We have plenty of time."

The cold air rushing through the window stung my face. Where the hell was Wagner taking us on the coldest day of the year?

"Süleyman, could you turn the heat on?"

"The heater isn't working."

As we sped shivering through the deserted streets, Süleyman's anger and frustration seemed to fill the car. It was exactly 3:52 when we pulled up in front of the hotel.

The professor was waiting in the lobby, in his black coat and a black fedora. He stood and gave me a very formal and very grave greeting, and then picked up his violin case and a small wreath of white flowers. A ribbon on the wreath bore the words *Für Nadia*.

Outside, Süleyman held the passenger side door open for the professor, and I went around and got in on the other side. The professor's manner was very solemn, almost gloomy, and I didn't know what to make of it.

"Where are we going, professor?"

"To Şile."

"Where?"

"Şile."

Şile was a resort town on the Black Sea coast. It was a considerable drive, and would be completely deserted at this time of year. I was sure he must have got the name of the place confused.

"Professor, do you know where Şile is?"

"Yes."

"And you want to go there at four o'clock on a cold winter morning?"

"Yes," he said irritably. "I want to go to Şile."

Süleyman turned around and asked me what was up.

"He wants to go to Şile."

"What?"

"Yes, you heard me. If I'd known I'd have brought my bathing suit."

We drove off, across the Fatih Sultan Mehmet Bridge to the Asian side and along the Ankara highway. The only vehicles on the road were trucks, and after we took the Şile turnoff we had the road to ourselves. No one spoke as we drove through the forest, and there was a palpable air of tension in the car.

I'd been to Şile with Ahmet once. It could have been a nice resort town, with its picturesque fishing port and restaurants overlooking a beach that stretched out into the distance, but it wasn't. There was something squalid about it. We'd had too much wine with lunch and ended up having a fight, and didn't speak the whole way back. I'd sworn I'd never go back to Şile, but here I was, and in the middle of winter at that.

What was this madman planning to do up here, and were those creepy security agents right to be suspicious of him? Was he going to flash a coded signal to a Russian submarine lurking off the coast, or had he buried some Nazi treasure out here during the war?

The American businessman in the seat next to me woke up a little while ago and tried to start a conversation with me. He asked me what I was writing. I wanted to tell him it was none of his business, but I'm trying to learn how to be nicer to people. So I just told him that it was something personal, something I had to do for my own sake. I was polite and friendly, but still managed to get the message across that it was in fact none of his business and that I wanted to be left alone.

It's time to get up and walk around a bit again. Perhaps I should ask the flight attendant for some coffee. Or maybe I should take a little nap. Just for half an hour.

CHAPTER 6

As we sped along through the forest in the gray light of early morning, the professor took out an old map and began examining it. Then he turned to me and said, "Could we slow down a bit?"

I told Süleyman, and he slowed down. Then the professor said we needed to stop and back up a little. So we backed up about 500 feet until we reached a narrow dirt road that branched off to the left.

"OK, this is it. Tell him we need to go down this road."

So I told Süleyman, and I saw him raise his eyebrows slightly in the mirror.

"Where are we going, professor?"

He gave me a blank look and just said that there was something of a personal nature he had to take care of. I began to feel decidedly uneasy. As we bumped along, the professor kept peering out the window as if he was looking for something. Or someone.

After a while the woods thinned out, then ended, and we were climbing a barren slope of sandy, pebbly soil. The track we were driving along deteriorated and we could only inch along.

"If the car gets stuck in this sand we'll never get out of here."

I didn't say anything, and neither did Professor Wagner. Then, at the top of the slope, the sea opened out before us, dark, stormy and forbidding, with huge waves crashing against the rocks, sending up plumes of spray and receding in cascades of foam. Black clouds raced in off the sea like invading horsemen. Here we felt the full force of the wind, and the car seemed to shudder. Süleyman stopped the car, but the professor motioned for him to keep driving, so we began inching forward again until the track petered out altogether about twenty yards from the sea.

"This is as far as we can go."

I didn't bother to translate this for the professor. I don't know if he would have heard me anyway, he was looking around in an almost agitated manner, as if he were trying to find something. There was nothing at all on the beach except an abandoned building back up on the ridge a little to the left. It was either in ruins or unfinished, with a small, glassed-in porch in front. A large, rusting sign announced it to be the Black Sea Motel. There was another smaller shack behind it with a tin roof that had been partly blown off.

The professor picked up his violin and the wreath and for a moment seemed at a loss for what to do. Then he looked out the rear window and said, "Can we back up a bit, up to the top of that ridge?"

Süleyman muttered to himself and put the car in reverse. He put his arm on the passenger seat and turned to look out the rear window, but just as he started to reverse the engine stalled. He tried to start it again several times, but it didn't respond at all. Then finally it turned and sputtered and we began to reverse slowly.

About halfway back up the ridge the professor asked us to stop again. Süleyman looked at him with a mixture of irritation and puzzlement. The professor took a deep breath, gave me a look that seemed almost fearful, but also somehow resigned and deeply sad.

"Forgive me, but I must ask you to leave me alone here for a little while. If you could continue on back over the ridge and wait for me there, I'll come join you when I'm done."

"And then?" I asked.

"Then...well...Then we'll probably go back."

When he opened the door, a gust of cold wind blew in. He climbed out slowly with the wreath and the violin, closed the door, and then stood there waiting for us to leave. Süleyman gunned the engine, either out of impatience or to keep the car from stalling, and the car lurched back. As we reversed, I watched the professor walk toward the sea, struggling against the wind, until we were over the top of the ridge and I could no longer see him.

As soon as the car stopped I got out and walked to the top of the ridge. Then, shivering in the cold, I watched the professor walk toward the sea, to the point where the highest waves washed onto the beach. Then he put down his violin, took a few more steps forward, and tossed the wreath into the waves. He stood there for a few moments with his hands clasped in front of him, then turned, and started back. When he looked up and saw me he seemed annoyed, so I went back toward the car.

Süleyman was leaning against the hood, smoking a cigarette. I held my hands over the hood to get some of the warmth from the engine.

"What's he doing?" he asked irritably.

I just shrugged my shoulders. We stood there in silence for a while, and then, just as I was about to get back in the car, Süleyman flicked his cigarette away and started striding up to the ridge. I followed, worried about what he might do.

When Süleyman reached the top of the ridge he stopped and turned to me with an expression of disbelief. I joined him and looked down at the beach. There, in front of the crashing waves, his black coat flapping in the wind, the professor was playing his violin as he looked out to sea.

Süleyman shook his head and started back toward the car, and I began slowly making my way down to the sea. When I was about halfway to the sea I could hear the music intermittently, and it grew stronger the closer I got. I stopped when I was just close enough to hear it clearly. The professor was playing an exquisite, lyrical melody that reminded me a little of Schubert's *Serenade*.

As I stood there, at the same time entranced and not quite believing what I was seeing, I heard the car drive up behind me and stop. Then I heard the engine sputter and die. I turned around just as Süleyman was getting out of the car.

"Why did you turn the engine off?"

"I didn't turn it off, it just stalled," he answered irritably. "There's no point in trying to start it when it's this hot. I'll try in a little while."

Just then the music stopped. The professor hesitantly played a few more notes; then he stopped again.

Süleyman swore under his breath, got back into the car, and slammed the door. The professor started playing again, but when he reached a certain point he faltered. Again and again he started from the beginning and played until he reached that passage, but somehow couldn't get past it.

I decided to get out of the wind, and as I sat shivering in the back seat of the car I saw that the sky was getting progressively darker. A few snowflakes began to drift down, then more and more, until snow began to stick to the windshield.

I got out of the car, wrapped my scarf round my head and began to struggle across the sand. Why the hell had I worn high-heels? But how could I have known that we'd be on a deserted beach in a snowstorm?

When I reached the professor I became alarmed. His face was completely drained of color and looked almost deathlike. Snow had begun to settle on his hat and his shoulders.

"Professor," I shouted. He didn't hear me.

"Professor, professor, hey, Mr. Wagner! Please come back to the car."

I began to shake him by the arm. "Hey, professor!" The breaking waves crashed onto the beach, and I could see the white flowers from the professor's wreath bobbing and swirling in the foam.

I tried to take his violin, but couldn't pry in from his frozen fingers. Then I started trying to drag him toward the car. It took all my strength to pull him along a few steps, but he kept turning to look back out to sea. As if he was searching for something out there among the heaving waves. Then, suddenly, he pulled his arm free and started rushing toward the water and I almost had to tackle him to get him to stop and turn around. Süleyman finally came out to help me, and each taking an arm we were able to march him along step-by-step. As we pulled him along, he kept muttering something, but I couldn't quite make out what it was. Something about a storm, about a storm arriving and then leaving. At one point he turned to me with a wild, desperate look in his eyes and said something in German. Then he tried with all his strength to break free and rush back toward the waves. If Süleyman hadn't been there I don't know if I would have been able to hold him. Then he seemed to lose his will altogether. He went limp, and we almost had to carry him the rest of the way. We managed to get him into the back seat, and I climbed in beside him while Süleyman rushed around and got behind the wheel. But when he turned the key in the ignition, the engine wouldn't start. It just made a kind of whirring noise and then stopped.

Meanwhile, the professor had started to tremble. He'd gone completely pale and his breathing was very shallow and I was afraid he would die at any moment.

"Come on Süleyman, do something, the man's dying!" I shouted.

He kept trying, but the engine wouldn't respond. We were out of the wind, but it was very cold in the car and the snow was getting heavier.

"OK," I said, "I don't think he's going to make it unless we can get him somewhere warm. I'll need your help, let's try to get him up to that building."

It wasn't easy getting him out of the car and putting his arms around our shoulders so we could drag him along. He was completely limp, a dead weight, and much heavier than I would have thought. The Black Sea Motel was farther than it had seemed and the ground was rough and my high heels made the going even more difficult. But we finally got him up the steps to the glassed-in porch and got the door open. There were a few battered tables and some plastic chairs, and a primitive seascape was painted on the back wall. We sat the professor in one of the chairs and I went and banged on the inner door.

"Hello! Is anyone there?"

I heard a shuffling sound inside, then a key turning in the lock, then the door opened and a scrawny boy in a heavy, hooded overcoat peered out. There was something strange about his face, his very angular features. He looked both old and young, sinister and innocent.

"Listen, we need your help. I think this man is dying. We need to get him warm."

He gave me a baffled look and said,

"We're closed. We're closed for the winter. This place is only open in summer."

"We just need to keep him warm until we get our car going."

"Well, there's no heat here."

"What do you mean there's no heat?"

"I mean there's no heat. This place is only open in summer."

"Who are you and what are you doing here?"

"I'm the caretaker. I stay here to keep an eye on the place."

"Well, how do you keep warm, you must at least have some kind of stove."

"I have a little electric heater, but it broke last night. I have to bring it in to Şile to get it repaired, but the bus doesn't start running for another hour or so."

"Can we at least put him in one of the rooms? We can lie him down on a bed and cover him with blankets."

"I don't know about that . . . Abdullah might get angry."

"Who's Abdullah?"

"He's the owner."

"Where is he?"

"He's in Istanbul; he only comes out in the summer."

"Well, don't worry about Abdullah. Let's get him into a room."

The boy hesitated, then went over to a small desk, opened the drawer and took out a key. Süleyman and I got the professor to his feet, dragged him inside, struggled up the stairs with him, got him into what had to be the most depressing room I'd ever seen, laid him on the bed, and covered him with a rough woolen blanket.

"Is there any chance of getting the car started?" I asked Süleyman.

"Not without a mechanic. It might even need to be towed. The only thing I can think of is to walk up to the main road and try to hitch a ride into town."

"That will take hours. What if I called someone out from Istanbul?"

"That will take hours too. I think our best bet is for me to get into Şile."

"I'll go with you," the boy said, "I have to go in anyway."

After they'd gone I went to see how the professor was doing. He didn't look at all well and he was still shivering.

The blanket wasn't going to be enough. I had to get him warm somehow. But how? Then an idea occurred to me. I took the blanket off: then took off his shoes, his wet coat, his trousers and sweater and shirt; turned him on his side and bent his knees; then stripped to my underwear; lay beside him and drew the blanket up over us; and put my arms around him. At first I felt so cold that my chest tightened and my teeth started chattering, but slowly I began to feel a little warmer. But the professor's thin, bony body was still cold. He wasn't showing any signs of coming around, either, and I began to worry. I turned him around and switched positions to warm the front of his body, and continued to switch positions every half hour or so.

I must have dozed off at one point, because the next thing I knew I heard the door open and someone walk in. I opened my eyes and looked up, and there was Süleyman, looking at us with an expression of disgust on his face.

"What the hell is going on here!?"

And with that he turned and stormed out of the room. I called out after him but he didn't answer.

A few minutes later I heard the sound of the Mercedes driving off. The sound gradually faded and then died away. Now we were stuck here in the cold in the middle of nowhere. And on top of that, Süleyman was going to tell everyone at the university that he'd caught me in bed with the elderly professor.

I got up and dressed and took my phone out of my bag. I'd left it on silent and had missed several calls, all of them from Kerem. I called him back right away, worried that something had happened to him. He answered right away.

"What's happened, Kerem? Are you all right?"

"They're here!" he said excitedly.

"Who's there?"

"Those men?"

"Which men, Kerem?"

"You know, you told me. The three men!"

I felt a mixture of anger and apprehension that those creeps were in my house with my son.

"Is the man with the mustache there, Kerem?"

"Yes."

"Can you put him on the phone?"

As soon as I heard his voice I started giving him a piece of my mind, asking him what right he had to come into my house and talk to my son.

"We were just paying a friendly visit."

"Get out of my house!" I said.

"First tell us what you've been up to."

"We're not up to anything. Just get out of my house!"

"If you're not up to anything what are you doing up there?"

"Where?"

"In Şile."

I was taken aback.

"How do you know?"

He laughed and said, "From your cell phone. We can tell where you're calling from."

"I want to talk to my son," I said.

He passed the phone to Kerem.

"Are you OK?"

"Yes. This is actually kind of fun."

"Good. I'm out of town right now."

"Yes, I heard. You're in Şile."

"I'll tell you about it later. It's going to take some time for me to get back, but I'll call someone and ask them to come to the house."

"My father?"

I thought a while. "I'm not sure yet."

In fact Ahmet was the first person I'd thought of calling. After all, he was the boy's father. But I just didn't want to deal with him right then because I knew he'd act as if I was asking him a favor or something. I also didn't want to try to explain the situation to him.

So I called my brother for the first time in years. When he answered he was completely taken aback.

"Maya?"

"Yes, Necdet, it's me."

"Wow... hello."

"Necdet, I'm calling because it's an emergency and I need your help."

"What is it, what's happened?"

"I'm in Şile. I left Kerem alone and there are some security agents in the apartment with him now."

"Security agents?"

"Yes."

"Are they military or civilian?"

"I have no idea."

"Well, what are they doing at your house?"

"I'll explain, but could you please go to our place now and make sure Kerem's OK?"

There was silence for a while. Then he said, "But I've got guests."

"Necdet! This is important, think about what might be at stake here."

At this veiled remark he said, "All right. I'll head over right away."

I took a deep breath and said, "Thanks. I'll try to get there as soon as I can."

"What do you mean you'll try? And what are you doing in Şile in the middle of winter?"

"I have a guest, an American professor. He asked me to bring him here but the car broke down and we've been stranded at a motel. There's no one here."

"Why didn't you say so? I can send someone to get you."

"Thanks Necdet, I would really appreciate that. I'm at a place called the Black Sea Motel. It's hard to describe where it is though. It's at the end of a dirt road before you get to the town itself."

"Don't worry, they'll find it," he said. "I'll give them your number."

After hanging up I went to wake the professor. Some of his color had returned but he still didn't look all that well.

I shook him gently and called, "Professor, how are you doing? Do you think you can get up?"

He opened his eyes briefly, then shut them again, reached for my hand and began murmuring again, something about the storm, and Nadia. No, he wasn't saying storm, he was saying something that sounded like "sutuma," whatever that was. Nadia was on the sutuuma.

"She was so close but I couldn't reach her. There were moments I was sure I could see her. There was nothing I could do, there was nothing I could do."

"Professor, can you hear me? Can you try to get up?"

He kept murmuring to himself, "It's all my fault. Nadia, forgive me, forgive me."

He was choking on the words, his voice raspy; and, a few times, I heard him whimper. Small, silent whimpers. He kept begging, "*Mein Schatz*, forgive me!"

He opened his eyes again and looked around in bewilderment.

"Where are we?"

"We're still on the beach, or rather at the motel on the beach. You fainted from the cold so I brought you here. Someone's coming to get us. Please get dressed, professor."

Only then did he realize he was naked, and he didn't understand why. As he slowly got dressed he kept giving me puzzled glances.

"Yes, professor, I undressed you and put you to bed," I said. "I thought you were dying and I had to do something to save your life."

"What kind of thing?" And then without waiting for an answer, he added, "Thank you."

I helped him get dressed and then helped him down the stairs. The boy who'd let us in had lit a small fire just outside the door to the glassed-in porch, and was warming his hands over it. He stood when he saw us, but just then a large black car drove up.

A man got out and called, "Maya Duran?"

"Yes?"

"Your brother sent us to get you."

Meanwhile the driver had got out as well.

"How quick!" I said. "I thought it would take you at least two hours to get here from Istanbul."

"But we didn't come from Istanbul," the driver said. "We weren't very far away and we got going as soon as the colonel called us."

I thanked them, and they helped me get the professor into the car.

"Who are these people?" asked the professor.

"They're going to take us back to Istanbul."

"What happened to the Mercedes?"

"It broke down, professor. That's why these men came to get us."

We were just about to move off, when I asked them to wait a moment while I went and gave the boy some money. Then I got back in the car and we drove off. The professor dozed off again, and I gazed out the window feeling glad to be warm again.

My brother was probably at my apartment by now, and I had every confidence that he would be able to deal with the situation. It might seem strange that I didn't call the boy's father, but anyone who knew Ahmet would understand. He was such a completely spineless person, probably because his father had been so overbearing.

My former father-in-law was a fairly well-known politician and a complete racist with romantic, fascist ideas about the pure, noble, and superior Turks who'd migrated out of Central Asia. Indeed, the political movement he belonged to had once openly supported the Nazis. And he'd dominated Ahmet so much that Ahmet was never able to develop his own character. Ahmet had remained weak and timid, unable to take risks or to confront anyone, and ready to betray anyone if it meant he could avoid taking a stand.

I was exhausted, and all I wanted was to get home, hug Kerem, and get into a hot bath. I didn't want to think about Süleyman and the things he was going to say to people. I took out my phone and called my friend Filiz, who was a doctor at a hospital near the university.

I told her the situation and she said we should bring the professor straight to the hospital. She wasn't there herself, but she'd call and tell them to expect us.

Then I woke the professor and said, "We're almost back in Istanbul. These gentlemen will take you to the hospital."

"To the hospital?"

"Yes. You're not well and you should see a doctor."

"All right. But what about you?"

"I'm going home. I'm very tired, I'm exhausted. I'll come and see you tomorrow."

"Who are these gentlemen?"

I was just about to answer when the man in the passenger seat said in fluent English, "We're friends."

They were going to drop me off first. I whispered in the professor's ear: "Professor, who is Sutuuma?"

He gave me a puzzled look and didn't seem to understand. Then he started nodding off again so I shook his arm gently.

"Professor, who or what is Sutuuma?"

He twisted his lips and then murmured, "It was a ship. From Romania..."

"Why did you keep saying, 'Forgive me, Nadia'? What happened?"

"Did I...say so?"

His face turned from pale to white, he closed his eyes, and spoke with a very low voice.

"No, no, no," he whispered frantically.

So I didn't insist. There is no need to force an old and devastated man.

They pulled up in front of my door as if they'd been there many times before. I said goodbye to the professor but his eyes were closed and I don't think he heard me. The driver got out and opened my door for me. I thanked them both for their trouble, and they very graciously told me it had been their pleasure to be able to help.

I opened the apartment door somewhat apprehensively, not knowing what to expect. Neither my brother nor the security agents were there, but Kerem, sitting on the couch with a huge bag of potato chips on his lap, greeted me cheerfully. He was in such a good mood that he didn't push me away when I hugged him.

"Where's your uncle?"

"He left. He said for you to call him tomorrow."

"And what about the other men?"

"Uncle Necdet spoke to them for a while. I couldn't hear what they said. Then they left. Uncle Necdet told me that there was nothing to be afraid of and that you'd be home soon and then he left. Mother, what's going on? Who are these men?"

"Can we talk about it tomorrow, Kerem?" I said. "I'm exhausted. And pass me the potato chips."

I was famished, I hadn't eaten for almost twenty-four hours, and I began devouring the potato chips. I was always telling Kerem not to eat these disgusting things, but at that moment they seemed delicious. Kerem laughed and told me to leave some for him, but I just shook my head and kept stuffing my mouth.

Then I took a long hot shower, put lip balm on my lips and night cream on my face, wrapped myself in my bathrobe, and went straight to bed. Just before drifting off I thought about the professor and hoped he would be all right. Then I fell into a deep, sound sleep.

CHAPTER 7

I woke at seven from a dreamless sleep, feeling better than I had for some time. Indeed, to my surprise, I realized that I felt quite happy. I was also very, very hungry.

I didn't get up right away, but lay there for a while thinking, trying to piece things together and wondering why I felt the way I did. I had no reason to be happy. In fact I had quite a few reasons to feel worried. I knew that Süleyman was going to start spreading gossip about me as soon as he got to work. He was going to tell everyone about finding me and Professor Wagner naked in bed together. I knew that he would exaggerate and add invented details, that he would tell the story in a way that would put me in the worst possible light. And I could just imagine how delighted those fat, miserable, sour-faced witches in the administration building would be to cackle to each other over this juicy item. On top of this, Wagner might be seriously ill, and I had those creepy security agents trying to intimidate me. Yet somehow, at that moment, none of it bothered me. I also thought about Kerem, and how cheerful he'd been. I hadn't seen him smile like that for a long, long time. What was happening to us?

I went to the kitchen, put on water for tea and took the *sucuk* out of the fridge. *Sucuk* is the classic spicy sausage that the migrating Turks brought from Central Asia and that was adopted throughout the Middle East and the Balkans. Originally made from horsemeat, it is now usually made from beef, though Christians in the Caucasus and the Balkans also use pork. Every region in Turkey has its own variation on the *sucuk*, and my favorite is the Kayseri version, which contains much more garlic than others, and allspice instead of the more common cumin. I sliced the *sucuk*, placing the slices in the frying pan over a low heat. There was no need to add any oil or butter, because the *sucuk*'s own fat would soon come oozing out.

Then I started making the tea in exactly the way my grandmother had taught me. As soon as the water had come to a boil I turned off the flame and waited. There is a nonsensical nursery rhyme I had to recite to myself; I think the time it takes to recite this is exactly the length of time the water has to cool. Then I would hold the kettle about a foot and a half above the teapot and pour the water into the teapot in a slow trickle. When I asked her why she did this she said it had to do with oxygenating the water, and for a long time I accepted this. I later learned that it had to do with bringing the water to exactly the right temperature to bring out the full aroma and flavor of the tea. Adding the water slowly, in a trickle, also allowed the tea to release its aromas more fully. I did all of this not simply because it made for better tea, but because the ritual made me feel connected to my grandmother, made me feel as if in a way she was still with me, and this always calmed me and gave me strength.

Then I broke the eggs over the *sucuk*. Not just any eggs, not supermarket eggs, but what they call village eggs. Of course I knew these eggs didn't come from any village. I knew exactly where they came from. I bought them from an old Bulgarian woman who sold them on the street corner. She raised chickens in the garden of her little house above Bebek, and whatever she fed them, or whatever else she did to make her chickens happy, they were the best eggs I'd ever been able to find in Istanbul. The yolks had such a deep, rich, golden color.

I filled two glasses with tea and put them on the table, and by now the kitchen was filled with the irresistible smell of frying eggs and *sucuk*. Then I took the frying pan and brought it into Kerem's bedroom.

I stood for a moment watching him sleep. He looked so innocent, so vulnerable, and I felt a wave of tenderness wash through me. Then he sniffed the air, opened his eyes, and sat up.

"What's going on?"

"I cooked breakfast. Go wash your face and hands and come to the table before it gets cold."

He smiled and jumped right out of bed, and right then I realized why I felt happy. Kerem and I had become close again. His moodiness, his depression, his distance and unavailability had all been a tremendous weight on me, perhaps even more than I'd realized. It had darkened every aspect of my life. I supposed that Professor Wagner had unwittingly brought us back together, and I was grateful to him for this and hoped that he was recovering.

At the table, Kerem cheerfully told me about his adventure the previous evening as he dug into his breakfast.

"They were completely thrown off because I wasn't scared of them at all. I just said, 'Oh, you must be the men my mother told me about, come on in.' They just looked at each other and then came in. The guy with the mustache asked if they could take a look around, and I asked if he had a search warrant. He asked how I knew about search warrants, and I just said what, you think I'm the only kid in the world who doesn't watch television? That got a laugh out of them. Then I said they could look around as much as they wanted, we didn't have anything to hide."

He paused to finish his sausage and eggs.

"Later they asked if the computer was yours or mine. I said it was mine and that at the moment I was using it to do some important research on the internet. He thought that was funny and was all, like, research, huh? What are you researching, kid? I said I was looking into the

German professors who came here during World War II, and particularly into Maximilian Wagner. This surprised him and he asked me how I knew about this stuff, and I just said you'd asked me to look into it. That was when your call came, and Uncle Necdet got here within a few minutes. They knew who he was right away and they were very intimidated by him. I really had a lot of fun with the whole thing."

As I looked at him, at his face and his eyes, it struck me how very much he looked like my grandmother.

"So, what did you find on the internet?"

"I don't know that much about the period so a lot of it doesn't make sense to me, but I printed a bunch of stuff and put it in a folder. You can look it over when you have time."

"Thanks. Meanwhile there's something else I'd like you to look up. A ship called Sutuuma or something like."

"I'll need more to go on than that."

"That's all I have. Except that the ship came from Romania."

"A ship from Romania. Sumuta?"

"I'm not sure, but I think it was Sutuuma."

He repeated the word to himself several times.

After I'd sent him off to school and cleaned the kitchen, I called Filiz to ask how Wagner was doing. The news wasn't good. She said he was in pretty bad shape, but they'd have to do some more tests before they could say anything definite.

I opened the window to air out the house a bit. It was still cold, but not nearly as cold as it had been the day before, and I wished the professor had picked today to go to Şile.

Then I put on my dark blue suit and a white silk blouse, put on my makeup, and got ready to face the world.

My first stop was the military base in Maslak. I told the guards at the gate that I was there to see Colonel Necdet Duran.

"Is he expecting you?" they asked.

"Yes," I said. "I'm his sister." They were respectful but still called to confirm, and then told me that someone would come to escort me to my brother's office. While I waited, I looked around at the carefully manicured lawns, spotless paths, and freshly painted buildings. A squad of soldiers marched past in step, and here and there officers walked briskly, their shoulders squared, their backs perfectly straight, their uniforms flawlessly starched and ironed, and their shoes highly polished. Everyone saluted everyone else they passed, but I didn't see one person smile.

The military in any country is a world of its own, but here it was particularly so. The officers lived a privileged life in their own gated compounds. They had their own supermarkets, where everything was much cheaper because it was subsidized and tax free; their own restaurants, nightclubs, and even hairdressers and barbers, all staffed by conscripts who were subject to the strictest discipline, and again, of course, all offered at very low prices. They also had their own summer resorts in the best locations all along the coast. These establishments were open only to officers and their families, and they tended to socialize only among themselves. Even the socializing was done according to military rules. There was a rotation of who was to entertain whom, officers wives were expected to take turns at inviting other wives to tea, and the order of service was determined by the husband's rank. A colonel's wife was always served her tea before a lieutenant's wife.

The officers were able to continue their education while they served, then retire in their early forties and start a new career in a firm that was run or owned by former officers. They were able to continue to use all the military facilities, and because all their friends and colleagues were former officers, they never really moved into the real world, but continued to live in an isolated world of privilege where they could continue to feel superior to everyone else.

In the early years of the Republic, one of the most important functions of the military was to indoctrinate conscripts with the ideology of the new regime. They could bring in young men from every corner of the country and teach them what it meant to be a modern, Republican Turk. They were taught how to behave and what to think and believe. For some young men, this even involved learning Turkish for the first time. Over time this led senior officers to come to think of themselves as the ultimate fount of Republican idealism. They felt they knew better than everyone else, and therefore they felt superior to everyone else. They also came to see themselves as the ultimate guardians of the Republic, with a duty to eliminate any threats to the regime. They regularly purged the officer corps of anyone whose political or religious leanings were suspect. And they also regularly staged coups whenever they felt the nation's politics was heading in the wrong direction.

Before long, a young officer appeared and very politely asked me to come with him. He led me to a building not far away, up to the second floor, and knocked twice on an office door. I heard my brother call "Come in," and the officer showed me in and closed the door behind me. My brother got up from behind his large mahogany desk and came over to me. He kissed me on the cheek and sat me down in one of the two chairs facing each other in front of his desk. He sat down opposite me. There were some fresh flowers in a small blue vase on the coffee table between us. I noticed that he had a silver-framed picture on his desk of himself with his wife and children. The office was unnaturally clean and well-ordered, as if here even inanimate objects were afraid to break military discipline.

My brother looked very dapper in his uniform.

As soon as I was seated a private entered and stood at attention.

"Bring the lady sweetened Turkish coffee. I won't have anything."

I was touched that after all these years he remembered how I drank my coffee.

"Thank you so much for helping me out yesterday, Necdet."

"How Kerem has grown," he said smiling faintly. "He's really filling out. He behaved with a lot of poise yesterday too."

"Who are those men, Necdet?"

"As you said, they're security agents."

"You mean from the National Intelligence Agency?"

"No!"

"Military intelligence?"

"No!"

"Well, where are they from then?"

"They're part of some kind of special unit."

"Well, what do they want from us?"

"They're interested in that German professor, not you."

"What do they want from him?"

"I can't tell you."

"He was in Istanbul fifty-nine years ago. Is it anything to do with that?"

"In a sense."

"Is it about some kind of crime?"

"You could say that."

"What kind of crime?"

"I can't say."

At that moment the private knocked on the door and brought in a tray with my coffee and a glass of water. The coffee, in an elegant white porcelain cup, had exactly the right amount of foam on top, and smelled delicious. There must, I thought, be a very strict military method of making coffee. Exactly so much coffee, exactly so much water heated to a specific temperature. No one was ever allowed to vary the method even in the slightest degree, but I had to admit that the coffee was perfect.

"Come on, Necdet, I have a right to know about something that's causing me so much trouble."

"It would be better if you forgot all about it and didn't see Professor Wagner again."

"All right, I promise I won't see him again if you just tell me what it's all about. Or is he a spy?"

"No!"

"Did he steal something?"

"No."

"Murder?"

He hesitated a moment, then said, "I suppose you could call it that."

"Necdet, is the professor a murderer?"

"No!"

"Well, what's the problem then?"

"Maya!"

He stood up, exasperated, paced around a bit, then went and stood behind his desk and put his hands on it.

"Maya, stop pressuring me! I can't tell you anything. I can only say that it's better for you and your son if you just walk away from this right now."

"OK, but one last question. Don't raise your eyebrows like that. If the professor isn't a murderer, then why are they interested in him?"

My brother thought for a while. He seemed to be considering how best to put what he was going to say. Finally he spoke in a hushed voice: "The worry is that the professor might stir up the past and bring a crime to light."

This confused me even more. If the professor was not guilty and, quite to the contrary, he was trying to bring an unsolved murder to light, then what could be wrong with that?

My brother came over to see me out. He held me by the shoulders—he was a head taller than I—and looked me in the eye.

"Now look Maya," he said. "There's one thing I want to make clear. I rushed to your help when you phoned in desperation yesterday evening. But please don't do it again. The boy has a father, talk to him. You're a grown woman, take care of your own son. We live in different worlds. Don't get me involved in this business."

"Aren't you my brother?"

"Yes, I'm your brother, but we live very different lives and have very different views of the world. Please, let's just stay away from each other."

The way he said this, almost hissing through his tight lips, and the cold look in his eyes hurt me even more than his words. This was not the Necdet I'd grown up with. It was as if his body had been taken over by some alien being.

It was clear that he was scared. I could feel the fear behind his anger and the way he looked at me. But this didn't give him the right to hurt me, and I gave in to the urge to hurt him back.

"Necdet," I said. "I have to tell you something. Those men know about our grandmother."

His jaw dropped.

"Are you serious?"

"Yes. They threatened me with it."

He swore under his breath and looked away for a moment, then turned back to me.

"OK then, goodbye Maya."

"Necdet, don't worry. They've probably known about it for years but it hasn't kept you from being promoted. That means no one has any doubt about your patriotism."

"Do you really think so?"

"Yes," I said. "I'm sure of it. Otherwise you wouldn't be in the position you're in now. They must know you're enough of a nationalist to say that your own grandmother has tainted blood."

"You still haven't forgotten that?"

"I haven't forgotten at all, Necdet," I said. "And I'm curious. Do you still think that way?"

"I can't worry about what happened before I was born. And what happened before the Republic is certainly not my problem. I'm a Turk and my duty is to defend this country."

"No offense, Necdet, but I'd rather you were the kind Turk who rescued our ancestors than the kind of Turk you are."

"Is that how you thank me?"

"I didn't mean to upset you, Necdet. It's better if we just never talk about this again. Thank you very much for everything you've done."

He looked at me anxiously to see whether I was making fun of him or not.

I put out my hand and touched his arm. I felt like drawing close to him. But the uniformed arm remained impassive.

"Necdet," I said. "I can't repay you for what you've done for me and Kerem. I thank you with all my heart. Please give my greetings to Oya and to the children."

He paused for a moment as if he didn't know what to do. He was upset that I'd reminded him about the tainted blood remark.

"If only you knew," he muttered between tight lips.

"What are you talking about, Necdet?" I said.

"You don't know anything. You follow the latest trend without thinking."

"Who, Kerem or me?"

"No, you and your friends."

"Which friends?"

"Your 'intellectual' friends."

"Necdet, I don't understand what you mean, who are these friends and what don't we know?"

He spoke with the weary expression on his face of people who are continually explaining the same thing.

"You go on and on about the Armenian question without realizing whose game you're playing."

"Necdet, I'm just talking about my grandmother."

"Well, why don't you talk about your maternal grandmother?"

"What's that got to do with it?"

"It's got everything to do with it, but it doesn't suit you."

At that I lost my patience.

"Necdet, please, stop talking in riddles! What happened to my grandmother, what don't I know? Come on, tell me what happened? Why are you so angry?"

The vein in his temple was throbbing and his jaw was clenched.

"All right then, come back in and sit down," he said. He took my shoulders, propelled me toward the chair I'd just left, and sat me firmly down. Then he sat and leaned back in his chair.

"The thing that you don't know," he said, "Is this country's recent history, what happened in the past, what happened to us…"

"Then tell me, I'm all ears!"

"People are always talking about the Armenians as if they're the only ones who suffered in this country, as if they're the only ones who were killed."

"I'm only talking about grandma. I don't have anything to do with any trend..."

I shut up when I saw the impatient expression cross his face. After all there wouldn't be any point in what I was going to say.

"Why do you ignore the suffering of the Balkan Turks, the Anatolian Turks, the millions of people who died or were driven from their homes? When the Western powers were breaking up the Ottoman Empire, everyone in this country suffered. Armenians, Greeks, Jews, I agree, but no one talks about the five million Ottoman Muslims who also died. Isn't that unjust?"

"All right, I hear what you're saying," I said. "But that doesn't mean I can't remember my grandmother."

"But it prevents you from remembering your maternal grandmother!"

"Why should it?" I said. "And besides, what happened to my maternal grandmother?"

We hadn't had the chance to see very much of my grandmother Ayşe because she lived quite far away, in Antakya. We saw her only once every couple of years during our summer vacation. I remember her as a warm-hearted woman who didn't speak much and had an air of sadness about her. My grandfather Ali was like that too. They were like kind and generous strangers who treated us very well. I remember that she had very fair skin and a broad, almost Asiatic face, and that he was a taciturn man with a dark complexion and sunken cheeks who smoked one cigarette after another.

Their house was only a few miles from the Syrian border; it was always much hotter there than it was in Istanbul, and the food my grandmother made was much too spicy for me. Except for one dish called *oruk*, which was made from cracked wheat and ground beef. It was delicious, and it was one of the few things she made that I could eat, so she made it for me all the time. The garden was full of pomegranate trees, and my grandmother used to squeeze pomegranate juice for us. I remember one day my grandfather picked a pomegranate that weighed almost a kilo, and maybe I remember it because it was one of the few times I ever saw him express pure joy. When we left, our car would be loaded down with jams and pepper paste and pomegranate juice, and jars of very hot red pepper.

"Or was our mother's mother Armenian too?" I asked.

"No," said my brother. "She was a Crimean Turk. And our grandfather was, as you know, from Antakya."

"Well, what is their story?"

"I'll tell you," he said. I never thought that what he was about to tell me would shock me so much. As I listened to my brother I realized once again that I'd never really known the people I thought I knew. What a strange country this was, every household had a secret, a story.

My grandmother had been born and raised in the Crimea, and was an adolescent at the outbreak of World War II. The Crimean Turks were one of a number of groups that had been severely oppressed by Stalin. Thousands of them were killed during the collectivization, the intellectuals were all arrested and executed, and thousands died of starvation when their food was confiscated. By the time the war started, half of their population had either died or been deported to Central Asia. So when the Germans invaded Russia the Turkish government persuaded them to fight on the German side. Even though Turkey was neutral, the government was terrified Russia would invade and did what they could to support the Germans against them. So they helped organize the Crimean Turks into what was called the Tatar Legions that fought under German command. Many of them had actually been conscripted into the Red Army and had been captured by the Germans. They were in prison camps and really had no choice but to do what the Germans told them. But when the tide turned and the Germans began to retreat they had no choice but to flee their homeland with their families. The Soviet NKVD sent special units to arrest and execute any Crimean Turks who were suspected of collaborating. Entire villages were being rounded up and sent to Siberia. So they left with the German army and were settled in northern Italy.

"So our grandmother was with them?"

"Of course, I'm telling you her story. When she was a young girl she and her family fled with thousands of Crimean Turks in fear that they would be massacred as soon as the Red Army arrived.

"When the Allied forces entered Italy they had to move again, and were settled in the region of Ober Drauburg near the River Drava in Austria. But their troubles didn't end there. When the British army entered Austria they were taken prisoner and this time transported to the Dellach camp. They thought that as British prisoners they'd be safe and that they might be allowed to go to Turkey and start new lives there, but unfortunately it didn't work out that way.

"In 1945 the camp commander received orders from London that all the inmates were to be sent to the Soviet Union. The British were going to hand them over even though they knew it meant they would be shot. The Crimean Turks pleaded and begged, but to no avail. Then, when they realized that there was no escape, that there was nothing they could do, three thousand of them decided to commit suicide rather than be sent back. They all jumped into the icy river, the women first, holding their children by the hand, and then the men. The remaining four thousand were loaded into cattle cars, the doors were nailed shut and the train was sent on its way."

"You mean, our grandmother was among them."

"Yes, in the train with her mother and father. Several of her relatives had died after jumping into the river.

But they had reason to hope. They'd heard that because all the rail lines and rail bridges into Eastern Europe had been destroyed, they were going to be sent through the Balkans to Turkey, and then through Turkey to the Soviet Union. Conditions on the train were inhuman; there was no ventilation and little to eat or drink. It took days to reach Turkey, but as they neared the border their spirits rose. They were sure that the Turkish government would take pity on them. That they'd let them free, or turn a blind eye and let them escape. After all, the Turkish government had encouraged them to fight the Red Army. But no, the Turkish soldiers assigned to guard the train wouldn't even allow them to open the doors to get some air.

"Over the next few days, conditions on the train deteriorated and people were starting to die. They begged the soldiers to help them, to at least let the most ill go free. The soldiers were sympathetic but they were under strict orders and there was nothing they could do.

"Our grandmother didn't give up on trying to convince the soldiers to help them. She focused on one soldier named Ali who seemed to be the most sympathetic."

"Would that soldier be our grandfather Ali?"

"Let me tell the story. As they neared the Soviet border they began begging the soldiers to at least shoot them rather than let them be shot by the Russians. Then, one winter morning, they reached the border crossing next to the Kızılçakçak reservoir. The Turkish soldiers got off, and the train began moving across to the Soviet side, where Russian soldiers stood waiting. At the last moment, the people in one of the carriages managed to break open the door, escape, and jump into the reservoir. The Soviet soldiers stopped the train as soon as it was on their territory, opened the doors, herded everyone out, and then lined them up and shot them right then and there, within sight of the Turkish soldiers who'd been guarding them. As for the people who jumped into the lake, they all drowned. And that was the end of the Tatar Legions and their families."

"But what about our grandmother?"

"Well, this is the interesting part. Our grandmother was one of the people who jumped into the lake, but a soldier dove in after her and rescued her."

"You mean our grandfather!"

"Yes. Ali from Antakya. He rescued a young girl, brought her to Antakya and married her, taking out a false identity card for her in the name of Ayşe."

"Why a false one?"

"Because if the government had found any survivors they would have sent them to the Soviet Union."

"Necdet, is this all really true?"

"Yes, unfortunately every word of it is true."

"And what happened to her mother and father?"

"They were shot at the border."

"That means both of our grandmothers concealed their true identities. So many secrets in one family. It's hard to believe."

"That's exactly the point. Just about every family in Turkey has secrets like these. A lot of people aren't even aware of their family secrets. When the Empire collapsed people fled here from the Balkans, the Caucasus, North Africa, and the Middle East, and there were also soldiers fighting on nine different fronts. It was inevitable that millions of families would be affected."

"Well, but we call them all Turks."

"We don't use the term solely in reference to the Turks from Central Asia, we also use it for all the people who fled here because nowhere else was safe. It refers to all the people who came together to build a new nation and a new life."

"But don't you think that the Crimean Turks were betrayed by our government. Just as the Armenians were betrayed?"

"Well, yes, but I'm a soldier, it's my duty to serve and protect the state, not to question it. Both the Crimean Turks and the Armenians made the mistake of siding with an invading army, and they paid the consequences for that."

"But what about the women and children?"

"Maya..."

"Yes, you're right, there's no point in us arguing about this."

As the young officer waiting at the door took me back to the main gate I was still reeling from what I'd heard, but I was thinking more about the file I'd seen on my brother's desk. It was a yellow, official file, marked TOP SECRET, with MAXIMILIAN WAGNER written underneath.

CHAPTER 8

I got a taxi right away, but even though the traffic wasn't at its worst, it took me an hour to get to the hospital. The sky was overcast and threatening more rain or sleet or snow, and as we drove along to the sounds of arabesque music from the driver's radio, I kept worrying about what kind of reception I was going to face when I got to the university. How much had the gossip been exaggerated and twisted as it passed from person to person, and how many people had heard by now? I was also still digesting the story I'd heard about my mother's mother, and wondering what it was about Wagner that had everyone so worked up.

The hospital was, as always, very crowded. Throngs of worried, desperate relatives, sick children, frail old men and women, victims of accidents and fights, people in pain waiting hours to be treated. Everyone looked poor and desperate and unhealthy. That is, it wasn't only the patients who looked unhealthy, but the friends and relatives who'd brought them as well. These were the people who been forgotten, betrayed and left behind by the system. Anyone who could afford private insurance went to one of the sparkling fancy new hospitals that had sprung up in recent years. It was only the poorest who had to come to crowded, grimy, dilapidated public hospitals like this. The doctors and the staff were dedicated and talented and did the best they could, but they were fighting a losing battle with ever-diminishing resources and an ever-increasing patient load. The paint was peeling and there were patches of damp on the walls and ceilings. The equipment was antiquated and supplies and medications were in short supply. And it didn't look nearly as clean as a hospital should.

These, I thought as I looked around, were the people the politicians claimed to care about and represent whenever there was an election. But as soon as the politicians came to power they immediately went about filling their own pockets and enriching their friends. Even the so-called religious parties were no different. They'd spend a fortune to repave roads in wealthy neighborhoods, but the hospital wouldn't even get a new coat of paint.

I took the elevator up to the third floor and told the nurse behind the desk that I was there to see Filiz. She paged Filiz, who, within a few minutes, came clicking down the hallway in her high heels. She kissed me on both cheeks then brought me to her office and offered me tea.

"So," I asked, "How is he today?"

"He's doing quite well. He was able to eat breakfast this morning. His respiration, pulse and blood pressure are back to normal, but he still has a bit of a fever. We're still waiting for the results of his chest x-rays."

"Good, I'm very glad to hear that."

And indeed I was genuinely glad. I'd grown fond of the man.

"He's been asking for you all morning," said Filiz with a mischievous smile, "He's very anxious to see you. How did you bewitch the man in such a short time? If he were a little younger, I'd say..."

"For God's sake Filiz, don't talk nonsense," I said. "Can I see him?"

"But you haven't finished your tea..."

"I don't want any more."

As we walked down the corridor she tried to get me to tell her more about Wagner. I just told her that he was the rector's guest and that I'd been assigned to show him around. She gave me a look that said she thought I was being evasive. I insisted that this was all I knew, and in fact that was the truth. Well, not quite. I did know a bit more than that, and perhaps I was being evasive, but I really didn't know why.

As we made our way down the corridor, I was struck by Filiz's confidence. Even the way she walked exuded self-assurance and control. We'd been friends for years, but I usually met her in different settings where she was just an ordinary person. But here, where everyone was feeling anxious and out of place, she was part of a small elite. She was one of the people with answers, one of the people whose knowledge was sought, one of the people who could give orders that would be obeyed immediately.

He was in a small, dingy room with three other men. He was in the bed nearest the window, in a hospital gown with a drip attached to his arm. He looked pale and his hair was tousled, but his face lit up when he saw me.

"Ah, it's you. I was worried I'd never see you again."

I smiled.

"Why, professor?"

"I thought you might be angry with me after all that trouble I caused you yesterday."

"No, professor, I wasn't angry, but I was a bit annoyed because I didn't understand what was going on."

Filiz left and I pulled a chair up next to the bed.

"How are you feeling, professor?"

He smiled but his voice was a bit weak.

"Fine, not bad. I slept through the night."

"You slept through the day too."

He continued sheepishly. "Yes, I vaguely remember. In that motel room, wasn't it? When I woke up I was half naked."

"Yes."

"Did I ask you if it was you who had undressed me?"

"You asked me and I said yes I had."

"I apologize."

"There's nothing to apologize for, professor. If I'd left you in that state you would have died."

"Most probably... You saved my life."

After that there was silence. The room was filled with that awkward silence between two people who don't know what to say to each other. I realized that we were avoiding each other's eyes. Whenever our eyes met, one of us looked away.

I wriggled in my seat. "I'll leave you in peace. I'll come back and see you later."

"All right, thank you again. Can I ask you something?"

"Yes, professor?"

"Where's my violin?"

I paused as I tried to remember.

"I picked it up on the beach, I was holding it as we dragged you to the car. No, you were holding it. I remember that you refused to let go of it. It must be in the car."

"It would mean a lot to me if you could find it."

"Don't worry."

I walked over to the door and was just about to open it and go out when I heard him say, "A strange thing happened yesterday."

I turned and looked at him.

"In my sleep I thought it was Nadia beside me. She put her arms around me. I could feel her as if she were alive, I could even smell her and feel her kiss my shoulder."

He turned and looked out the window.

"It was as if all those years hadn't passed, as if we were young again."

"Who is Nadia?"

He turned and looked at me for a moment, and then said, "I'll tell you later. You deserve to know."

After I left him I looked around for Filiz, and when I couldn't find her I walked for a while in the garden. It was unsettling to have been mistaken for Nadia, for a woman I'd never met. It was also unsettling to think about having embraced a stranger's naked body.

I'd only been to bed with two men so far: my husband Ahmet and Tarık. Wagner had been the third, and this experience had given me an odd sense of peace, a peace that had nothing whatsoever to do with sex. The feel of his body next to mine had woken a deep tenderness within me. What Süleyman had found obscene had been perhaps the most genuine moment of decency I'd ever experienced. I wouldn't have thought it possible to lie still with my arms around someone for so many hours, but yesterday I hadn't been aware of the passage of time at all. I also have to confess that at one point I began to kiss him on the shoulder.

It had been completely different with the other two men I'd been to bed with. With them, there'd been sex, but not this tenderness and peace. With them it had been almost the opposite of intimacy. I'd been physically joined to another person but at the same time felt completely alone. Nor, I have to say, did I experience much physical pleasure.

I left the hospital grounds and caught a taxi on the main street. It was killing me to pay as much as I was for taxis, but what could I do? I was also feeling stressed because I'd lost half a day and was going to have to spend the afternoon rushing to catch up.

No one I passed on my way up the stairs and down the corridor to my office treated me any differently than usual. Hasan the tea man, Suat Tunç the assistant rector, and Professor Suna Kalaycı all gave me friendly greetings. I glanced at the pile that had accumulated in my in-box, then picked up the phone and called the rector's secretary to ask if I could get in to see him. Even that grumpy old bitch was pleasant and helpful. I sensed none of the scorn I'd expected from her, and she even smiled when I passed her on my way into his office. So it seemed Süleyman hadn't told anyone. Yet somehow rather than making me feel relieved this worried me. I had the sneaking suspicion that he was going to try to use what he knew to his advantage.

The rector was on the phone, and waved for me to sit down. He turned to me when he'd hung up.

"How's it going?" he asked.

"I'm afraid Professor Wagner got sick and I had to put him in Çapa Hospital."

"What's the matter!? What happened?"

"It's nothing serious. He just got a severe chill. I thought that because of his age it was better to be cautious."

"Oh, good! How is he now?"

"He's fine. But I'm not sure when they're going to discharge him. We might have to change his plane ticket."

"Oh, that's no problem, we can take care of that. The important thing is that he get the rest and care he needs."

"There's something I need to say, but..."

"Go ahead."

"For the past few days I've had to do a lot of running around for the professor, and I've had to take a lot of taxis."

"I understand. Süleyman took the Mercedes to the mechanic. This time it needs some major repairs. Tell the general secretary to assign you another car."

"Thank you."

Just as I was going out the door he called me back

"Wait a minute, there's something else I almost forgot."

"Yes?"

I walked back to his desk.

"I've been invited to a reception at the British consulate this evening but I'm not going to be able to make it. I'd like you to go in my place."

"Wouldn't it be more appropriate for one of the assistant rectors to go?"

"You're right, but when I told them I couldn't come they asked for you."

"Me?"

"Yes you, and by name."

"There must be some mistake."

"No mistake," he said, and handed me an envelope. "It says formal attire."

Back in my office I opened the thick envelope that had been addressed in an elegant hand. Below the royal coat of arms was a gracious invitation to attend a reception that evening at 7:30. RSVP and black tie and evening gown. I was flabbergasted. I'd never been invited to anything like this, and I had no idea why I was being invited now. I was pleased, and at the same time terrified. I wouldn't know anyone there, and I had no idea how you were supposed to behave at this kind of thing. But why would they invite a lowly clerk like me, and me specifically? And was I going to be resented for this by the people who were usually expected to stand in for the rector?

I looked at my watch. It was already after three, and I had to get moving. I went to the general secretary and told him the rector had authorized a car for Professor Wagner. He grinned and ogled my breasts. A lot of men do this on the sly, but this man enjoyed making it obvious that he was looking. I ignored him.

Ten minutes later I was climbing into the back seat of a navy blue Ford Focus. The driver was a polite young man called Ilyas who'd driven me once or twice before. I told him to take me home, and we made fairly good time because the rush hour hadn't started yet. But just as we were nearing my street I changed my mind and gave him another address to go to.

Mehmet the hairdresser expressed surprise and pleasure to see me during office hours. I'd been going to him for years and we'd developed a nice, comfortable relationship. I knew what he could do and he knew what I liked, so we didn't have to waste time discussing, and I was never disappointed. He was also a genuinely good-hearted person, one of the very few I knew.

"I'm in a terrible hurry. I'm going to a reception at the British consulate this evening."

"In that case let's put your hair up, Maya!"

"Do whatever you like," I said. "I have every confidence in your taste."

The hairdresser's was full of women having their hair colored, having manicures, pedicures, and waxing. I seemed to be the only woman with black hair. One the assistants turned my chair around, gently pushed my head back, and washed my hair in a small basin.

Later, while I was having my hair done and sipping my coffee, I called Filiz at the hospital and learned that the professor's condition was improving. They would keep him one more day for observation and would probably discharge him the following day.

Mehmet created a wonderful chignon, but I wasn't used to wearing my hair up and felt naked with my neck exposed like that.

"The necklace will do the trick."

It was getting dark as I left, and the street was filled with people doing their evening shopping. I bought some cheese pastries from the patisserie on the corner, and then, feeling like a rich woman, sauntered to my chauffeur-driven car.

When I got home I found Kerem at his computer, but he didn't have his usual air of gloom. When he heard me come into his room he looked up and smiled.

"You'll never believe what I've found."

His printer was churning out paper and there was already quite a pile.

"Look," he exclaimed. "Did you know that Einstein wrote a letter to Atatürk?"

"No, I didn't. But what has this got to do with us?"

"Not with us but it does have something to do with Maximilian Wagner."

I promised that I would read it all when I came back in the evening, and then I put the pastries on a plate and went into the shower, taking care not to get my hair wet. Then I went into the bedroom and put on the black dress I'd worn two days ago when I'd had dinner with Wagner. I put on my makeup and then took my grandmother's necklace out of the safe and put it round my neck. When I looked in the mirror, I was very pleased by what I saw.

When Kerem told me how good I looked, which was something he never did, I felt even more pleased.

"You look just like a model in one of those magazines."

"Don't do any more research," I said. "You've given me more than enough to read for the time being. Why don't you watch television or something?"

He rubbed his eyes, and it was clear that he was very tired. Indeed, he seemed happy to have an excuse to get away from the computer. But before he turned off his computer he wanted to show me some of the printouts he'd kept separate from the others.

"Look, this is what I found out about that ship."

The first page was headed:

"Confidential GENERAL DIRECTORATE OF SECURITY, MINISTRY OF THE INTERIOR Number: 55912-S /13 September, 1941"

"What's this? Is it about that Romanian ship? The Sutuuma?"

A smile of pride spread over his face.

I was curious and wanted to read it right away, but I didn't have time, so I put it in the bedroom and, once again feeling like a rich woman, went and got into the chauffeur-driven car that was waiting for me.

The British consulate, which is very near the Pera Palas, is a large, imposing building, a palace really, built as an embassy when Istanbul was the capital of the Ottoman Empire. I held out my invitation to the guard at the consulate gate and he respectfully opened the gate. I climbed the marble steps and entered a large hall lit by chandeliers, where a valet dressed in black took my coat and led me upstairs.

The hall was quite crowded. The consul and his wife were standing at the entrance greeting guests as they entered, shaking hands and exchanging a few words of banter. Some, clearly, were old acquaintances, but they were no less gracious to those they didn't know. When I gave him my name he smiled, but when it was clear he had no idea who I was, I added that I was from Istanbul University. He shook my hand vigorously, turned to his wife to say, "The professor is from Istanbul University," and she smiled warmly and shook my hand as well. I didn't think it the right moment to correct them and say that I wasn't a professor, so I just smiled.

Everyone, the men dressed in dinner jackets and the women very elegantly turned out, stood chatting in small groups while waiters circulated with trays of drinks and hors d'oeuvres. I took a glass of red wine and a little meat ball with a toothpick in it, and as I ate the meatball I realized I was very hungry. I hadn't eaten since the eggs and sausage this morning, so I began taking something from each of the trays of hors d'oeuvres that passed within my reach.

I was contemplating a large tapestry on the wall when the consul called for everyone's attention and made a short speech. When he'd finished everyone applauded, and more food and drinks were served. I wandered around, and once or twice approached one of the groups and tried to join in, but it was as if I were invisible. So I grabbed a glass of champagne and took an interest in the paintings and tapestries on the wall. As I was contemplating a large and dramatic painting of a naval battle, I became aware that someone was standing behind me looking at the painting over my shoulder. I turned and saw a tall, slim Englishman with horn-rimmed glasses.

"Are you bored?" he asked.

"No, it's all very lovely."

"You don't seem to know many people here."

"In fact I don't know anyone here."

He smiled politely.

"But I know who you are."

"You mean that you know I'm from the university."

"No, I mean I know who you are."

I smiled.

"Well then, in that case what's my name?"

"Mrs. Maya Duran," he said, bowing slightly.

"How do you know who I am?"

"Haven't you noticed that a lot of people seem to know who you are lately?"

"What do you mean by that?"

"May I offer you another glass of champagne?"

He took my empty glass and signaled to one of the waiters to bring me another. As soon as I'd taken my glass he lifted his.

"To the famous Maya Duran."

"Who are you?"

"Forgive me. I'm the consular attaché, Matthew Brown."

He took a card from his jacket and presented it to me with a flourish.

"I'm not a professor," I confessed.

"I know."

"I'm not the rector's assistant either. I'm a simple clerk."

"I know."

"Then why did you invite me to this party?"

"Because I wanted to talk to you."

"About what?"

"About Professor Maximilian Wagner."

"What do you want to know about Wagner?"

"What he's been up to, why he came to Istanbul."

"Why should I tell you?"

"Of course, you don't have to tell me anything. We are just having a friendly chat."

"He used to teach at the university and he came back for a visit. The rector invited him to give a talk while he was here. That's about it."

He lifted his eyebrows for an instant and lowered them.

"That's not all," he said.

"That's all. At least that's all I know."

"In that case what were you doing in Şile yesterday?"

"Now I'm going to ask you something. Why is this man so important?"

He became serious and looked at me thoughtfully.

"It's better if you don't know," he answered.

He said it so firmly that I understood I wasn't going to get anything more out of him.

My head was aching and I was in a daze from all these questions.

"If you'll excuse me, I have to go. Good evening."

"I'll see you to the door," he said.

We passed through the noisy crowd and went downstairs. A valet brought my coat and Mr. Brown kindly helped me put it on. Then he saw me to the car.

Before I got in he said, "Mrs. Duran, if you tell us what this man is up to, you'll be doing the British government a favor that we won't forget."

When I didn't answer he said, "You know that a friend in need is a friend indeed. You have my card. Please call me."

He helped me into the car, gently closed the door, and bade me farewell.

As we drove off down the lively, brightly lit streets of Istanbul, I unpinned my hair, took off my high heels, opened the window, and let the wind blow on my face. I had no idea what was going on, what I was involved in, and why so many people were suddenly interested in me, and I was becoming increasingly uneasy. I was alone and had no one to turn to. I couldn't trust my brother, my ex-husband, or the rector and there were no friends I could rely on. My only ally was a young boy surfing the internet.

As we passed the Pera Palas Hotel I realized that I wanted to confront Wagner and get him to tell me what it was all about, but he was still in the hospital. I must have been frowning because Ilyas asked me if I was all right.

"It's nothing, Ilyas. I've just got a bit of a headache."

"If you like I can find a pharmacy that's open."

"Thanks, I've got some aspirin at home. Thank you, Ilyas, you're very thoughtful."

"Thank you."

When I entered the house, I took off my shoes and picked them up. Kerem was still at the computer.

"I keep finding more and more stuff."

"We're not writing a book, all we need to know is who Wagner is."

"Where is he now?"

"He's in the hospital now, but they're letting him out tomorrow."

"When is he going back to America?"

"Probably in a few days. Why?"

"I want to ask you for something."

"In return for all your research?"

"No, but I've spent so much time on this man I want to meet him before he leaves."

"Why?"

"Well, I've never met anyone that important."

"Important in what way?"

"He has to be important if he has all these spies after him."

In the kitchen I took two Alka-Seltzer from the cupboard, dropped them into a glass of water, and watched them fizz. If I'd had a migraine I would have taken Relplax, but I knew the difference between a regular headache and one that would turn into a migraine.

Then I took a hot shower and held my neck under piping-hot water for a long time. I also washed my hair; I decided I didn't want to keep the chignon.

In the shower, as I thought about Matthew Brown and wondered why he was interested in Wagner, I found myself whistling, and was surprised to realize I was whistling the introduction to the lyrical serenade Wagner had been playing on the beach. He'd played it over and over again so many times it had imprinted itself in my mind. Then I stopped whistling at the same point where he'd stopped, again and again. He'd never managed to get beyond that point.

I took Kerem's printouts and said good night to him. Then, as I lay in bed reading them I found myself becoming completely absorbed.

My neck is stiff from writing for so long, or rather from copying and pasting, collating, and working on what I've already written. My right side is beginning to ache. I need to get up and move around a bit. We must be about halfway across the Atlantic by now, and I'm anxious to finish by the time we reach Boston. Most of the rest of the story is already in place, I just have to pull it together and fill in some details, so it shouldn't be too difficult. But my laptop's battery is running low and I have to figure out what to do about this.

I go over to the flight attendant sitting in the front and start a conversation with her. I ask her how long they stay in America, when they make the return journey, how they cope with jet lag. She must be bored, as she's happy to answer.

They usually lay over for three days after a transatlantic flight. Another team flies the plane back. Jet lag tends to be worse flying back to Europe than flying out to America. Some pilots and crew use melatonin to regulate their sleep, but she, Renata, prefers not to. In the meantime, was there anything I'd like? She could get me a plate of chilled fruit if I wanted. By the way, was I a writer? She'd noticed I'd been writing since the plane took off.

I tell her that I'm writing about one of the German professors who immigrated to Turkey during World War II. She says she's never heard about anything like that, and I smile and say that few people have. Then I thank her, say that a plate of fruit would be wonderful, and ask her if it would be possible for her to charge my laptop.

"Of course," she says.

We go back to my seat together, I give her my laptop and she takes it back to her station and plugs it in. Now I'll eat the fruit and get a little sleep while the battery is recharging. Thanks Renata.

CHAPTER 9

Your Excellency,

As Honorary President of the World Union "OSE" I beg to apply to Your Excellency to allow forty professors and doctors from Germany to continue their scientific and medical work in Turkey. The above mentioned cannot practice further in Germany on account of the laws governing there now. The majority of these men possess vast experience, knowledge, and scientific merits and could prove very useful when settling in a new country.

Out of a great number of applicants our Union has chosen forty experienced specialists and prominent scholars, and is herewith applying to Your Excellency to permit these men to settle and practice in your country. These scientists are willing to work for a year without any remuneration in any of your institutions, according to the orders of your Government.

In supporting this application, I take the liberty

to express my hope that in granting this request your Government will not only perform an act of high humanity, but will also bring profit to your own country.

I have the honor to be,

Your Excellency's obedient servant,
Prof. Albert Einstein

Kerem's notes at the bottom of the page said that this letter, signed by Einstein, had been written on 17 September 1933, and sent to the prime minister of the Turkish Republic. I was curious about what OSE stood for, so I turned on my laptop and did a search on the internet.

What I learned was that the OSE was an international organization to aid Jews. It had originally been founded in Russia as a charitable society and later, when it was headquartered in Paris, it had become active in helping Jews living under the Nazi regime. I also learned that Albert Einstein had served as honorary president.

A lot of Turkish websites had articles about "Einstein's letter to Atatürk," but I learned that the letter had been addressed not to Atatürk, who was president of Turkey, but to the prime minister, and that it had probably not been written by Einstein himself, who had already left for the United States by that date. It seems he had signed a number of blank pages before he left.

There were notations in Turkish on the letter indicating that it had been received and read by the prime minister and then passed on to the minister of education. After consulting with the minister of education, the prime minister decided to turn down the request and sent the following letter dated 14 November 1933:

Distinguished Professor,

I have received your letter dated 17 September 1933 requesting acceptance by Turkey of 40 professors and physicians who cannot conduct their scientific and medical work in Germany anymore under the laws governing Germany now.

I have also taken note that these gentlemen will accept working without remuneration for a year in our establishments under our government.

Although I accept that your proposal is very attractive, I regret to inform you that I see no possibility of rendering it compatible with the laws and regulations of our country.

Distinguished Professor, as you know, we now have more than 40 professors and physicians under contract in our employ. Most of them find themselves under the same political conditions while having similar qualifications and capacities. These professors and doctors have accepted to work here under the current laws and regulations in power.

At present, we are trying to found a very delicate organism with members of very different origins, cultures, and languages. Therefore I regret to say that

it would be impossible to employ more personnel from
among these gentlemen under the current conditions
we find ourselves in.

    Distinguished Professor, I express my distress for
being unable to fulfill your request and request that
you believe in my best sentiments.

However, Atatürk took a personal interest in the matter and intervened, believing that these professors could make a valuable contribution to Turkey's modernization. Indeed, Turkey ended up accepting a total of 190 professors, first from Germany, then from Austria after the *Anschluss* of 1938, and then from Prague after the 1939 Nazi invasion.

When the first group of scholars arrived, Atatürk invited them to a banquet given in honor of the Shah of Iran at Dolmabahçe Palace, and welcomed each of them individually. Professor Alfred Kantorowicz even treated the Shah's teeth, and the ophthalmologist Joseph Igersheimer wrote him a prescription for a new pair of glasses.

I drifted off to sleep thinking about these people who had been uprooted, forced to live different lives—like my grandmothers—and that these were the lucky ones, because so many others had had their lives snuffed out. For what?

CHAPTER 10

I woke the next morning with the papers spread all over the bed and my laptop still on beside me. All these things that I hadn't known a few days ago had taken over my life. Wagner, the Sutuuma, Nadia, spies...

I thought about the white Renault. I hadn't seen those three men for a while. Had they decided to stop following me? Had my brother warned them off me? Perhaps he'd taken over the case. Could he be having me watched now?

I'd seen Wagner's file on his desk. Had he just received it or had he been involved from the beginning? But when I'd called from Şile he'd acted as if he didn't know anything. Indeed, he'd seemed surprised.

Whatever the truth was, I still had to get on with my daily life. Get Kerem out of bed and give him breakfast, get dressed, and get myself to work.

I didn't have the strength to make an elaborate breakfast. I was feeling lethargic and my joints were aching, and I would have liked to stay home and watch television or read all day. So instead of eggs and sausage we had corn flakes.

Kerem never paid much attention to the time in the morning because I always pestered him to be on time for the school bus. He didn't have to think about it because he knew I'd make sure he was on time. But that morning he was surprised because I didn't say anything at all.

He was dawdling over his breakfast, but after a while he noticed something was wrong and looked at his watch. Then he looked pointedly at me, but I didn't pay any attention and continued reading my newspaper. He seemed worried, but didn't say anything.

Then after looking at his watch again, he asked, "What day is it today?"

Without lifting my head from the newspaper I said, "Friday."

Then after a moment, and without looking up, I asked, "What's the matter?"

"I mean it's not the weekend. There's school."

"Yes," I said, absentmindedly and turned a page of the paper.

He waited me out as long as he could, then got up and said, "What's the matter with you? I'm going to miss the school bus. There's two minutes to go."

"Is that so," I said. "I had no idea."

He ran to the hall and began to put on his coat. He tried to behave like an angry man and the more he did, the more childish he seemed. I went over to him and laughed.

"No need to hurry. I'm taking you to school today."

"You?"

"Yes," I went and looked out the window. Ilyas was already there. I called Kerem over and showed him the Ford Focus waiting outside the front door. Ilyas was leaning against the car smoking a cigarette.

"There," I said. "That's our car and that's our driver."

"Shit!" he said, then immediately put his hand over his mouth.

"Am I going to go to school in a chauffeur-driven car like the rich kids?"

"Yes."

"Why did the university give you a car? Is it because of Wagner?"

"Yes."

"I'm beginning to like this man more and more."

I had one more surprise for him but I wasn't going to tell him yet. We went out and got into the car. Ilyas opened the door for me. Kerem sat on my left, and glanced out the window to see if any of the neighbors were watching. He was enjoying this. As we approached the school he began to smile, and I took advantage of the situation to kiss him on the cheek before he got out of the car.

As soon as I got to my office, I settled down to deal with all the work that had piled up in the past few days.

Then, at lunchtime, I went to the faculty dining room. Not because I was hungry, but to see Nermin, a friend who worked in the archives and always ate lunch in the faculty dining room. I found her at her usual table, and when she saw me she looked up and smiled.

"Maya! I haven't seen you for ages."

We made small talk over lunch, and then at one point I told her I needed to find some information on a guest I was showing around.

"Professor Wagner?" she asked.

"Yes," I replied.

"Of course," she said. "We have a separate section about foreign professors who've worked at our university. Come and have a look whenever you like."

"May I come after lunch?" I asked.

She could only nod and blink because her mouth was full.

Half an hour later I was in the archive library, where Nermin told me they were in the process of entering hundreds of thousands of files into the computer system.

"Have the files on the foreign professors been entered yet?"

"No, unfortunately we haven't got to them yet. You just wouldn't believe how many documents there are."

She led me down an aisle through walls of documents.

"Here you are," she said. "Everything you're looking for will be here. I'm sorry but I'll have to let you get on with this by yourself. I'm swamped."

I was only too happy to be left alone. I began to read the names of the files. Ernst Reuter, Fritz Neumark, Paul Hindemith, Alfred Braun, Ruth Sello, Robert Anhegger, Maximilian Ruben, Ernst Praetorius, Rudolf Belling, Carl Ebert, Margarete Schütte-Lihotzky, Julius Stern, Bruno Taut, Hans Bodlaender, Eduard Zuckmayer, George Tabori, Alfred Joachim Fischer, Clemens Holzmeister, Martin Wagner, Gustav Oelsner, Erna Eckstein, and Ernst Engelberg... The list went on and on. Most of these professors had stayed in Istanbul, though a few had gone to Ankara.

I found the following in one of the files.

The professors who fled to Turkey from Nazi Germany formed the backbone of Istanbul University. The University Reform drawn up by the Swiss medical professor Albert Malche was implemented in 1933. The university's Ottoman name, Darülfünün, was changed to Istanbul University.

The new Turkish Republic was ten years old, and the regime's effort to westernize relied on German scholars in such disciplines as law and medicine to compile libraries, codify teaching methods, and train archaeologists. There were also professors of botany, geology, chemistry, and biochemistry. The professors would be allowed to lecture through interpreters for the first three years, after which they would be expected to lecture in Turkish. The German professors were to be paid a salary five times higher than that of their Turkish colleagues.

Despite earning a relatively high salary, many of these professors had difficulty adjusting. Some had difficulty learning Turkish and dealing with their own cultural prejudices. Many of their Turkish colleagues were resentful of their presence and of their much higher salaries. There was pressure from the German authorities and from the many Nazi sympathizers, both German and native, who were present in the country at the time. Despite this they laid the foundations of the Turkish education system, and some of them stayed in this country for decades and were even buried in Turkey.

The graves of Curt Kosswig and Professor Dr. Erich Frank were next to each other in the Aşiyan Cemetery by the Bosporus. The renowned architect, Bruno Taut, was laid to rest in the Edirnekapı Cemetery, and the archaeologist, Clemens Bosch, in Feriköy.

Professor Fritz Neumark established the School of Economics and remained in Turkey for nineteen years. After returning to Germany he served twice as the rector of Frankfurt University. Ernst Reuter established the Urban Settlement and City Planning Institute and served as an advisor to the government in Ankara, and in 1947 returned to Germany to become the first mayor of occupied Berlin.

Professor Ordinarius Wilhelm Röpke was a famous economist; Professor Ordinarius Umberto Ricci was a faculty member of the University of Rome; Professor Bruno Taut was the founder of the Bauhaus School; Professor Clemens Holzmeister, an urbanologist; Professor Kurt Bittel, an archaeologist... The list went on.

There were hundreds of names, but Professor Ernst Hirsch, who became a Turkish citizen in 1934, popped up again and again. His book, *Pratik Hukukta Metot,* was still used as a reference by Turkish lawyers. Erich Auerbach, one of the greatest names in literary criticism, wrote his work *Mimesis* in Turkey. I noticed the files all contained handwritten notes indicating whether the subject was Aryan, Jewish, or mixed.

I still hadn't found anything on Maximilian Wagner, so I concentrated on trying to find his file. It took some effort before I finally found it. But as soon as I pulled it out, something about it seemed wrong. All the other files had been quite thick, but his contained only two sheets of paper.

The first was an official report that Aryan Maximilian Wagner, a German national and a lecturer at Istanbul University, had been arrested by Turkish security authorities and later deported. The report also stated that he had been declared persona non grata by the Cabinet, and that a copy of the document had been sent to the National Security Agency.

The second document stated that a Mr. Scurla, personal representative of Adolf Hitler, had come to the university to investigate Professor Wagner, and had denounced him to the rector as a British spy who sent coded messages in the form of musical scores.

Nermin was busy so I just waved goodbye to her and went back to my office. There was still a lot of work for me to catch up on, but I couldn't focus enough to even begin, so I just sat and had a coffee and tried to pull my thoughts together. So, Maximilian Wagner had been a spy after all. It didn't quite fit. That is, it didn't feel right. But of course, how well did I know him? I liked him, but did my liking him mean he couldn't be a spy? Besides, being a spy against the Nazis during World War II didn't make him a villain either. And what about Scurla? Had Wagner really been using musical scores as code? I supposed it was possible. But then did his violin have anything to do with this? It seemed strange that he would bring his violin with him on such a brief trip. Had the piece he'd played by the raging sea been part of a coded message? But if so, who had the message been intended for? There'd been no one there to hear it. Except me. Perhaps he'd been symbolically completing a mission he'd failed to accomplish during the war. No, nothing about it made sense.

Kerem would be home by now. I phoned Ilyas and asked him to pick Kerem up and bring him to the university. Then I called Kerem to tell him that Ilyas would be picking him up. He immediately thought something was wrong.

"What's the matter? Has something happened?"

"No, there's nothing wrong."

I folded my arms on my desk, rested my head on them and closed my eyes, imagining myself in Artvin, on the Kafkasör Plateau, in the Kaçkar Mountains. I was struggling through the snow, surrounded by white mountain peaks, the cold air causing a slight ache in my chest. Two years ago I'd taken a camping trip in the Kaçkar Mountains, and it had been one of the most magical experiences of my life. I remembered the frozen waterfalls that looked like fantastic ice-sculpture, the wooden houses perched here and there on ledges that seemed impossible to reach. I'd felt so happy, clear-headed, and healthy that I didn't want to leave, and I'd brought three pine saplings back to Istanbul with me as a memento. Two of them had died but one was still growing in my living room, and I always felt a special warmth in my heart when I saw it.

A little later the janitor came in with my mail. I didn't open all the envelopes but just glanced at them. There was nothing important. Then the telephone on my desk rang. I picked it up. Gizem, the trainee who'd just begun working in the rector's office, was on the other end.

"There's a call for you from the Russian consulate. I'm putting it through."

I was greeted by a male voice speaking Turkish with a heavy Slavic accent.

"Maya Duran, I wish you good day."

"Good day."

"I am your humble servant, Arkadi Vasiliyevich, the cultural attaché to the Russian embassy."

"Yes, sir?"

"If it is convenient, I should like to visit you."

"What is this visit about?"

"I should like to meet you in connection with your university."

"Would your visit have anything to do with Professor Maximilian Wagner?"

He paused, clearly taken aback, then continued in a mixture of Russian and Turkish, "Er... *pajalusta*... more to do with the university. If you would allow me, let me explain the reason for my visit when I arrive, tête-à-tête."

"Is Monday afternoon at three convenient?"

"Yes, madam, I shall impose upon you."

We hung up. What an important person I'd suddenly become. An hour later I went down to wait for the car. I waited twenty minutes for them, and it was ten past five by the time we got to Çapa Hospital.

The professor was looking much better. His color had returned and his face had more life in it. He gave me a big smile when he saw me.

"I've brought you a visitor," I said, and brought Kerem in.

The professor straightened up a little in his bed and shook hands with Kerem.

"Is this your son? What a nice surprise. Does he speak English?" And then he asked, "What's your name?"

"Kerem."

He was clearly shy about speaking English. He actually got high grades in English and he had a good teacher, but he'd never spoken English outside the classroom.

The professor asked if he took English at school.

"Yes."

They were both struggling to find something to say.

"How are you feeling today?" I asked.

"I'm feeling great, even better than before. In fact they're letting me out tomorrow."

"I'll come get you tomorrow and bring you back to the hotel. What day are you thinking of flying back?"

"I'd like to go Sunday if it's possible."

"I'll see what I can do."

We looked at each other for a moment, and he smiled. I turned to Kerem.

"Well, say goodbye to the professor, we're leaving now."

Kerem shook hands with the professor, and almost in a whisper said, "Bye, bye."

He held on to the professor's hand for a moment, looked him in the eye and asked him in Turkish, "Are you a spy?"

I was so embarrassed I blushed.

"Professor, Kerem is saying goodbye to you."

Wagner chuckled, "I understood that word," he said, "Don't worry, he has the right to ask."

He turned to Kerem and said in Turkish, "*Hayır!* No!" rolling the *r* at the end of the word. Then he turned to me.

"Did you find my violin?" Wagner asked. I'd completely forgotten.

"I'll look into it right away, don't worry," I said. On the way back I explained the situation to Ilyas.

"Do you have Süleyman's telephone number?" I asked him.

"Yes, I do," he said.

"The professor left his violin in the Mercedes. Could you pick it up tomorrow?"

"Certainly."

When I got home I took some food out of the fridge, heated it up, and set the table.

We ate without talking and then withdrew to our rooms.

I turned on my laptop, and when it was warmed up I started looking up Scurla. I hadn't expected to find anything so quickly, but on the first page of results I found a Herbert Scurla who'd lived in Istanbul from 1937 to 1939. He had been minister of education of the Reich in 1934, and was in Istanbul as a representative of the German Office of University Exchanges. Interestingly, he later became a leading member of the Communist Party in East Germany and also had a successful career as a writer.

A Turkish site had a piece about Scurla's mission having been to try to persuade the Turkish Minister of

Education to deport the refugee professors back to Germany in exchange for their replacement by another group of professors approved by the German government. The Turkish government declined this proposition, and the refugee professors were allowed to continue in their posts. The report that Scurla presented to Hitler on his return was discovered in a Nazi archive in 1987.

When Hitler began the Second World War, he was not pleased that scholars fleeing Nazi terror in Germany and Austria took refuge in Turkey and were allowed to work there. Herbert Scurla, Undersecretary for the German Foreign Ministry, came to Turkey in 1939, met with the Minister of Education, Hasan-Ali Yücel, and conveys the message, "Send these scholars back to us and we'll send you Germany's most brilliant brains."

However Turkey declined Hitler's proposition and the professors continue their work. The report Scurla presented to Hitler on his return was found in 1987 in Nazi archives.

This meant that his conclusions about Maximilian would be included in this report. With a little effort I learned that the archive in which the report had been found was in Bad Arolsen, near Kassel, and that it had been filed under ITS, for International Tracing Service.

So, how was I going to get a look at this report?

I turned off my laptop and took the family photograph album out of the walnut chest I kept at the foot of my bed. The album, bound in embossed leather, with fading pictures protected by tissue, had always held a deep fascination for me.

I stared at the photographs of my maternal grandparents. My grandmother had a broad face, clear skin, prominent cheekbones, and slightly slanted black eyes. My mother had inherited her features, and to a lesser extent I had as well. My grandfather Ali was a thin man with sunken cheeks and a rather large nose. Now, looking at their faces after so many years, I felt a deep sadness at never having really known them, never having known their story. And also at the realization that there was so much more I would never know. All I had was the outline of a story, and I would never know the details. I would never know anything about either of my grandmothers' families, their parents and grandparents and siblings. Like so many people in this country, I would never be allowed to know my family history beyond two generations.

I tried to picture them as they were when they were young, my grandmother as a prisoner fleeing from a train and jumping into an icy lake, and my grandfather, the young soldier who'd fallen in love with her, jumping in to save her without a second thought. If he had hesitated, none of us, my brother and me, my brother's children, and Kerem, would ever have existed.

How many people in this country had felt it necessary to hide their true identities as both of my grandmothers had done? How many people, like my brother, were terrified that their history of "tainted blood" might be discovered? How much better it might have been if we'd all been allowed to be who we are, if we'd been free to build a multiethnic, multicultural society. We'd been so imprisoned by the nationalist myth promulgated by those who felt that in order to create a nation they had to create a national identity. Yet the myth was so fragile that those who felt their existence depended on it had to resort to violence and intimidation to protect it. What strange logic they used as well. "If you call me a murderer I'll kill you." What a disaster it would be if it was discovered that the president of the Republic had Armenian ancestors!

Maximilian knew nothing about my mother's mother, yet had it not been for him, I might never have learned her story. Tomorrow I'd pick him up from the hospital and bring him to the hotel. Then I'd get him to tell me his story. He'd told me I had the right to know, and I felt I did. After all I'd been through because of him, he had to tell me.

It was only nine o'clock, so I decided to spend some time on the internet reading about what Germany had been like in Maximilian Wagner's youth. I started with the political and economic crises of the early twenties, when Germany experienced a period of hyperinflation and the German mark lost so much value that it was being traded at 4.2 million to the dollar.

At the moment, Turkey is struggling with high inflation and the worst economic crisis in recent times, and though it isn't comparable to the situation that had existed in Germany after World War I, it is still serious. The day Professor Wagner had arrived in Istanbul, the prime minister had a strong disagreement with the president, and as he left the Presidential Palace he told the crowd of reporters outside that the greatest crisis in the history of the Republic had commenced. As soon as he spoke those words the crisis began in earnest. Overnight, the Turkish lira lost a third of its value and began trading at 1.7 million to the dollar. Banks failed, thousands of businesses—both large and small—went bankrupt, and everyone who still had money did everything they could to get it out of the country. Foreign investment and loans dried up. The stock market crashed, businessmen were arrested, or committed suicide, or fled to countries that did not have extradition treaties with Turkey. New Zealand became a very popular destination, and the people of Tanzania were surprised by a sudden influx of wealthy Turks.

The situation was quickly moving toward what Germany had experienced in the twenties. I'd given all my savings to Tarık to trade on the stock market, and even though he insisted my money was safe, I was sure I no longer had anything to fall back on. This was causing me considerable anxiety, because Ahmet never paid the child support or alimony he was supposed to. Every time we met he had another excuse, so I was left carrying the burden of feeding and clothing Kerem and sending him to school.

In Germany, anger at the loss of savings, jobs, and security had led people to begin listening to Hitler and his National Socialist German Workers Party. The Nazis were skilled at manipulating the people's anxiety, and no one could foresee what the party's growing power would lead to. Even after Hitler came to power in 1933, people were still blind to the true nature of his "movement."

One of Hitler's first acts after forming a government was to pass the "Law for the Restoration of the Professional Civil Service." The aim of this law was to purge government agencies of Jews and replace them with Aryans, and particularly with those Aryans who were loyal to the party. Jewish professors, judges, notaries, and civil servants were suddenly dismissed from their positions.

The sense of insecurity in Germany led to increased support for the Nazi party, just as the sense of insecurity here has led to increased support for the Islamist party. In Germany, those who were disappointed in the old regime and those who felt their country had been unjustly punished by the victors of World War I began to flock to the party, and there were many others who sympathized without becoming active members. Even those who had previously supported other parties began to wear Nazi lapel pins, to the astonishment of their friends.

Adolf Hitler moved step-by-step, according to the rules of the system, and even the most influential individuals and institutions supported him wholeheartedly. Looking back, it's hard to understand how an entire nation could be so blind and acquiescent, but, then again, it's easy to imagine the same thing happening here. No one listens to the few lone voices who point out how the Islamists are taking over the judiciary, the upper levels of the police, the schools, and, indeed, the entire government bureaucracy—how they're already pushing ahead their agenda in the major cities whose administrations they control. On 23 March 1933, before he had been in power for two months, Hitler managed to get the Enabling Act passed in parliament, giving his government unlimited power. How long will it be before something similar happens here?

CHAPTER 11

I dreamt I was swimming in a clear, blue sea. The sun was bright and sparkling on the water. High mountains rose behind me, and there was an island not too far in the distance. The water caressed my skin like silk, and when I looked down I could see the sandy bottom. I felt so light, so full of life, I felt as if I could swim forever.

Then, suddenly, the sky clouded over and the water grew dark and murky. I could no longer even see my own legs. Just as I thought this, something grabbed my leg. I couldn't see it, but I knew it was a hand. A thin, bony hand, but strong. No matter how hard I tried to kick myself free it wouldn't loosen its grip, but dragged me down into the water. Then another hand took my arm, and I could see that it was my grandmother pulling me down. Not my grandmother as I'd known her, her face was white and gaunt and her hair was spread out around and above her head, swaying and dancing like a creature with a life of its own.

I woke with a start and looked at the clock. It was almost nine. It was Saturday, and I stretched, luxuriating in the knowledge that I didn't have to rush out of bed. I had the whole day in front of me. First a nice shower and a good breakfast, then to the mall to take advantage of the last of the winter sales. I'd have a leisurely lunch there, then go to the hospital, fetch Wagner, and bring him to the hotel. I was glad I didn't have to go to the university.

When I pulled open the curtains I was delighted to see that it was bright and sunny out. It happened like that in Istanbul sometimes. After weeks of rain and snow and wind without even a glimpse of the sun, there would suddenly be a balmy, spring-like day. And when it did happen, and especially if it happened on a weekend, hundreds of thousands of people who'd been cooped up would pour out into the streets. They would stroll along the shore of the Bosporus or the Marmara Sea, or in the Belgrade forest. Cheerful groups would crowd onto ferries and have picnics on the islands. In the evening, the smell of fried mussels and grilled fish would waft from seaside restaurants, and the people of Istanbul would sip ice-cold *rakı* as they watched the sun set behind the mosques of the old city.

An hour later Kerem and I were sitting at the kitchen table eating breakfast with sunlight streaming in through the window. The moment was perfect, one of those rare moments when I was utterly content to be where and who I was. And just then the doorbell rang.

It was Ahmet; he was taking Kerem for the weekend. In fact he was supposed to take Kerem every weekend, that was our arrangement, but he usually didn't. He usually didn't even bother to call and cancel either.

He just stood in the corridor with a wary expression on his face. I looked at him, and it struck me how much he'd aged. His hair was thinning, and his face had taken on that look of disappointment and resignation that men often get in middle age.

"Well, what are you doing these days?"

"Nothing," I said, "I'm trying to earn money to pay for my son's school and to keep this house."

Then I called out, "Kerem, come on, get ready, your father is going to wait for you downstairs in the car."

Just as I was closing the door, I saw Ahmet lean forward. At the last moment he lifted his eyebrows as if he were going to say something, but it was too late; whatever it was he could say it to the front door.

Kerem was ready. I put a twenty in his pocket as he went out. "Don't show it to your father, ask him for whatever you want, let him buy it. Don't you dare buy anything. You can spend the money next week."

He left without a word. No thank you, no goodbye.

That's how it was in our family.

I cleaned up the house a bit and then went to the mall. I had a coffee, bought some clothes that were on sale, and then went to the bookshop to ask if they had any books on the German professors who'd come to Turkey in the

1930s. The clerk looked on her computer, said yes, and led me to the history section.

"Yes. This is it."

She slipped a book into my hands. A thick book with a pink cover. It was titled: *My Memories—the Kaiser—Weimar Republic—Atatürk's Nation*, Ernst. E. Hirsch. It had been translated by Fatma Suphi and published by the Turkish Institute for Scientific and Technical Research. I recognized Hirsch's name from the archives, and felt very pleased to have found the book.

I paid for the book and then sat in the bookstore café, ordered a coffee and a sandwich, and looked at the book's back cover.

Professor Hirsch left Germany in 1933 and worked as guest lecturer at Istanbul University's Faculty of Law from 1933 to 1943, and at Ankara University's Faculty of Law from 1943 to 1952. The views and observations relating to the declining years of the Weimar Republic, Hitler's rise to power, the attitude of the law makers, and the first thirty years of Atatürk's Turkey that appear in My Memories, *will intrigue everyone who is interested in recent history and political and social life. This book also presents a picture of how our university system has evolved.*

At the beginning of the book was a full-page photo of the professor. He was not looking at the camera but had his head turned to one side as if he were trying to remember something, an elderly man with spectacles and slightly thinning gray hair, in dark clothes and a tie. The caption read, "A life beyond the boundaries of time." Hirsch was born in 1902 and died in 1985. So he was quite a bit older than Wagner. I immediately flicked through the index to see if Maximilian Wagner's name appeared. It didn't.

Hirsch quoted Goethe at the beginning of the book.

Vergänglich sind der Erde schönste Gaben.
Nur was wir, außer dem Bereich der Zeit,
gewirkt als Geister auf die Geister haben,
das ist und bleibt in alle Ewigkeit.

Even the greatest blessings on earth
Pass with our thoughts that go beyond the boundaries
     of time.
Only He thinks
About the impression we make,
He endures to eternity.

The first chapter was titled, "Never Forget Where You Came From" and was about Hirsch's childhood. I skipped this and flipped ahead to the Hitler years. At this point my coffee and sandwich arrived. Everything he said fit with what I'd read over the last few days. What had happened when Hitler attained unlimited power after the Enabling Act was passed, and how deeply this had wounded Professor Hirsch. This is how he put it:

On 1 April, 1933, the NSDAP, the party, not a state authority, called for a boycott of Jewish shops, trades, lawyers, doctors, etc., with posters, "Germans! Be on your guard! Don't buy from Jews!" Those who were being boycotted were forced to hang these posters in their shop windows, their businesses, and at the entrance to their offices. And that is how the terror began.

What made the terror even more effective were the Storm Troopers on duty in front of the boycotted shops barring people from entering. Apart from the odd exception, the German people allowed the Jews to be terrorized and displayed no moral courage.

It was not the Kristal Nacht of November 1938, but the Day of the Boycott of Jewish Businesses of 1 April, 1933, that was the real German Day of Shame. This day when the German people's unwillingness to oppose the arbitrary acts of the NSDAP was revealed, increasing the audacity of the Nazis to do whatever they wished.

I had become so engrossed in Nazi Germany that it was some time before I heard my phone ringing in my bag. By the time I opened my bag and found the phone it had stopped ringing. When I looked I saw that it was Filiz who'd called and I immediately pressed the reply key.

"I'm sorry," I said, "I didn't hear my phone. When should I come and collect the professor?"

"That's why I phoned," she said. "The doctors thought that while he was in the hospital they might as well give him a check up; the results will be ready this evening. If you like, come then."

"All right," I said, "I'll come at six."

Then I phoned Ilyas and said, "Can you pick me up from home at five? We're going to the hospital."

"Very well, madam," he replied.

"Ilyas, have you managed to find the violin?"

"No, madam."

"Why? Didn't you ask Süleyman?"

"I asked him but he said it wasn't in the car."

"OK, thanks," I said and hung up. Yet another headache. In all that commotion we'd either left the violin on the beach or Süleyman was lying. I was sure that while I was dragging the professor to the car I'd tried to pry the violin from his hand, but hadn't succeeded. He'd been holding it too tightly. We might have left the case behind, but I was sure he'd been holding the violin. I just couldn't remember what we'd done with it while we were pushing Professor Wagner into the car.

I emerged from the shopping center and walked home. The streets were even more crowded than they'd been earlier. When I got home I undressed, got into bed, and continued to read Hirsch's book. I read until four.

> *We were faced with the fact that Hitler had won over half the votes. His party had seduced the people with indoctrination and demagogy, with bribery and corruption, trampling underfoot and destroying every standard of traditional value and putting forward a new set of values. But everyone who had witnessed the worthlessness of a large section of the press before 1933, who had observed the rude tone of political conflict, was able to understand that the constitutional take-over of the government was in fact a guise to attempt to outwardly legitimize a government coup.*

I closed the book and thought for a minute: this was the price of high inflation, broken national pride, and high unemployment—50 million dead.

Then I recalled what had happened here on 6–7 September 1955. It was a time of tension between Turkey and Greece over Cyprus. The president and the prime minister, together with leading members of the ruling party and senior military officers, devised a plot to terrorize the then considerable Greek population of Istanbul. First they staged a bombing at the house in Thessaloniki where Atatürk was born, and which, at the time, was serving as the Turkish consulate. A consulate employee who was working for the National Intelligence Agency placed a small bomb in the garden. It caused no damage except for one broken window. Yet the following day, newspapers in Turkey printed doctored photographs of the consulate in ruins, together with inflammatory articles inciting revenge against Greeks. It was later discovered that these doctored photographs had been prepared a week earlier.

Meanwhile, thousands of factory workers from several cities in Anatolia were brought to Istanbul by train, truck, and bus. In the afternoon, Nationalist student groups began a protest march from Taksim Square, and were soon joined by the factory workers. Greek-owned businesses and Greek homes had previously been marked with crosses, and the mob began systematically looting and destroying the shops. What they couldn't carry away, they simply tossed out into the street, and Istıklal Avenue was strewn with coats, hats, shoes, rolls of cloth, broken pianos, and washing machines. And shattered glass. After that they vandalized and burned Greek churches and desecrated Greek cemeteries, and then turned their attention to the homes. They broke down the doors and threw all the furniture out onto the streets. Thirty-seven people were killed, and there were hundreds of reports of rapes and beatings, and even of forced circumcision, particularly of priests. The looting and burning continued for nine hours before the army finally intervened. The Greek population of Istanbul before the riots was 70,000, and today it is less than 3,000. One of the senior officers who organized the riots later said proudly that it was "a successful special warfare operation." The U.S. secretary of state, John Foster Dulles, who was visiting Ankara at the time, urged the government to blame the rioting on communists.

I shuddered to realize how very similar this was to Kristallnacht.

As I lay in bed trying to find an excuse to linger a little longer, I saw the papers on my bedside table.

They had to do with the ship I'd asked Kerem to find out about the other day.

CONFIDENTIAL
GENERAL DIRECTORATE OF SECURITY,
MINISTRY OF THE INTERIOR number: 55912-S /
13 September, 1941

Upon your request of 4 September 1941, we are informing you that everyone who is to sail with the Struma will be allowed to leave after they have completed all emigration procedures. In the meantime, we will require a list of those Jews who have booked and are in labor camps to enable them to leave the country.

When the Romanian Iron Guards began actively persecuting Jews in 1938, many Jews began to escape from the port of Constanţa, hoping to reach Palestine. By 1939 the city had become a huge refugee camp with thousands of Jews lining up outside fly-by-night travel agencies that were selling tickets for what came to be known as "coffin ships." These ships were barely seaworthy, had few or no amenities, and were usually crowded to five or ten times their capacity. A few made it to Palestine, only for their passengers to be detained and interned by the British military police, but many did not. In December 1940, a Uruguayan registered ship called the *Salvador*, carrying 347 refugees, despite having a capacity for a maximum of 40 passengers, sank during a storm in the Sea of Marmara. A few of the passengers were rescued, to be deported back to Romania, but 203 drowned.

The Romanian authorities allowed these ships to continue to sail because it was a lucrative source of revenue; the refugees had to ransom their way out illegally, handing over everything they owned and signing over their property before they were allowed to board. And despite the knowledge that many of the ships did not make it, there was no shortage of demand. The slight chance of reaching safety was preferable to the near certainty of death in the camps.

The only problem was the availability of ships. There were plenty of unscrupulous shipowners willing to take part, but the Germans had requisitioned every available ship to transport food and livestock up the Danube to

Austria. However, an abandoned, Greek-owned ship called the *Macedonia,* which was seventy-four years old and measured fifty feet long and twenty feet wide, was rejected by German officials as unsafe even to transport cattle on the river. The owner of the *Macedonia* immediately seized the opportunity, had a few repairs made, registered the ship in Panama, and renamed it the *Struma*. He then made a deal with a ticket agency, which began advertising passage to Palestine aboard a luxury liner for one thousand dollars. The posters and brochures featured pictures of the Queen Mary.

Within days, 769 Jews had bought tickets. They included 269 women, many of them pregnant; 103 infants or toddlers; a number of professionals, including 30 physicians, 30 lawyers, and 10 engineers; a number of businessmen, merchants, craftsmen; and students and a select group of youth leaders. When they saw the ship, their disappointment was beyond description. It had only 100 bunks and a single toilet. The shipowner had prepared himself for this moment; he appeased the passengers by saying that as the ship he'd chartered flew an American flag it had to wait outside Romanian territorial waters. The *Struma* was only to take them as far as the liner. When they reached the open sea the passengers faced the harsh realization that they'd been tricked. There was no luxury liner waiting for them, but it was too late to go back to Romania.

They arrived in Istanbul on 15 December 1941. The engine had broken down and the hull was leaking. The captain requested permission to remain in the harbor until repairs were completed. The Turkish authorities, considering what had happened to the *Salvador*, generously granted this permission.

In view of the unbearable conditions on the ship, the Turkish authorities were willing to allow passengers to disembark while the ship was being repaired. However, it turned out that none of the passengers had entry visas to Palestine. As a compromise, the Turkish Foreign Office requested at least an assurance from Sir Adrian Knatchbull-Hugessen, the British ambassador in Ankara, that all the passengers would be issued visas to Palestine. The British refused to give any such assurance. The Turkish-Red Crescent, the American-Jewish Joint Distribution Committee in Turkey, and the Jewish community in Istanbul mobilized to feed the passengers, whose provisions had run out and who did not even have drinking water.

The *Struma* stayed in the Istanbul harbor seventy-one days, during which time the Turkish government conducted intense negotiations to find a solution. Despite the intervention of international organizations, the British government requested in a telegraph sent by the British High Commission in Palestine that the boat be prevented from reaching Palestine at all costs, stating that they thought the best solution was for the Turkish authorities to send the boat back to the Black Sea.

The colonial secretary, Lord Moyne, complained that the escape of these people would, "have the deplorable effect of encouraging further Jews to embark."

Thus the *Struma*, with failed engines a failed generator, and no radio, was abandoned to its fate in the waters off Istanbul.

I jumped up suddenly. I'd been so absorbed I'd lost track of the time. I hastily reached for my plaid skirt and white silk blouse.

CHAPTER 12

Ilyas had arrived early. When I looked out of the window I saw him leaning against the car, smoking a cigarette. He was a heavy smoker, but at least he didn't stink up the car the way Süleyman did.

After we set off I asked him about the violin.

"Süleyman says it's not there, madam. I asked him to take another look but he insists that it's not there."

This left me in a difficult position. I had to get the violin back, and now I'd either have to put pressure on Süleyman or go back to Şile and ask around if anyone had found it. It also made me uneasy that I hadn't seen or heard from Süleyman since he stormed out of the motel room. What was he up to?

"Where's the car being repaired?"

"A mechanic called Riza."

"Could we pay Riza a visit?"

"Of course, it's not far."

When we arrived at Riza's garage, I saw that the Mercedes had been raised. No one was working on it, and Süleyman didn't seem to be around. A man in overalls came out and asked in a friendly manner if he could help. I introduced myself, told him I worked for the rector of Istanbul University, and gave him my card. I explained that a visiting professor had left his violin in the car and I'd come to get it.

As I watched the Mercedes being lowered I remembered something interesting I'd come across in the past few days. One of the Germans who'd worked in Ankara was Ernst Reuter, and his son Edward, who'd grown up there, had gone on to become the chairman of the board of Mercedes.

When the car had been lowered, Riza opened the door. I made a thorough search, but there was no violin anywhere. I looked in the trunk as well, but it was empty except for a pile of rags in the corner.

Had Süleyman been telling the truth? Had we left the violin on the beach or at the motel? But it couldn't be in the motel.

"Did Süleyman take anything from the car?"

"I didn't see him take anything."

I thanked Riza and was just about to get into the car when I turned back.

"If it's not too much trouble, could I look in the trunk again?"

"Of course."

I opened the truck and reached for the rags in the corner. They were wrapped around something, and I knew at once it was the violin. I unwrapped it and showed it to the mechanics who'd gathered around.

"You've all witnessed this, haven't you?"

"Yes."

I turned to Ilyas.

"You see what Süleyman did?"

"Yes, madam."

We thanked Riza and drove off. We'd probably left the violin case on the beach, but at least we'd found the violin.

"Ilyas, do you know any music shops. I'd like to stop and get a case for this violin."

"Of course, madam!"

About twenty minutes later he pulled up in front of a store that sold musical instruments. I showed the man behind the counter the violin and said I wanted a case for it. He took the violin and looked at it appreciatively.

"This is a beautiful instrument, quite old and the workmanship is very good. I can get it appraised for you if you're interested in selling it."

"I don't want to sell it, I just want a case."

"Yes, of course, madam, but I'm afraid we don't have much of a selection. I doubt if we have one that will do this violin justice."

"It doesn't matter, I just need something to carry it in."

He brought out three that looked very much alike. I took one, put the violin in it, and went back to the car.

It was almost seven by the time we got to the hospital. Filiz gave me a hard time for being late, saying that Maximilian kept asking for me. Then she said there was something she had to talk to me about.

"What's the matter?" I asked, "Has something happened?"

"Well, I told you that we were going to give him a thorough check up."

"Yes?"

"While they were doing a CAT scan they found a lump in his pancreas. It didn't look very good. They spoke to him and asked if he would like further tests, but he said it wasn't necessary. He said he already knew that he had a tumor in his pancreas and that it was malignant."

"In other words, the man has cancer of the pancreas!"

"He seems to be handling it very well."

"How long do you think he has?"

"It's difficult to say. But probably not more than six months."

"So that means he came to Istanbul to say farewell."

"Yes, probably. Come on, don't keep him waiting any longer, but if he doesn't tell you himself, don't let on that you know about it."

"Don't worry Filiz," I said. "I won't say anything."

The professor smiled when he saw us.

"I thought you'd never get here."

He was already dressed in his suit and tie, with his hair neatly combed, and indeed he looked so healthy it was hard to believe he didn't have long to live.

He said goodbye to each of the people who'd helped him, and tipped the nurses and the orderlies. Then we went to the car.

"Oh, we have a different car and a different driver."

"The Mercedes is being repaired and this car is newer and less likely to break down. So this is our last evening, professor. Do you want to go straight to the hotel or are there places you'd like to see?"

"Of course, there are, but I didn't ask because I didn't want to put you out. I wouldn't mind seeing Sultanahmet Square one last time."

That, "one last time," wrenched my heart. I told Ilyas and he drove us straight down the tramline to Sultanahmet Square, where we got out of the car.

It was a magical spot at that hour, with the Hagia Sophia and the Blue Mosque all lit up and standing out against the night sky. I bought a bag of roasted chestnuts from a street vendor, and we sat on a bench and took it all in. We sat in silence at first, picturing all that had happened there, the Byzantine emperor riding with his procession to the gates of the Hagia Sophia, the Ottoman sultan arriving in front of the Blue Mosque, the Hippodrome filled with excited crowds watching the chariot races. Slowly, we fell into conversation, talking about this or that emperor or sultan, the palace intrigues, uprisings and mutinies, the ruthless cruelty exercised by those with absolute power. Byzantine princes who were blinded and exiled on the islands, how a sultan's brothers were all strangled the moment he came to power to avoid wars of succession. Grand viziers who rose to great power from humble backgrounds, only to be executed as soon as their power became a threat.

Would we—had we been granted such power and responsibility—have been more reasonable and compassionate? Probably not, we agreed. We would have been part of a system that would resort to anything to perpetuate itself, we would have been conditioned by this system, corrupted by it and by the power it granted us. And we would have had enemies. We went on to talk about the nature of power and of the machinery of oppression and the ways in which it had expressed itself through history, and how crimes against humanity were justified by the lopsided internal logic of systems whose only purpose was to perpetuate themselves at all costs.

At one point during a lull in the conversation—we'd been talking about the looting of the city by Crusaders in the twelfth century—he turned and asked, "Did you study history?"

"No, I studied literature. But I've always been interested in history, particularly the history of my city. But there are a lot of gaps in my knowledge of history."

I didn't tell him that I'd only learned about the history of Istanbul so I could seem knowledgeable to the visiting professors I had to show around.

"Such as?"

"Well, modern history in general, and your period in particular."

"My period?"

"The period during the war when brilliant scholars came to Turkey."

"Brilliant scholars?"

"Yes. Reuter, Neumark, Hirsch, Auerbach, Spitzer, you..."

"I knew all of them. Those are the people I used to meet for drinks at the Pera Palas."

"I spent the past few days reading about them in the university archives."

"In the archives? Is there a file there on everyone?"

"Yes, there is, and they're full of information, but I have to confess that the slimmest file is yours, professor."

"Why?"

"The intelligence service seized all your papers. There are only two documents left in the file."

"Which ones?"

"The document stating that you were deported, and the one stating that Scurla was making inquiries about you."

"Scurla?"

"Yes."

The professor was silent for a while, then stood up, and took a last look around.

"Come on, let's get back to the car and drive to the hotel. I have a lot to tell you. It's going to be a long night."

CHAPTER 13

As soon as we'd settled into the car I handed him the violin case.

"I found your violin."

He frowned at the case.

"But this isn't my violin!"

"Don't worry, it's a different case but it's your violin."

He opened the case and when he took out the violin he smiled and looked at it lovingly. I explained that the case had been lost in the confusion and that we'd probably left it on the beach. I didn't bother to tell him that Süleyman had hidden the violin.

He placed the violin carefully on his lap.

"I can't remember exactly what happened."

"Professor, can you tell me about Nadia?"

"I'll tell you on one condition."

"What's that?"

"Stop calling me, professor. Call me Maximilian, or Max for short."

"I have something to tell you, too, Max."

When we arrived at Pera Palas I told Ilyas not to wait. I would probably be there for some time, Max and I were going to have dinner together, and I could call him to come get me when I was ready to leave.

Max went up to his room for a moment, and I waited for him at a small round table in the bar. I ordered a white port and asked the waiter to reserve a quiet table for us in the restaurant. Now, finally, after all the mystery, I was going to find out who Max and Nadia were, why we'd gone to Şile, what that odd ceremony had been about, why all these spies were interested in him, and why he'd been deported.

I finished my wine and ordered another, and passed the time imagining the people who'd sat in this bar. Mata Hari. Kim Philby. The British ambassador to Bulgaria who'd narrowly missed being killed by a bomb because he'd come in here for a drink instead of going straight to his car. All the intrigues, all the stories we'd never know. By the time the professor arrived I was feeling a bit tipsy. He looked so dapper and so healthy that it was hard to believe he had only six months to live. I asked him if he'd like a drink, but he said he'd rather not, so we moved to our relatively secluded table in the dining room.

That evening there were Ottoman dishes on the menu. We chose artichokes in olive oil and lamb's shank in tomato with an aubergine sauce. We ordered the same wine we'd drunk the last time, a robust and fruity Anatolian Shiraz.

I could see that Max was ill at ease. He looked troubled, and I guessed that it was going to be difficult for him to tell me what he had to tell.

"This time last week I knew nothing about you and your friends," I said.

"Of course you were more relaxed then. I've caused you a lot of trouble."

"No, I'm very glad. You've opened new horizons for me."

He nodded, raised his eyebrows a little and bent his head slightly to one side.

"The other day I read something about a student from your time expressing gratitude to Hitler."

He looked at me in astonishment.

"Why?"

"He said that if it hadn't been for Hitler it would have been impossible to bring teachers of this caliber to Turkey. He was one of Erich Auerbach's students."

"Then he was very lucky. Auerbach was a truly remarkable scholar. You must have read his *Mimesis,* which he wrote while he was here."

"I'm afraid I haven't professor, sorry, I mean Max."

"But you studied literature at the same university. How could you have missed this masterpiece?"

"I've heard of it, of course, but unfortunately it hasn't been translated into Turkish. Which, considering what I've read in the past few days, seems odd."

"I think it's one of the most outstanding books on literary criticism. I'll send you the English translation as soon as I get back to Boston. Then you'll have a mission."

"What kind of mission?"

"To translate *Mimesis* into Turkish and bring the book back to the country where it was written."

I found the idea exciting.

"Yes," I said. "That would great."

"When you've read the book you'll realize how important it is, and what a service you'll be doing for Turkish readers and students. Will you promise to do this?"

"OK, I promise. But what makes this book so important?"

"There's no way I could give a brief explanation."

"So give me a detailed explanation then."

He smiled.

"That's hardly dinner table conversation."

"Why not?"

"Well, as briefly as possible Erich Auerbach and his colleague Leo Spitzer tried to methodize the notion of *Weltliteratur* or world literature. This was something Goethe had talked about, the notion of understanding literature as a product of human culture in general rather than of a specific culture. He learned Persian at an advanced age so he could read the great Persian poets Hafez and Saadi, as well as your common heritage Mevlana Rumi. This was the basis for his *West-Östlicher Diwan*."

"What do you mean when you call Mevlana our common heritage?"

"I mean that even though he lived in Turkey he wrote in Persian. If he'd written in Turkish the world would have known very little about him. The great Turkish poets Yunus Emre and Şeyh Galip are practically unknown elsewhere but Omar Khayyam, Saadi, Hafez, and Rumi are widely read. This is of course largely due to the spread of Persian culture and to Goethe."

"Yes, I suppose you're right."

"Anyway, Leo and Erich tried to methodize the concept of *Weltliteratur*. *Mimesis* was a broad study starting with the Old Testament and Homer—in other words two main sources of Western literature—and extending as far as Proust and Virginia Woolf. But in fact it focuses mainly on Western literature. After all its full title is: *Mimesis: The Representation of Reality in Western Literature*."

"Wait a minute, I'm confused. This book was supposed to be about world literature, it was written in Istanbul, but it doesn't examine Eastern literature?"

"Yes, it really only deals with Western literature. Erich was always complaining that he couldn't find the material he needed in Istanbul."

"That reminds me of an old story. Do you know of Imam Ghazali?"

"Of course!"

"After he'd finished his studies in Baghdad, Ghazali was on his way back to Tus when the caravan he was

traveling with was waylaid by bandits, who stole everything the passengers were carrying, including the single
small bag Ghazali had with him. Ghazali immediately
set out to track down the bandits and get his bag back.
It took him months, but he finally found the cave the
bandits used as their headquarters. He tried to force his
way in, and the guards were about to kill him when the
leader heard the commotion and asked what was going
on. Ghazali explained that he'd come to retrieve his bag.
The bandit asked what was in the bag that was so valuable he risked his life to get it back. Ghazali explained
that it contained notes he'd been given by his teacher in
Baghdad. The bandit gave him back his bag and said,
'Remember, knowledge that can be stolen from you was
never yours to begin with.'"

Max laughed.

We talked for some time about Auerbach's ideas, as
well as about the difficulties the translation might pose.
Wagner suggested some resources that might be helpful
to me, and said he could help me get the letters Auerbach
had written while he was in Istanbul. Then, during a lull,
I tried to bring the conversation around to what we were
supposed to be talking about.

"Was that student right when he said that Turkey
owed a debt of gratitude to Hitler."

"I suppose in a sense he is. Turkey was very foreign to
us and we knew almost nothing about it. All we knew was
that the Ottoman Empire had collapsed, and that in its

place there was a Republic that was attempting to make westernizing reforms. And we were quite a distinguished group, the cream of German academia. Except for me, of course. At the time there was only one medical school in Turkey, and its curriculum was very outdated. Atatürk wanted to westernize the university system quickly. The German professors undertook to do this, and their efforts still form the foundation of higher education here. For example, the conservatories still use the curriculum established by the composer Paul Hindemith."

"What was Turkey like when you first came here?"

"Well, it was still a relatively poor, agricultural society with a very small elite. The total population was only 17 million. What is it now?

"Over 70 million. There's one thing I'm curious about, Max. You came much later than the other German professors. All the Jewish and actively anti-fascist academics came in 1933, but you didn't arrive until six years later."

"Well, I was neither a Jew nor a Communist. I come from a Catholic bourgeois family."

"Well, then why did you leave Germany in 1939?"

"That's what I'm going to tell you. But I don't know where to start."

"Please start as far back as possible. From your childhood, your youth."

"Very well. But prepare yourself for a long story."

"I'm ready," I said. "There's just one thing I'd like to ask. Can I record what you say?"

He frowned slightly. I saw him hesitate a little.

"I have no particular reason," I explained. "It's just that I feel there'll be a huge vacuum after you've gone. I'll be able to fill that void only by listening to your voice and reading books from that period." I added laughing, "And of course translating *Mimesis*."

He laughed, too, and said, "All right. Go ahead and record it."

I took out my small digital recorder and pushed it to him across the white tablecloth. The flashing red light seemed to emphasize the importance of what I was about to hear.

That Saturday evening the restaurant was quite crowded. Veteran waiters in black darted swiftly among the tables, and there was a hum of conversation punctuated by the clinking of glasses and the occasional burst of laughter.

Professor Maximilian Wagner began to tell his story:

"As I said, I was born to a wealthy family with pretensions to nobility. I received a very good education. My father was a well-known judge and my mother had a modest career as a pianist. I spent my childhood and youth learning Latin, Classical Greek, philosophy, literature, history, and music. I became an assistant at the university when I was still quite young. I could say that I was happy and carefree. I got along well with my professors, my colleagues, and my students, and I spent much of my free time working with an amateur string quartet.

I had no sense whatsoever about what was to come. Yes, from time to time I heard about the right wing groups and a former sergeant called Adolf, but no one took this seriously and neither did I.

"Then I got to know a history student named Nadia. I liked her at once, but it took me some time to realize how attracted I was to her. I just became aware slowly that I was thinking about her more and more. I'd think about her as soon as I woke up in the morning, and getting dressed and making my way to the university became charged with sweet anticipation because I knew I would see her. She had no idea how I felt, of course, but at a certain point I had no doubt left that I was madly in love with her. This was 1934, a year after Hitler had come to power and passed that terrible law."

"The law about public office," I interrupted.

"Yes. This was a terrible, unexpected blow. My Jewish university professors were forced to leave their jobs. Meanwhile pressure had begun on Jewish students too. It became impossible for them to study. Nazi students at the universities terrorized them. Nadia insisted on continuing to come to the university. Then one day I saw some Nazis roughing her up in the garden and I went to rescue her."

For what seemed a long time he stared at the tablecloth in front of him. Then slowly, almost in a monotone, he continued telling his story. The little red light kept flashing, and waiters came and went, filling our glasses and clearing our plates. Sometimes he kept talking in spite of them, and sometimes he waited for them to finish, taking a sip of wine and looking off into the distance.

It was a difficult story to listen to, but I listened as attentively as I could, without interrupting and without making any movements that would distract him. At one point, though, I felt I couldn't take it anymore. I just stood up abruptly and went to the ladies' room without saying a word.

When I returned the table was empty. I was worried he might have been offended by my leaving like that. The recorder was still sitting there, its red light flashing.

He returned within a few minutes, though, looking somewhat refreshed. He was even smiling, and I thought that perhaps telling the story was a kind of catharsis for him.

"I'm sorry, Max," I said. "I interrupted your story."

"That's OK. I needed a break too."

We sat in silence for a few minutes, sipping our wine. I asked the waiter to bring us some fruit. Then, after he'd brought it, the professor continued his story in the same monotone, staring at the same spot on the tablecloth.

Meanwhile, the restaurant was slowly emptying, and as it grew quieter the professor's voice grew more audible. The waiters stood around near the kitchen door, looking bored, and as if they were eager to clean up and go home.

I gently put my hand on his. He continued without taking the slightest bit of notice. When he came to the end of a passage in the story he stopped and looked up at me.

"Don't take this the wrong way, but I think it's time for us to leave," I whispered. "We're the only ones left."

He glanced around. "Of course, of course."

He signaled for the bill. The headwaiter had the bill ready, and brought it to the table. Max wrote his room number on it and signed. I left a tip and we made our way to the lobby.

"I must hear the end of the story, Max," I said. "The bar is going to close soon. Would you like to go to another bar nearby?"

"No," he said. "Let's not go out at this hour, but, please, come to my room. There's a mini-bar."

This seemed the most logical solution. Kerem was staying with his father, so I didn't have to rush home. There was no harm in sitting in his room for an hour or two, but then it would be too late to call Ilyas. I'd have to take a taxi.

So we went to his room, we settled down in the comfortable armchairs, and Max got some brandy from the mini-bar.

After he'd poured us brandy he said, "There's a lot I could tell you about what Istanbul and the university were like then, but this doesn't seem the right time."

"You're right," I said. "I want to hear about Nadia. Were you able to find her?"

He nodded.

"I see."

We waited for a while in silence. Then we began to drink.

The story had reached the end of the 1930s.

The professor seemed to be gathering his strength to continue. When we'd finished our brandy, he called room service and asked them to send up a bottle of Martel. Then we sat in increasingly uncomfortable silence until it arrived. Then, after he'd poured us each a stiff drink, he picked up where he'd left off, and continued in the same monotone as before.

I immediately pressed the button of the recorder on the coffee table. The small red light began to flash.

At first I listened as I had before, without moving, but later I got up and paced around the room. He didn't even seem to notice, and kept staring at the floor as he talked. After some time, his voice began to crack, and when I looked at him I saw that he was exhausted.

"It sounds like you're close to the end. Once you're finished I'll leave and let you get some rest."

"No. It's not almost finished. The real story begins now."

"In that case, professor, please lie down. If you don't fall asleep, you can continue to talk. If you sleep, then you can give me a summary of the end of the story tomorrow."

At first he seemed to object, then he agreed. I helped him to get undressed and put on his pajamas and then got him into bed.

The professor was lying on the bed on his side and I was sitting on the chair nearby. He continued his story in a tired, bitter voice.

He kept taking me to Romania, Germany, Istanbul, and Ankara with different people. I felt the pain, the excitement and then the images that sprang to life before my eyes slowed down and began to scatter. And Max's voice fell silent. He was sleeping, breathing lightly but regularly.

I got up without a sound and looked out the window at the Golden Horn and the Saturday night traffic on Tarlabaşı Boulevard. I wondered if I should leave, but then thought that he might wake up and want to carry on with the story. On a whim, I took off my jacket and got into bed too. I hugged him from behind just as I had at the Black Sea Motel. I was also very tired. At first I thought he hadn't noticed me but then without changing his position at all, he said, "Thank you."

It's dark inside the plane. The blinds are down, so I don't know whether it's light or dark outside.

A few people are waking up in the seats around me. More and more people are getting up to go to the toilet.

I'll finish this chapter and then take a short break.

What are you thanking me for?" I asked.

"This will make it easier for me to tell the rest of the story."

"This isn't the first time I've embraced you, Max."

"Yes, I know, thank you for that too. You saved my life."

This time we were both dressed but I felt the same intense tenderness I had before. I rested my head against his back.

He was speaking almost in a whisper now.

I couldn't hear what he was saying anymore, but I knew the recorder would be picking it up.

I must have fallen asleep as he talked, because the next thing I knew my phone was ringing, and it was almost noon. It was Ilyas, asking when he should pick me up.

"You don't need to come to my house, Ilyas," I said. "Come to Pera Palas at two, we'll meet there and take the professor to the airport."

"Very well, ma'am," he said.

The professor was gone, but I could hear water running in the bathroom. After a while he came out wearing a white bathrobe. He smiled.

"How deeply you were sleeping!" he said. "Oh, that delightful sleep of youth..."

I got up too, had a shower, and felt better. The sleepless night, the drink, and the crying had given me shadows under my eyes and made my face puffy. I made a compress with the icy water. I didn't want to appear ugly to Max.

After that we ordered breakfast from room service. We drank our strong, black coffee and ate our breakfast looking out over the Golden Horn. After breakfast we packed his suitcase, and then he handed me an envelope.

"This is the letter I mentioned yesterday."

As I read the letter I felt a lump in my throat, and tears began to form in my eyes. Max had his back to me, as if he didn't want to see my reaction. Then he walked slowly to the bathroom.

I quickly copied the letter. He emerged from the bathroom just as I was writing the last words. I handed him back the original letter, then folded my copy and put it in my bag.

"I'll take good care of it, Max."

He smiled. We sat in silence for a while, and then went downstairs. The hotel bill would be sent to the university but he paid the extras, that is, the food, drink, and so on. He was holding his violin case. A bellboy brought down his suitcase and handed it to Ilyas.

We got into the car and left. We said nothing until we got to the airport.

The traffic was relatively light because it was Sunday.

He kissed me on the cheek as I bade him farewell at the terminal and said in a low voice, "Thank you. For everything." Then he walked away without looking back and disappeared into the crowd.

CHAPTER 14

I can't describe the emptiness I felt after he'd gone. The world suddenly seemed a different place. As Ilyas drove me home, I looked out the window at all the cars, all the houses. So many people, all with their own stories and pasts, their tragedies and triumphs, none of which I would ever know.

When I got home I sat down, and decided I would do as little as possible for the rest of the afternoon.

I took the recorder out of my bag. Everything that Max had told me was contained in this tiny device. I was holding an amazing story in my hand. I felt as though I was about to discover the secret of life.

Max had said that he would tell the whole story but there was something missing. An important part of the story; maybe the most important part. A secret that he couldn't confess even to himself. A secret that led to a lifetime of regret, and even to his cancer. I thought this secret was hidden in his unconscious mutterings in Şile when he kept repeating, "Forgive me, Nadia." Several times, I wanted to ask him about it in Pera Palas, but I hadn't dared to.

I'd learned so much in the past few days. About things that had happened in this country not that long ago, and what had happened in Europe within living memory. But I also realized I hadn't learned nearly enough and that I needed to know much more.

But what did it matter if I knew what my grandmother had been through in the context of historical events? What did it matter if I knew what had occurred on specific days 60 years ago, 100 years ago, or 600 years ago? What was I going to do with the knowledge of what the people Wagner spoke of had experienced in this city? It could only be meaningful as a story about people.

The people rushing around at the airport, the anxious drivers on the road, the overweight women at the university, the people shopping in the malls, all of them had their own stories. We take as much interest in their stories as we do in our own, as long as each story is taken on its own merit. Each story is, in the end, the story of human experience, of all of our lives slipping away.

As I sat there, I remembered how bored I used to get on Sundays when I was a teenager. My father would watch soccer games on the black and white television, shouting excitedly whenever his team scored a goal. My mother would either be cooking in the kitchen or doing the crossword at the dining room table. My brother would be out, and I would have been out too if there was anywhere to go.

I felt the same way that day. Max was gone, and with him had gone the excitement, stimulation, and curiosity that had made me feel alive. Soon Ahmet would bring Kerem home, and we'd go through the same routine day after day.

I'd travel the same roads, see the same people, hear the same gossip.

Perhaps the only thing that would make my life feel meaningful would be to get involved in Max's story.

There was also Süleyman. Had he intended to steal the violin, and if so would he take revenge on me for taking it back?

When Kerem came home he went straight to the computer. I told him that tomorrow was a school day and not to stay up too late. He just grunted OK to appease me, and I knew he had no intention of obeying me.

I didn't have the strength to get him away from the computer. I dragged myself to bed, but when I lay down I couldn't fall asleep. So after a while I turned on the light and began reading about the *Struma*.

Conditions aboard the *Struma* as it sat off the docks in Istanbul were grim. There weren't enough bunks for everyone, and there was little room to move around. There was no bath or shower, and only one basin for washing the infants. Nor was there any way to do laundry. Worst of all, there was only one toilet for 769 people, and there was always a line at the door. So people began to relieve themselves on deck. The deck became slippery with feces and urine and there was an unbearable stench.

The doctors among the passengers had to deal with hundreds of cases of dysentery without access to drugs, and two of the younger passengers began to suffer from severe psychiatric distress.

The days began at four or five in the morning, and people took turns filling buckets with seawater for whatever washing could be done. Fuel was rationed, and they were able to make tea and cook food only once every three days. The rest of the time they ate small amounts of fruit and nuts. The children were given half a glass of powdered milk and a single biscuit.

Jewish organizations in Turkey, Palestine, and the United States were doing whatever they could to resolve the situation. Simon Brod and Rifat Karako, two leading members of Istanbul's Jewish community, tried to persuade the authorities to allow the passengers to leave the ship and continue to Palestine overland.

The British government and its secret service made every effort to stop the Jews from going to Palestine and to keep the *Struma* affair out of the public eye.

Meanwhile, life aboard the ship went on, and the passengers did what they could to establish some kind of normalcy in their cramped and squalid conditions.

Two young people were married by the rabbi on the ship. Passengers arranged social activities to make the most of their time. Two musicians gave a concert every night. Classes in Hebrew literature and Jewish history were organized.

That winter was unusually cold, and fuel was rationed because of the war, but nevertheless the Jews of Istanbul built a fire on the shore to give the passengers moral support. They brought wood and tended the fire so that the passengers aboard the ship could always see it.

I fell asleep reading, and woke the next morning with the pages strewn across the bed. Then I launched into the same soul-crushing morning routine. But as soon as I got to work I sensed that something was different. The secretaries and janitors looked at me strangely and whispered among themselves. People suddenly stopped talking when I approached.

I assumed that Süleyman had been spreading his gossip. I didn't, in fact, really care. It was their problem if they got some kind of twisted pleasure from telling each other I'd slept with an eighty-seven-year-old man. Yet at the same time I just didn't feel I had the strength to deal with this kind of nonsense. Not now.

I sat down at my desk, looked at my overflowing in-box, then suddenly, impulsively, got up and walked out. I decided I wouldn't come back for at least a week, and I didn't give a damn about the consequences. I'd tell them I was sick, and if I had to I'd manage to get a doctor's note somehow. As I walked down the stairs, through the campus, and across Beyazit Square, I realized that the past week had changed me, changed the way I saw things.

As soon as I got home I phoned the rector's secretary to tell her I was ill and that I'd be out for a few days, and then hung up before she could say anything. The house was a mess, but I decided that I wasn't even going to try to do anything about it.

After sitting motionless for a while I phoned Tarık.

"Do you want to get together this evening?"

"Oh," he said cheerfully. "Has your old man gone?"

"Yes."

"OK," he said. "Should I pick you up at 7:30?"

"No, I'll come to you."

"All right," he said. "Bye!"

Then I drew the curtains in the bedroom, got into bed, and went to sleep. I slept until late afternoon, and was drinking a cup of tea when Kerem came in.

"How was school?"

He mumbled something that sounded like "fine" and went straight to his room. So, it seemed our relationship was back to what it had been.

I drew a bath and got in, leaving the tap on a little because I found it soothing to hear a slight trickle of water. I closed my eyes, surrendered myself to the feeling of the warm water, and tried unsuccessfully to get a grip on the events of the past week.

After that I got dressed and put on a little makeup. I ordered some grilled chicken wings for Kerem, left a little money on the table, and went out. It was eight o'clock.

Tarık lived in one of those new high-rise luxury apartment buildings. The security guard must have been told I was coming; he accompanied me as far as the elevator. When I went up and knocked on the door, Tarık opened it himself. He was alone; in other words he'd sent his maid away.

His apartment was furnished in a cold, minimalist style. There was no wood, patterned fabric, or curtains to give it a feeling of warmth. Everything was white, and most of the furniture was metallic. But he was on the 27th floor and had a wonderful view of the Bosporus. I stood for a moment taking it in, the passing ships, the twinkling lights on the far shore, the Bosporus Bridge, the illuminated facade of the Kuleli Military Academy.

"Let's have a glass of wine," I said.

"I've got some white port for you."

"Thanks, but tonight I feel like red wine."

He always had good wine. That evening he served a very nice Italian wine called Amarone. He poured it into huge glasses. After we'd finished our first glass he kissed me, but I pushed him away. When he asked what the matter was I just said I wasn't in the mood.

He didn't persist. He just asked, "What's happened to you?"

"I don't know," I said, a little ashamed.

It was true. I didn't know what I was doing or where I wanted my life to go.

Later, sitting at a glass-topped metal table overlooking the Bosporus we ate sushi that Tarık had ordered from Istanbul's best Japanese restaurant.

"So, your old man's gone," he said.

"How does he come to be mine?"

"Just kidding, honey."

"That's OK then."

"What was he like?"

"It would take too long to explain."

"Why?"

"In fact there's nothing to explain. He was pretty much like all the other visiting foreign professors."

I didn't want to talk about Max to Tarık. Somehow I felt as if this would be a betrayal of Max.

"Now tell me how you can be so cheerful?"

"Why shouldn't I be?" he asked.

"We're in the middle of a serious economic crisis. The lira lost a third of its value in a single day. People are going bankrupt, committing suicide, banks are collapsing, businesspeople are getting arrested. You're in the money business, how can you be so relaxed?"

"Because I'm smart."

"What does that mean?"

"Well, let's just say I've learned a few things."

"What kind of things?"

"It's easy to learn, but you need strong nerves."

He gave me a supercilious smile. He loved talking about this kind of thing.

"You can't move with the crowd and you can't panic."

"Meaning?"

"When everyone buys, you sell, when everyone sells, you buy and you don't panic."

"Is that what you're doing? Hasn't the stock market hit bottom?"

He laughed out loud and took a sip of wine.

"No, on the contrary we're all making money."

"Me too?"

"Of course. You've been making more money than ever. While you were showing the professor around you were also getting rich."

"How did this happen?"

"Everyone was scared out of their wits, buying foreign currency and trying to smuggle it abroad."

"What did you do?"

"I didn't buy any foreign currency. I left it all in Turkish lira."

"Are you crazy? When the lira is losing value so quickly..."

"This is the secret," he said. "Let me put it simply. The Turkish lira became so unpopular that overnight interest rates rose to 9,000 percent."

"So?"

"I invested all my clients' money, as well as yours and my own, in interest-yielding Turkish securities. Just think, you're earning 9,000 percent interest every night."

"But against foreign currency..."

"The situation can't continue the way it is. The exchange rates will balance out. But even with today's rates you've made a lot of money."

"How much?"

"At least twice as much as last month. But be patient, I'll make a lot more money for you. Most people don't know this, but the biggest profits are made in times of crisis."

I did the math in my head, and realized that if I tripled my money I might not have to work anymore.

Tarık raised his glass and said, "To Maya, one of the new rich."

"Don't use that phrase, I hate it," I said.

"Which phrase?"

"New rich. The *nouveau riche*."

"I don't know French."

"It means, new rich. But it's used for rich upstarts, social climbers."

"For goodness' sake," he said, "Stop this nonsense, rich is rich, there's nothing old or new about it!"

Tarık was not one to appreciate nuance of any kind. All he cared about was making money and living his version of the dolce vita. Max and Nadia's story, my grandmothers' stories, these would mean nothing to him. Even if I did my best to explain, he'd understand nothing about what I'd been through in the past week. But at the same time, being with him had done me good. It had lifted me out of the gloom I'd felt myself sinking into. And learning that I was getting rich had certainly cheered me up as well.

He insisted on taking me home that evening.

I was feeling better when I entered my dark apartment, the only light filtering from Kerem's room.

I wondered what Max was doing at that moment. He was probably sleeping because he hadn't slept the night before. Despite his age and illness he was a very strong man.

Then it struck me. I knew what I had to do to get over the feeling of emptiness, to give my life meaning. I had to put together what the professor had told me and begin by writing Maximilian and Nadia's story. I pressed a button on the recorder. This time it was the green light that came on, and Professor Wagner's voice filled the room.

MAXIMILIAN AND NADIA'S STORY

The year was 1934. A tall, slender tutor in a perfectly tailored suit strode purposefully but gracefully toward a small crowd that had gathered in the courtyard of the Munich University Law School. His face bore a stern, almost angry, expression.

Everyone noticed him at once. Indeed, people tended to notice Maximilian Wagner wherever he went.

Young women noticed him because he was handsome and gallant. The Nazis noticed him because he epitomized their ideal of the master race. Professors noticed him because he was an intelligent, hardworking, and original thinker who had reached his position at an unusually young age.

The students in the courtyard moved out of his way as he marched toward a group of about a dozen Nazis who had surrounded a young woman. When he reached them, they stopped tormenting her at once and turned toward him.

German students were still always impeccably respectful to their tutors. Even if he was only slightly older than them, he was still their tutor, and they all knew that he had a brilliant career ahead of him, and that he would play a leading role in the new Germany that would dominate the world.

The young woman, disheveled and trembling with fear and impotent rage, remained in a defensive position, crouching slightly with her arms raised to protect her face. The young tutor held out his hand to her. The students parted to make way for her, and she stepped behind Maximilian without taking his hand. She stood straight now but, mortified at being the center of attention, she didn't look around.

"But you're an Aryan German. Why are you protecting a Jew?" asked one of the Nazi students.

"I'm stopping an injustice. Don't forget that this is a law school." Maximilian replied confidently.

At that, they dispersed, muttering.

Within a few moments they were alone in the courtyard. Maximilian turned and caught the girl's eye. She gave him a shy and somewhat admiring look.

"Are you all right, Nadia?"

"Thank you very much, I'm fine now of course."

"Come, let's have coffee."

As they walked, he found himself amazed that he'd been able to act with such calm confidence. He'd been trying for months to establish a relationship with her, but he'd always been too awkward and shy even to get started. He'd thought about her every moment of every day, and had felt so charged with exhilaration when he was near her that he could barely put one foot in front of the other without stumbling. But then, he hadn't done what he'd done to win her favor. He'd done it because it was the right thing to do, and hoped it was something he would have done for anyone.

As they left the campus together, Maximilian sensed with tremendous joy that a new chapter in his life was beginning. That afternoon, for the first time, they sat at a table together over coffee and Bienenstick cake. Nothing in the world was more important to him than being close to Nadia, and being alone with her at that moment made him happier than he remembered ever being, but he was also aware that the situation was quite grim. Nadia realized that she could no longer study at the university, and she was heartbroken.

"I can tutor you privately. I hate what's happening and I can't stand to see a student as promising as you be shut out like this."

Nadia stared at the table gloomily.

"As those Nazis said, you're an Aryan German. What makes you want to take a risk like this?"

"Being German doesn't mean having to behave like an animal with no conscience. This country is going through a very bad period right now, but I believe the German people will come to their senses and stop putting up with this kind of nonsense."

Nadia gave him a look of hopelessness, as if there was so much she would like to say that she knew this kindhearted young man couldn't possibly understand. Then she gave him a smile of gratitude and slowly shook her head.

"Please. If not for your own sake, then for mine, so that I can ease my conscience. This nonsense won't last long, and then you can take your exams and keep studying at the university."

"I don't know what to say."

"I don't think it's safe for you to come to the campus anymore. The Nazis are getting more and more violent. They're even threatening some of the professors."

Nadia tried unsuccessfully to keep her doubt and fear from showing on her face.

"Since you feel it's too dangerous for me to set foot on campus, I presume you don't intend to tutor me there."

"No...I mean yes, I don't intend to tutor you there."

"Then where?"

He smiled happily and put his hand on hers.

"Don't worry, I know a place where you'll be perfectly safe, where no one will touch you."

A few days later, in his study at home, Maximilian felt a thrill of anticipation as he looked around to make sure everything was just right. He'd put out glasses of fruit juice and a plate of cookies, and had covered them with napkins.

When his mother passed down the hall he ran out and asked her, "Does my jacket match my trousers?"

"Yes, Max, I already told you, you look fine."

"Yes, but...should I take off my jacket? The weather is warm....If I just wear my shirt and trousers...Should I put on a darker shirt?"

"Hmm, yes, maybe you should wear one that's a little darker."

He rushed to his bedroom. His mother called after him.

"Max! What is this girl's name?"

"Nadia! She'll be here any minute—please show her in if she comes while I'm in my room?"

"Of course," she said.

Then she glanced at the clock in the hall. There was more than half an hour before the lesson was to start. She laughed affectionately.

From then on Maximilian tutored Nadia twice a week. They also began to see each other more often outside lessons. They met whenever they could. Nadia rarely proposed they meet, but she accepted Maximilian's invitations.

One weekend afternoon, the harmonious sound of four instruments filled the hall. Two violins, a viola, and a cello. Maximilian and his friends met every week to play music, and for some weeks Nadia had been coming to listen to them.

That day they were playing Schubert's *Serenade*. As the music flowed, the young girl got up, opened the door, and went out onto the balcony. The balcony looked out over the back of the university, and she could see part of the empty courtyard. They'd thought it would be safe for her to be there on the weekend. Nadia stood perfectly still on the balcony, her back to the young musicians.

Max joined her on the balcony when the piece was over. He took her by the shoulders and gently turned her toward him, and as he did so, he felt a sudden ache in his heart. The girl's beautiful eyes were filled with tears. Without saying a word she looked into the young man's eyes, and then put her arms around his neck and began to sob. After waiting for the girl's sobs to subside Max asked, "What's the matter?"

When she didn't answer he asked, "Is it because the composer is Austrian, like Hitler?"

Nadia was unable to speak.

"I'll explain later," she said.

A few days later when he was tutoring her at home, Max asked again what had upset her.

"This may be hard to understand, but when I hear such beautiful music played so well, I feel sad as well as happy. It somehow seems to transcend the human and I fall into a kind of trance. How can man create something so exquisite? It's like the voice of God."

Nadia didn't come to the quartet's practice the following weekend. Max explained why, and they talked about how some people were more affected by music than others. They recalled that Tolstoy, the composer of the *Kreutzer Sonata,* couldn't listen to music when he was writing or when he was feeling particularly sensitive. He would feel like a leaf caught in a storm and his feelings would be shaken to the core. Like him, Nadia did not perceive music as beautiful sounds, but as something devastating.

Then Max told them that he was going to compose a serenade for Nadia. From that day on, he would devote his life to this, and he would put all of his heart and musical talent into it.

Max and Nadia began to spend more time together. They went to restaurants and strolled in the park hand in hand. They made an interesting—indeed striking—couple: a slim, willowy girl with long black hair and green eyes next to a tall, blond man. Nadia was like no one else; she looked both northern and southern.

However, they no longer went to concerts together. Once, when they'd attended a performance of Beethoven's Fifth Symphony, Nadia had sat gripping the arms of her seat with sweat pouring from her brow. Max had finally had to lead her out of the hall under the disapproving gaze of the audience. Every moment Max spent with her, he grew more deeply enamored of her, but he also began to realize that she was very highly strung and subject to storms of emotion that made her tremble like a leaf.

Maximilian was rereading Goethe's *The Sorrows of Young Werther*. He'd liked the novel when he'd read it as a boy, but he hadn't understood why it had caused such an epidemic of suicides among young people. Now, though, he realized that one had to be in love to fully appreciate the novel. He thought about her constantly. He thought about her when he lectured at the university, and he saw her face when he played the violin. She was the last thing he thought about when he went to sleep and the first thing he thought about when he woke. The only thing that kept him sane was composing the *Serenade*. At times it seemed madness to try to emulate one of the greatest musical works of all time, but he kept at it, working for hours at his mother's magnificent Bösendorfer piano.

Schubert had written his *Serenade* one afternoon in 1826 while sitting with friends in Zum

Biersack garden. He flipped through a volume of poetry that had been sitting on the table, and when one poem caught his attention he said, "Such a sweet melody has just come to me, if only I had a sheet of staff paper with me." One of his friends drew some staves on the back of a train ticket, and Schubert wrote his great piece right there and then, with waiters rushing back and forth and fiddlers wandering from table to table.

Maximilian knew that if he titled his piece *Serenade* it would be compared unfavorably to Schubert's work, yet he felt compelled to do so nevertheless.

(The world that Maximilian is describing is so foreign to me I have trouble believing it's real. If I hadn't heard the story from him myself, I would have found it terribly overstated: people committing suicide over a novel, young men pining for their sweethearts and composing serenades for them. I couldn't see anyone behaving like this today. I couldn't imagine Ahmet or Tarık or even Kerem behaving like this. Perhaps it was the spirit of the times.)

Maximilian's mother, Hannelore, was an accomplished pianist. Music was an essential part of the education of wealthy children, and she was no exception to that belief, having received a musical education and provided one for her son. When Maximilian had finished his composition, he showed it to her and asked if they could play it together. He played it on the violin and she accompanied him on the piano, and together they worked out several problems of rhythm and harmony.

Nadia joined them for dinner that evening, and they had a pleasant meal together, avoiding talk of politics, the tension in the country, and what was being done to the Jews. Afterwards, over coffee, Hannelore mentioned that Max had composed a beautiful piece of music. Then Hannelore sat down at the piano and Max picked up his violin and they began to play. Everyone else sat in silence as the room filled with the deeply enchanting music.

Maximilian's father, Albert, listened with great pleasure, but Nadia became quite agitated, and she had to bite her lips to keep from weeping. She was swept up in a storm of emotion but did her best not to show it. When the piece was finished everyone applauded.

Maximilian stood and said, "This may be the first time anyone has made a proposal of marriage with his mother's help, but here goes. Nadia, will you marry me?"

This was too much for Nadia, and she covered her face with her hands and ran into the garden. Max's family watched in astonishment as he ran out after her. He searched for her in the twilit garden, and when he found her in the gazebo, he wrapped her in his arms and pressed her head against his shoulder.

"I'm serious Nadia, please marry me," he said, and kissed her on the lips for the first time.

The following evening Max's parents sat him down for a painful and awkward talk, yet nothing they said could get through to him. It was clear that they were not opposed in principle to his marrying a Jewish girl, and that they were only thinking of his happiness, but this made no difference to him.

"I know how painful it will be for you not to go through with this marriage," his mother said.

There was a long silence.

"But still," Albert continued, "compared with the pain that you would suffer over the years if you were to marry…"

Maximilian just listened without answering, waiting for his parents to finish.

The scene was repeated several times over the next few days.

"They won't leave your wife alone and they won't leave her parents alone either, they won't miss any opportunity to punish her for marrying an Aryan," Albert warned his son.

"We don't know what kind of country this will be for your children to grow up in either," his wife added. "They could face a lifetime of persecution."

That evening Maximilian answered his parents for the first time, "I'm going to marry Nadia. She agreed yesterday evening."

His mother was at a loss for words. She looked at her husband for help. He just sat there, deep in thought, leaning forward with his chin resting on his hand. Then, suddenly, he sat up.

"In that case, we'd better start planning your wedding!"

His wife looked at him as if he'd gone mad. Then Max began to laugh. Then his father and finally his mother began to laugh too. All three of them laughed long and loud. With tears in her eyes, his mother said, "I knew anyway that he wouldn't give up. He's a Wagner too. I know this family only too well. When they have got something into their heads..."

Later, when they'd calmed down, Albert said, "You'll have to move to another city, as far away as possible, and conceal the fact that Nadia is a Jew. As Frau Wagner, she'll be above suspicion."

They all agreed to this, and soon afterwards they visited Nadia's family. They were originally from Romania and lived above her father's tailor shop in a dilapidated building in the suburbs. Since the boycott, their circumstances had been diminished.

They were happy with the announcement, but also quite anxious.

A few weeks later Max and Nadia had a small wedding ceremony in the Wagner's garden, and were married according to the rites of the Roman Catholic Church. Afterwards, however, after all the guests had left, the two families held a Jewish wedding.

Nadia and Maximilian stood under the chuppah. The two families poured wine into their goblets, blessing them according to Jewish tradition, and broke the glasses. Texts were read from the Old and New Testament; they wore the *kippah* and read the *ketubah;* and observed all the traditions, including "the seven blessings."

Then the bridegroom took his violin, and Hannelore sat at the piano, which had been brought out into the garden and illuminated by candles. As they played, tears like jewels rolled from Nadia's eyes. When the music had ended and the applause had died down, Maximilian announced that he had titled the piece *Serenade für Nadia*.

This wedding was a ceremony that couldn't normally take place under Nazi administration. Nadia's family was very pleased. The Roman Catholic Wagner family had behaved with tolerance and had given their consent to everything.

A short time after the wedding, Maximilian began work at Heidelberg University and they moved to that beautiful city. There, they soon established a pleasant life for themselves.

Nadia's official name was Deborah, and they all agreed that for safety they would use this name. Frau Deborah Wagner was a good German name.

There were no Jews at the university to which Max transferred. In fact there were none left at his old university either. A few of his friends had gone to Istanbul, and in the letters that came via Marseilles, they spoke of being content there.

They lived a comfortable and respectable life as Mr. and Mrs. Wagner, and only when they were alone at night did they give voice to their fear and anxiety. They could not believe how bad the situation had become. They had believed that the Third Reich would fall within a few years, but on the contrary, it had become stronger. There were rumors that Jews were being sent to concentration camps.

Nadia's family had made a sudden decision to flee to Romania, and Max and Nadia were relieved because they felt they would be safer there. More and more people were supporting the Nazis, who could carry out their policies of persecution with impunity. Few dared to criticize them, and those who were allowed to do so were being manipulated to create an illusion of democracy.

Then the Nazis seized on news of an assassination in Paris to move their agenda forward. A seventeen-year-old Polish boy shot a member of the German embassy staff in revenge for the murder of his parents. It was presented as a Jewish attack on the Nazis, and they turned it into a propaganda tool. The explosion that Max and "Deborah" had feared began on the night of 9 November 1938, which would be remembered thereafter as

Kristallnacht. By morning, thousands of Jewish businesses had been looted, synagogues had been vandalized, Jewish graves had been desecrated, hundreds of people were injured, and ninety-one Jews were killed. The rising sun and the flames of burning buildings were reflected in the shards of broken glass that covered the streets.

Professor Maximilian Wagner and his elegant wife walked hand in hand toward the university.

"You can still change your mind, darling. We can go back if you like, I'll take you home."

"Oh Max, I have to go this time. Even you said I don't go to enough of these things, and it would look odd if I missed one that was in your honor."

Maximilian had become very popular at the university as his career advanced, and he regularly attended the semi-official celebrations to honor promotions and successes. Tonight's celebration was in honor of his recent publication.

At the cocktail party, people greeted each other politely and spoke affably to one another. A lady from the university went up to the rostrum and announced the occasion for the evening's celebrations, and then invited the rector to say a few words.

The rector made some remarks about Professor Maximilian Wagner's work. As he came to the end of his talk, he raised his voice to expound on the superiority of scholars of the German race. He congratulated Maximilian Wagner, an exemplary scholar and an exemplary German.

Just at that moment the waiter, standing with a bottle in the middle of the hall, popped open the champagne and, as the champagne spouted from the bottle, sounds of applause rose in the hall. The rector joined the other professors and drank champagne. Everyone came over to Maximilian to congratulate him.

The lady from the university went up to the rostrum again to end the ceremony and read a message from the ministry of education. As soon as she had finished, everyone in the hall shot out their right arms and shouted: "Heil Hitler!"

Deborah felt tense. She wondered if anyone had noticed she hadn't given the salute. In the meantime the disagreeable woman at the rostrum repeated some of the words in the message. The people in the hall once again took their glasses in their left hands and began to shout, "Heil Hitler."

This time Deborah stuck out her arm with force. She did so with such violence that she hurt her shoulder. She shouted with all her might: "Heil Hitler!"

Bending her arm at the elbow, she drew it back and thrust it out again in an even more violent salute. She shouted so fiercely that her throat hurt: "Heil Hitler!"

Maximilian Wagner went over to his wife, gently took her arm and lowered it, then put her hand on his shoulder and gently led her to the door.

They went out without saying goodbye to anyone, but no one paid any attention. Everyone understood this German lady's feelings, her excitement, and her pride in her husband's success. Indeed, after they'd gone people even smiled at her fervor.

As soon as they were home Nadia said, "I'm sorry, darling."

Max leaned down and tenderly kissed his wife on the cheek.

It was their habit in the evenings to discuss what was happening as they read the newspapers in the back room, the room furthest from the neighboring apartment. They laughed bitterly about articles such as the one that claimed Jews could be recognized by their smell.

Max put down the paper and looked lovingly as his wife.

"Perhaps the man is right!" he exclaimed. "I know you by your scent too. It always intoxicates me."

This time Nadia didn't laugh.

"They're looking into Aryan and Jewish marriages, Max," she said. "They've already started in other cities. They won't let us live here anymore."

"I don't know, my love. They haven't done anything like that at the university yet. They see us as the most trustworthy group. There's no danger yet."

Nadia leaned forward and cradled her head in her hands. She knew from the way people were talking in the streets and the markets that the situation was becoming even more dangerous. She knew that her husband always tried to comfort her and understate the danger, but she knew that day by day they were closing in. She also knew that, as loving and well intentioned as he might be, there were things he didn't see or understand, that he wasn't as sensitive to the mood as she was. She'd heard talk about people who'd pretended to be German, and knew that there was a lot of suspicion about this. There'd even been Germans arrested and sent to camps because they'd been denounced as Jews.

She couldn't stand to live with this constant fear anymore. She was terrified by the thought of being sent to a camp, of being separated from her husband. Indeed, she was just as worried about how he would survive without her. And, on top of this, she was pregnant. Of this she was certain, it was at least two months.

Despite Max's confidence, she was sure there were suspicions at the university. She could feel it. It seemed as if their friends there had begun to avoid them. Nor did she believe that academics were as trusted by the regime as he seemed to believe. These people didn't trust anyone, and they were naturally suspicious of cultured and intelligent people. Max had refused to swear an oath of loyalty to Hitler and believed his position would keep him safe, but she wasn't so confident it would. No, their position in Germany was becoming impossible.

They'd spent hours talking about this, and both of them realized they'd long since made the decision to leave. Yet they still behaved as if they were trying to decide. They'd even talked about it with Max's parents, who'd agreed that it was best for them to go abroad.

"But where will we go, where can we live?" asked Nadia.

"Istanbul... We can make a new life for ourselves there. After all, we have friends there."

Maximilian's father had friends in high places and was able to take care of the passports and visas. They sold the belongings they couldn't take to a dealer on the far side of town who didn't know them. Max resigned from the university, ostensibly for family reasons.

One Saturday they boarded the train and began their journey to Paris. The last thing that Max did before setting off was to mail a letter to the rector from the station. Nadia had tried to dissuade him, but he wouldn't listen.

Max saw this letter as something he was bound by honor and conscience to send. It denounced the Third Reich and proclaimed his abhorrence of Hitler's racist policies and his pride in his Jewish wife.

Nadia kept insisting that it would be dangerous to send the letter. "What if something goes wrong, Max?" she said, "What if they get hold of the letter before we leave the country? And is it really necessary to make these men angrier than they already are? I ask you, indeed I beg you, don't send that letter. Tear it up and throw it away."

But for some reason Max, who was usually very sensitive to Nadia's wishes, couldn't bring himself to listen to her. From what he said, this was above all a matter of principle. This was a way to raise his voice against the regime that had destroyed the great nation of Germany that he loved so much and to show them he wasn't afraid of them. "Please don't insist," he said to Nadia. "This matter is more important to me than you could imagine. Don't be afraid. After all, we're getting on the train. By the time they get this letter we'll long since have arrived in Paris."

As the train set off for Paris, Maximilian and Nadia talked excitedly about staying one week there, and then boarding the Simplon Orient Express and traveling to Istanbul. They were happy to be starting their new life. They sat down at a table in the train's pleasant, elegant dining car.

"To a wonderful future!"

Maximilian was drinking champagne. He was in a celebratory mood. But Nadia drank only water because she was pregnant, and she wouldn't be able to relax and truly celebrate until they were safely out of the country. She'd also had a tension headache for the past few days.

Nadia had introduced herself as Deborah to a couple of people they met on the train. They were very nearly at the border and soon she would be able to say, "Nadia" with pride to anyone who asked her name.

The station at the border was full of Nazis. They looked like packs of wolves with their high-peaked hats, swastikas, and leather coats.

Maximilian held out their passports and visa documents to the Nazis. He felt relaxed because everything was in order. The Nazi who was checking them didn't give them a second look. He simply stamped the documents and gave them back. He then wished Maximilian a good journey and began to walk away with the other officer. They even touched the peaks of their caps politely to "Frau Wagner."

Perhaps those men would be the last Nazis they ever saw in their lives. Well, they weren't going to miss them, were they? They didn't even glance back at them but continued their conversation. Meanwhile the pudding they'd ordered arrived.

However, Nadia kept rubbing her temple. Max filled a glass with water.

"Come on, take your medicine, my love, before the pain gets worse."

"I don't have it with me, it's in my suitcase. I'll go and get it later."

"No, I'll get it for you." Max got up and massaged his wife's temple a little. "You'll see. Once we get to Istanbul, you won't have headaches any more. I'm sure the headaches are from tension."

He touched his wife on the shoulder and went off. Their compartment was three cars ahead, and it was easy to walk there because the train wasn't moving. When he entered the compartment, he opened Nadia's case and began to search for the medicine. At that point the train started moving. Finally he found the medicine in her toilet bag. The train was gathering speed as he made his way through the three cars to the restaurant car. He sat down at their table. Nadia wasn't there; she must have gone to the bathroom. As he waited he took a sip of his champagne. He put the medicine beside the glass that he'd just filled with water.

The train was forging through the darkness of the night. After leaving Nazi Germany behind, the rattle of the train seemed more cheerful. They were now in France. They would not go back to Germany as long as those people remained in power. He would give Nadia the life she deserved in a neutral country; he would give her the happiness and security she deserved.

Time passed, but there was still no sign of Nadia. He noticed that people were giving him strange looks. Finally he went to the toilet and knocked on the door.

"Nadia are you all right, darling?"

A little later the door opened and a smart gentleman in a bow tie came out. Maximilian went to the waiter.

"Do you remember the lady I had dinner with?"

"Of course, Mr. Wagner!"

"Well, where is she?"

"The Gestapo came and took Mrs. Wagner off the train at the border."

"What?"

"Yes, that's exactly what happened. After you left they came and took Mrs. Wagner."

It was as though the waiter felt a secret pleasure in saying this. There must be a cruel Nazi concealed under this polite front; the situation seemed to amuse him greatly.

"In other words you're saying my wife stayed in Germany?"

"Yes, Herr Wagner, I'm afraid so!"

"I want to go back."

"You can't, Herr Wagner! It's a fair way to the next station."

Maximilian ran to the engineer in horror, but nothing he said made any impression on the man. So he went and pulled the emergency brake in the corridor. The train came to a sudden jolting halt. The conductor rushed up and shouted "What are you doing, Herr Wagner. You've stopped the train in the countryside in the middle of the night! Even if you get out here there's nothing you can do."

That was when Maximilian saw the train's doctor immediately behind him. The doctor stabbed a syringe into Max's arm. That was the last thing he saw before he lost consciousness.

When Maximilian came to, he was lying on the bed in his compartment. His head was aching. When he tried to get up, he realized that he was handcuffed to the bed.

What had happened was terrible. Unbelievable. He was on French soil and Nadia was at the mercy of the Gestapo. He wanted to go back immediately. He began to shout and scream again. The door opened and a security guard came in.

"Let me go!"

"Don't worry, we'll let you go in Paris. We had to sedate and handcuff you because you posed a threat to the safety of the train and the passengers."

"Release me!"

In Paris he got off the train and immediately called Germany. But his father sounded strange on the phone, as if he was having a conversation with someone else.

"Father, what are you saying, I don't understand?"

"Yes, my friend, I'll call you as soon as I can."

"Father, I'm in Paris now. Do you know about what happened on the train?"

"Of course, it's a deal. Very well, we'll do that. It's best you go there. Yes, that's the best place."

"Are you trying to tell me not to come back, Father? I can't come in any case. The letter to the rector…"

"The Gestapo is here," his father's voice whispered. Then he continued in a normal tone.

"Yes Kurt, we'll talk again as soon as you arrive."

"I understand, Father. I'll go ahead to Istanbul. Father! Please find Nadia!"

There was nothing to do now but wait for the Istanbul train. For days, he wandered in despair through the streets of Paris. He didn't eat, he didn't drink, and he didn't rest. He hoped that if he wore himself out he might be able to sleep on the train and reach Istanbul without going mad. He wanted to live. He had to survive for Nadia.

A group of people, most of them Jews, was waiting for the train at Sirkeci station in Istanbul. Professor Wagner's news had arrived ahead of him, and his friends had rushed to the station to meet him. They'd expected a grieving, exhausted man, but were not prepared for what they saw. The commotion died down as soon as he stepped off the train, and they began to behave as if they were at a funeral. They each greeted and embraced him in turn, and muttered a few words of heartfelt consolation.

Max was determined to save Nadia. He would do whatever it took, even if it cost him his own life. If he had to, he would go back to Germany, and he was even willing to try to assassinate Hitler.

Maximilian couldn't talk about his grief to his friends. But there was no need for him to do so because it was obvious. Most of the professor's acquaintances in Istanbul lived in the district of Bebek, by the sea. First they settled him into the Pera Palas Hotel. A few weeks later they rented a small flat for him near the university. He wouldn't need a larger place until Nadia came.

The first thing he did was to arrange all of Nadia's things. He ironed her clothes and hung them in the closet, put away her shoes, and arranged her perfumes and creams in front of the mirror on the dresser. He hung their wedding photos on the walls.

Everything was ready. All that was missing was Nadia. Maximilian went back and forth to the university like a robot, taught his classes, and started learning Turkish. He concentrated on finding out where Nadia was, but this was very difficult under the circumstances. Despite his influence, Max's father could do nothing either; he couldn't reach Nadia. He himself was in danger now because he had a Jewish daughter-in-law, and his standing had diminished.

When Max met people he knew, either new acquaintances or old friends, all he could talk about was Nadia. They talked mostly about the war. Just about everyone in Turkey, and indeed the whole world, could think about little else.

Turkey had remained neutral, and tried to remain on good terms with everyone, including the Germans. Atatürk, who had died the day after Kristallnacht, had been replaced as president by İnönü, who resisted Churchill's pressure to enter the war. But there were many influential people in and out of the government who supported Hitler and who celebrated news of German victories.

Turkey was exporting chromium to Germany. A "German Information Office" was set up in Istanbul and was extremely successful in its propaganda. The German expatriate community would meet at Teutonia-Haus and give parties in the garden of the consular residence in Tarabya. Maximilian and his friends were ostracized by them, and people from Max's circle had no place there. Indeed, the German government was putting pressure on the Turkish government to return the Jewish scholars. Adolf Hitler sent a special representative to prepare reports about them and influence the Turkish government:

His name was Scurla.

Max went about his life, keeping busy at the university and with various social engagements, but the only thing that mattered to him was to find Nadia and rescue her. In time, his efforts to do so brought him to Notre Dame de Sion.

Notre Dame de Sion was a French Catholic girls' school in the Harbiye district and, at the time, one of the most prestigious girls' high schools in the city. Some of his students and colleagues were graduates of the school, and he had been there once for the wedding of a Turkish colleague.

He returned later when he learned that they were involved in efforts to help Jewish refugees. He told them Nadia's story, and they told him sadly that all they could do was to pray for her. But he did learn that there was a certain Father Roncalli who might be in a position to help.

Father Roncalli, later to become Pope John XXIII, was then the Vatican Apostolic Delegate to Turkey and had become very popular not only among Turks, but also among all the religious minorities in the country. He was the first Catholic priest to say Mass in Turkish and had become involved in rescuing large numbers of Balkan Jews, partly with the help of Franz von Papen, the German ambassador to Turkey.

Papen was a former chancellor of Germany and had been instrumental in bringing Hitler to power, and as ambassador to Austria had played a leading role in the *Anschluss*. Later he fell out of favor with the regime and several of his close associates were killed; it was proposed that he become ambassador to Turkey to keep him away from the center of power. Atatürk objected because he'd known Papen during World War I and considered him untrustworthy, but after Atatürk's death his posting was approved. Papen's mission was to do his utmost to keep Turkey from joining the war on the allied side, and, if possible, to convince the Turkish government to join the German invasion of Russia. He was also charged with developing ties with the Arabs. Yet, interestingly, Papen helped Roncalli to save the lives of as many as 24,000 Jews. Later, during the Nuremberg trials, Roncalli testified in Papen's defense, and he was acquitted.

One day Maximilian went to the magnificent building behind Notre Dame de Sion to meet Father Roncalli, whom he found to be a gentle, kindhearted man. Indeed, he found it very easy to talk to him, and was able to tell him the entire story.

"I'm Catholic, Father," he said. "My wife is a Jew and is about to give birth any time now. But

I don't know what conditions she's living under, I don't even know if she's alive. In the name of everything sacred, I beg you to help me. I'm about to go out of my mind."

Roncalli put his hand on Max's, looked into his eyes, and said, "I understand, my son. I understand your grief and I'll do everything I can for you."

Then in a low voice he explained that he had given baptismal certificates to Jews through priests, interpreters, and merchants traveling to Europe, and had been able to save thousands of lives.

Maximilian couldn't keep still while he was listening to the priest. He got to his feet, paced the room, sat down again, looked entreatingly at the priest, touched his hand, and then got to his feet again—he couldn't contain himself.

Father Roncalli said, "What I need from you is to find out where your wife is and to figure out a way to get the certificate to her. And also, of course, you have to be sure she'll agree."

"What do you mean, father? Why wouldn't she?"

"Some Jews prefer to die rather than receive a baptismal certificate."

"I'm sure that won't be a problem. She's a rational person. If you can give me the certificate, I'll find out where she is and get it to her."

In contrast to Maximilian's restless excitement, the priest was calm and spoke in a measured tone.

"But I have to swear you to secrecy because thousands of lives are at stake."

Max swore that no one would hear of it. Then they went downstairs, where Roncalli told his assistant to get Nadia's details and fill out her baptismal certificate.

Before leaving, Max had one more thing to ask.

"Perhaps I'm asking too much but I wonder, if you asked Papen, would he be able to find out where my wife is?"

"I'm afraid I can't do that, my son," said the priest. "May God help you."

Max left with a strong sense of gratitude, and also of accomplishment and hope. He now had a baptismal certificate in Deborah's name, which represented a way to get her out of Germany. If he had to, he'd go back under a false identity to search for her. He couldn't manage this on his own, but he had many friends among the German professors in Istanbul.

One afternoon he took a walk with Erich Auerbach through Sultanahmet Square. Erich, who'd been living in Istanbul since 1935, was a quiet, serious person who minded his own business and whom everyone respected. Max trusted him, admired his character and generosity, valued his opinions, and did not hesitate to confide this latest development.

Erich didn't say anything right away, and they walked for a while in silence. Then, without turning to Max he said, "Perhaps Schummi can help you."

It was clear that he wasn't sure about this, but because Max knew Erich never said anything he didn't mean, it was enough to give him hope.

"How?" he asked. "How can he help, what can he do?"

"Schummi" was Albert Eckstein, a respected pediatrician who had been hired by the Turkish Ministry of Health in 1935 after he lost his job at Düsseldorf University. He worked at the Numune Hospital in Ankara and was consulted by the most influential politicians and even by Papen and other German diplomats.

Erich told him that when the minister of agriculture's five-year-old daughter came down with emphysema and was sent to a hospital in Vienna, Atatürk asked Schummi to go and supervise her treatment. This was after the *Anchluss*, and Schummi was naturally reluctant to go, but Atatürk gave his personal assurance that a Turkish attaché would stay with him the entire time.

Schummi went to Budapest by train, and continued from there to Vienna in the company of a Turkish diplomat. At the hospital he found the girl on the verge of death, but the doctors refused to perform surgery because they believed it would be a waste of time. He insisted and, to everyone's surprise, the surgery was successful and she began to recover.

Schummi was very depressed by what he'd seen in Vienna and by the racist attitudes of the Austrian doctors, but he did manage to obtain Turkish diplomatic passports for a Jewish doctor and an anti-fascist nurse whose Jewish fiancé had disappeared.

"Thank you very much, Erich," he said, "You've been a great help."

He'd already resolved to go to Ankara and meet Schummi when Erich said, "Wait! I haven't finished yet. There's a reason I'm telling you all this."

"Go ahead."

"Schummi has become so popular in Ankara that cabinet ministers, Papen's wife, and even some leading Nazis have consulted him."

"Really?"

"Yes. This will be useful. Schummi was recently consulted by Maitzig, the German trade attaché, who everyone knows is running an extensive network of Nazi agents in the region."

"I've heard of him."

"Schummi went to his house and treated his child, and as he was leaving Maitzig stopped him and said, 'Thank you very much, Dr. Eckstein. Perhaps there might be something I can do for you. Do you have any relatives in Germany?' Schummi said, 'They're all dead. Thanks to you, they're all dead.' He also refused the payment he was offered, saying that Maitzig's money was filthy."

The next day Max got leave from the university and went to Ankara by train. Dr. Eckstein was clearly very busy, but he graciously made time for Max and invited him to his office for coffee. Max told him his story as briefly as possible.

"I don't know which concentration camp my wife is in, whether she's alive or dead, or about to give birth, but here's the baptismal certificate. Please, doctor, a family's life is in your hands."

"I really want to help you, but it would be humiliating for me to ask Maitzig for any favors."

"It's a matter of life and death. Help me, I beg you."

Maximilian closed his eyes and waited for a while. Then he continued, "Give me a letter and I'll speak to Maitzig."

"No!" said Dr. Eckstein. "That would amount to the same thing." Then he looked at Maximilian. "I can't promise, but perhaps there's a solution."

Professor Wagner held his breath and waited.

"Mrs. Papen will be coming here in a little while," continued Eckstein. "Perhaps I can take the opportunity to ask her a favor."

"You are a remarkable person, doctor," Maximilian said. "I'll never forget this."

"Well, we don't know yet if anything will come of it."

Professor Wagner handed him the baptismal certificate and stood up.

"I'll wait in the garden. I'd be grateful if you could spare me a few minutes after you've seen Mrs. Papen."

Maximilian wandered in the garden among the crowds of desperate Anatolian villagers. Soon a black car arrived with a police escort. Mrs. Papen got out, and the director of the hospital came rushing out to greet her.

Max waited, and waited... He tried to squat like the Anatolian villagers but within a few minutes his legs were aching. He couldn't understand how they were able to sit like that for hours on end.

After a while Mrs. Papen was escorted to her car by the director, and Max made his way anxiously to Schummi's office.

They looked at each other for a while without speaking. Eckstein seemed quite tired and he didn't look well. Max was afraid to ask him anything because he didn't know if he could cope with the disappointment if it hadn't gone well.

"Professor Wagner," said Eckstein. "I've done my part. I gave your wife's baptismal certificate to Mrs. Papen and asked her to look into it. She promised she'd do what she could. All we can do now is pray that it works."

They looked at each other in silence a little longer. After taking a breath, Eckstein continued: "I wish from the bottom of my heart that you and your wife will be reunited."

Maximilian didn't know how he could ever thank him. He shook Eckstein's hand, and then left the room without saying another word.

That evening he boarded the train and returned to Istanbul. He went straight to Erich and told him what had happened. Now he could do nothing more but wait.

He felt extremely grateful to Auerbach, to Eckstein, and to the other Jews who'd supported him. Germany had destroyed their lives and killed their relatives; but even so they didn't hesitate to help him.

The days dragged past as he tried by various means to get whatever information he could. He did learn that Nadia's parents had been killed in Romania. They'd been in a large group that had been herded into a building. Later people were released a few at a time. But in fact they weren't being released, and they were hung on metal hooks as soon as they came out.

Then, about three weeks after his return from Ankara, he finally got news of Nadia. She'd been sent to Dachau, where she'd lost her baby. With Papen's help she'd been released from the camp, given her baptismal certificate, and sent back to Romania.

That was all he'd been able to find out, but he was overjoyed to know she was alive and out of the camp. Now all he had to do was find out where in Romania she was and get her to Istanbul, which seemed easy compared to what he'd already done.

He wanted to set off for Romania at once, but he couldn't because Romania was allied with Germany and he faced arrest there, which wouldn't do Nadia any good. But everything was on track, and soon he'd be able to get Nadia to Istanbul and help her forget what she'd been through. That evening he was in such good spirits that he took out his violin and played the *Serenade* for the first time since he'd left Germany.

He was interrupted by his downstairs neighbors, the Arditis, Sephardic Jews whose ancestors had come to Istanbul five hundred years before. They said they'd heard him playing, and asked if he wouldn't mind them coming in and listening to him. Maximilian bowed respectfully and invited them in. He waited for them to settle in their chairs and then picked up his violin and played the *Serenade*.

Then he told them the story of how he had composed the piece and what had happened to

Nadia. Unable to speak, Rober Arditi signaled to the professor to play the piece again. As they listened to the *Serenade* for the second time, tears poured from their eyes.

When Maximilian put his violin down on the table, Mr. Arditi slowly got up and left the room. His wife, however, began to talk warmly. She said that when Nadia arrived, she would help her, show her Istanbul, and make sure that she didn't feel out of place.

Her husband returned a few minutes later with a bottle of red wine. They drank to Nadia. They were upset that Nadia had lost her baby, but they all decided that this was not the time to think about that. After all, the Wagners would have more children.

The Arditis were very hopeful about finding Nadia in Romania. Rober Arditi had business connections in Romania, and they might be able to help get Nadia out. But where should they look for her?

Max shared the scraps of information he'd managed to gather, and Mr. Arditi wrote down the names of Nadia's parents, where they were from, and the names of former acquaintances he might be able to contact.

From then on he began to spend more time with the Arditis. Rober kept him informed of everything he was doing to find Nadia, and did whatever he could to keep Max's spirits up.

One day Mr. Arditi came running up the stairs in a state of excitement. He'd located Nadia. She'd gone back to her hometown and begun to work with a Romanian tailor her father had known. But she wasn't safe. More and more Jews were being killed in Romania, and they had to get her out as soon as they could.

Max wrote a letter to Nadia, put it in an envelope with all the dollars he'd been able to save, and gave it to Arditi, who said he'd make sure it got to Nadia, together with the names of a few people who could help her get to Istanbul.

A month later they received news from a merchant in Romania. Nadia had received the money and letter and was coming to Istanbul on a ship that was to sail from Constanța.

The ship was to sail in five days. If the trip lasted two days, Nadia would be in Istanbul, in her home, beside Max in their bed, in a week at most.

Mrs. Arditi suggested decorating the house in honor of her arrival and arranging a welcoming ceremony. She would do all the cooking herself. Max was so overjoyed that he kept kissing the Arditis.

The next day he told his Turkish and German friends at the university. When Nadia arrived they would go see Father Angelo Roncalli and Schummi together. Every day Max had the house cleaned all over again, and he filled it with flowers.

He began counting the hours until the nightmare he'd been living would be over, but his excitement and anticipation were so strong that each hour was an eternity. When there were 74 hours left, he felt as if he couldn't stand it anymore, and when there were 17 hours left, it was simply impossible to sit still. Of course his estimation of the time passing was based solely on guesswork, and optimistic guesswork at that.

When he thought that there were 12 hours left, he hired a taxi and headed up the Bosporus as far as he could go, to a place called Telli Baba, from which he could see the confluence of the Bosporus and the Black Sea. It was a beautiful spot, with steep, wooded hills running down to the sea, but he was in no mood to enjoy the view and could think only of the ship. The taxi driver smoked one cigarette after another while Max scanned the horizon with his binoculars. At one point a squad of soldiers patrolling the area became suspicions and approached to warn them off, but when they heard Max's story they allowed him to stay.

Then, finally, he made out the silhouette of a ship approaching the Bosporus. Its approach was maddeningly slow. Much slower, in fact, than normal. A long time later, when he could make it out more clearly, he saw that it was a very old and dilapidated ship. It also appeared to have broken down, because a tugboat was towing it. Later, he could see that the deck was crowded with people, and then at last he was able to make out the name: *Struma*.

At last Nadia was in Turkish waters. The ship passed quite close, and at one point it was just below him. The people on the deck were tightly packed together, but try as he might he couldn't see Nadia.

Max had the taxi keep pace with the boat along the shore road. Then, when the ship dropped anchor off Tophane, Max went down to the shore with the taxi driver to see about hiring a motorboat to take them out to the ship and get Nadia. The taxi driver reached an agreement with one of the boatmen, and they jumped into one of the boats and sped off toward the ship.

The ship was listing, and looked as if it was about to sink. All Max could think of was getting Nadia off the ship and bringing her home. But the coast guard boats would not let them draw alongside the ship. They waved, blew whistles, and yelled, "Quarantine, quarantine!" They had no choice but to go back to the shore.

Max had assumed that there was a delay because of passport control and health inspections. Hours passed, and when nothing happened Max went to the port authorities. The director informed him that the *Struma*'s actual destination was Palestine, but because the engine had failed, it had stopped at the port in Istanbul.

"My wife was going to disembark in Istanbul, she wasn't going to Palestine. Can I just bring her ashore?"

"No," the director shook his head. "We've been ordered not to allow a single passenger to land or anyone to draw alongside the ship."

After so many days spent counting the hours this was almost too much for Max, but he pulled himself together quickly. The important thing was

that Nadia was in Istanbul. He would do everything in his power to get her ashore, and he was
confident he would succeed. He thought it would
take him two days at most.

But days passed and no one was allowed off
the ship. In the meantime passengers had hung up
cloth banners with phrases in French such as "*Sau-
ver Nous*" and "*Immigrants Juifs.*" Something very
strange was going on. Max felt as if he were about
to lose his mind. Nadia was so near but he couldn't
see her. He just couldn't grasp what was going on.

The next day he went to the university rector,
explained the situation, and asked him for help.
The rector suggested he speak to Sadık Bey, who
held a senior position in the port authority. He
even helped him get an appointment.

Sadık Bey welcomed him, offered him coffee,
and told him the story of the *Struma*.

The *Struma* had been built in Newcastle in
1867 and was registered in Panama. It belonged to
the Compania Mediterranea de Vapores Limitada,
which was owned by a Greek called Pandelis and
operated by a Bulgarian named Baruh Konfino.

In 1941, when 4,000 Jews were killed in
Iaşi in Romania, Jews began to look for ways
to escape the country. At that point, illustrated

advertisements appeared in the newspapers. The "luxury ship *Struma*" that was to sail from Constanţa to Palestine. The advertisements contained illustrations of the luxurious saloons and cabins of the *Queen Mary*. The fare was exorbitant, $1,000 per person, but 769 passengers were able to buy tickets. Because some families had only been able to collect $1,000, they had had to make a choice amongst their children and decide which of them would be saved.

The passengers were horrified when they saw the *Struma*. When they complained, the ship-owner allayed their fears by saying that the real ship was waiting outside Romanian waters. They only discovered that this was a lie when it was too late to turn back.

The ship was packed to many times its capacity. There wasn't enough room for everyone on deck, so the passengers were cramped in the stuffy hold and allowed up for air for only fifteen minutes at a time. The provisions were inadequate. They began experiencing problems with the engine almost as soon as they left Costanţa, and broke down completely as they were approaching the Bosporus. In reply to an SOS, a Turkish rescue ship towed the *Struma* to the harbor.

Sadık Bey told him that the ship could not continue to Palestine in the state it was in. "Well, what's going to happen?"

"We'll wait and see."

"But my wife was coming to Istanbul. I have to get her off the ship."

"I'm sorry but you can't."

"Why?"

"The government has given strict orders; no one is to leave the ship."

In the following days he learned more about what was going on from the newspapers.

The Turkish government believed that the refugees' real destination was Istanbul and not Palestine, and they had no intention of accepting 769 Jews. They wanted the ship to continue to Palestine after the engine was repaired. However, the British, who were then in control of Palestine, were determined to limit Jewish immigration for fear of antagonizing the Arabs. They pressured the Turkish government not to allow the refugees to proceed to Palestine, and rejected a proposal to allow the refugees to continue their journey overland.

Maximilian went to the docks every day with his binoculars in hopes of catching a glimpse of

Nadia. Meanwhile, he was growing increasingly frustrated and puzzled by all the intrigue and delay. None of it had anything to do with him and Nadia, and it seemed absurd that these people should suffer because of this ridiculous bureaucratic mentality.

Once again, Maximilian took the same taxi to the docks and scanned the ship with his binoculars. He waited on the shore and the passengers waited on the ship, and nothing was being resolved. The newspapers reported that two young people had jumped ship but had been caught and returned. Max had missed this; he still had to meet his classes at the university and wasn't free to spend his entire day on the docks.

At first no one but a few officials was allowed onto the ship. Later, some members of Istanbul's Jewish community were granted permission to do what they could to help the refugees. They brought the engine ashore to have it repaired and brought food and medical supplies to the ship.

Consequently, more information about conditions on the ship began to circulate. Max heard that the only toilet had become blocked and that disease was beginning to spread. There was little food or medicine and no fuel for heating, and the passengers were becoming desperate. Occasionally people on the shore could hear them shouting, begging for help.

Maximilian had little trouble learning that Simon Brod and Rifat Karako were the two people allowed to come and go to the ship.

He approached them through the Arditis, explained the situation, and asked Mr. Brod to deliver a letter to Nadia.

In the letter he'd asked her to stand at a specific place on deck at exactly three o'clock. He was in place; he'd been there for a long time, making a supreme effort not to look at his watch. When he finally did, he saw that there were two minutes left. He picked up his binoculars and looked, and yes, there she was!

She was much thinner and she looked tired, but she was still beautiful. Indeed, she stood out so much from the others that he was amazed he hadn't seen her before. Had she not been up on deck at all? Now, he couldn't take his eyes off her.

Nadia waved to Max and then blew him a kiss. She also had a pair of binoculars. He wondered whether the people who'd taken the letter had given it to her or if she'd found it on the ship.

Max began to wave and blow kisses. He yelled, "I love you!"

Yes, Nadia had definitely seen him; she was waving.

The next day Max found Simon Brod again. He couldn't contain himself. He took the piece of paper he gave him. It was something like a shopping list, a yellow piece of paper with Romanian words on it. When he turned it over he immediately recognized his wife's handwriting. It was written in excitement, in haste. "Wait for me! Nadia."

Brod told him that conditions on the ship were getting worse, and that they feared people might soon begin to die.

"Well, what are you going to do, Mr. Brod?"

"We haven't been able to get through to the Turkish government. The only thing is to repair the engine as soon as possible, fuel the ship, and send it on its way."

"But the British won't allow that either."

"Yes, our friends are lobbying in London. We're talking with the embassy here. It's a difficult situation and we're doing all we can."

The professor laughed out loud. His nerves were shot.

"This is worse than I thought. It drives me crazy to be able to see her but not reach her."

Max was at his wits' end. There was nothing Schummi could do to help him, but perhaps Father Roncalli could. Perhaps he could get someone with a baptismal certificate off the boat. But Father Roncalli told him that there was nothing he could do; that he'd already tried and failed to rescue people from the ship. Then one day as he was waiting by the docks, he saw a motorboat leaving the ship and bringing some people ashore.

So, it seemed that some of the passengers were being rescued. But what about those who remained on the ship? What about Nadia?

The following day he learned that a wealthy businessman named Vehbi Koç had managed to get Martin Segal, the Romanian representative of the Standard Oil Company, and his wife and two children off the boat. And two days later a motorboat brought a sick woman ashore. The professor learned from Simon Brod that the woman was about to give birth and she had been admitted to the Or-Ahayim Hospital in Balat because she was bleeding. At the request of his friends from his own university's medical school, he got an appointment with Or-Ahayim's chief physician.

The hospital was on the banks of the Golden Horn. Max told the chief physician that his wife was on the ship and that he'd like to see the lady who'd been brought to the hospital. Again, he was struck by how sympathetic and obliging all the Jews he'd sought help from had been. After all, he was a German and they had reason not to trust him.

When Maximilian tiptoed into her room, the woman was sleeping with a drip attached to her arm. She'd had a hemorrhage and miscarried. He just stood there, without disturbing her, waiting for her to wake up. She had a fine-featured face with dark hair and fair skin. Her face was very thin, her cheeks sunken, and she had black circles under her eyes. Looking at her, Max understood more fully how bad things were on the ship.

Finally the woman awoke. Her name was Medea Salomovici, and fortunately she spoke German.

Her eyes rested for a moment on Maximilian's face, as if she were trying to remember who he was.

"I'm sorry, Mrs. Salomovici, I'm afraid I woke you up."

The woman gazed at Max a while longer without responding.

She looked at him for a long time, and then in a barely audible voice said, "Hello, Herr Wagner!"

The professor was stunned. How could she know who he was? She said something else, but he couldn't make it out so he leaned in closer.

"Nadia helped me a great deal," she said. "She did everything she could to ease my pain." She took a breath. Then she took Max's hand and fixed her huge black eyes on his.

"She always talked about you. She showed me your picture, that's how I recognized you. Save her from that hell as quickly as you can. I can't tell you how bad things are, people are going to start dying. My husband is on the ship too."

She began to weep inconsolably muttering again and again that Nadia would die if he didn't save her, that her husband was going to die and there was nothing she could do to help him.

Maximilian left the hospital with a sense of deep hopelessness, yet he was determined to remain strong. He couldn't give up; he couldn't allow himself the luxury of despair. He had to do something. He had to fight for Nadia.

The newspapers were following the negotiations between the Turkish and British governments. The latest development was a statement by

Winston Churchill that on no account would the ship be allowed to continue on to Palestine.

Exactly seventy days had passed. Maximilian was watching as usual through his binoculars when he saw a large number of policemen board the ship. Something was happening. The passengers began to resist the police, who were herding them into the hold. Then they cut the anchor and a large tugboat started towing the ship away. They turned the bow and started towing it up to the Black Sea. How could they do this? How could they tow the ship to sea without an engine or an anchor?

The taxi driver, Remzi, who'd been with Max all this time and who'd begun to see Max's mission as his own, let out a cry of alarm, took Max by the shoulders and shook him, then pointed to the ship, as if Max hadn't seen.

They drove along the shore road, keeping pace with the ship, until they could go no further. They watched it being towed into the Black Sea, and then to the east, in the direction of Riva and Şile.

Max wanted to take the next car ferry to the Asian side and try to continue to follow the *Struma,* but the taxi driver dissuaded him. They wouldn't be able to find their way in the dark, nor would they be able to see the ship. On top of that, they wouldn't be able to get back because the car ferries stopped running in the evening. Max agreed reluctantly to set out at four in the morning, and thus made a decision that he was to regret deeply for the rest of his life.

After a long, hellish, and sleepless night, they took the first car ferry and headed north toward Şile. When they reached the sea they followed the coast, and Max got out from time to time to scan the horizon with his binoculars. Finally, at Yom Point near Şile he saw the *Struma*. It looked abandoned, and the tugboat was gone.

They went down to the shore to the same spot he would visit fifty-nine years later with his violin. There were some fishermen nearby, and he ran over to see if he could get them to take him out to the ship. The sea was rough and they were reluctant, but he was able to offer enough money to convince one of them.

The taxi driver said he would wait on the shore, so Max got into the boat and they started struggling out through the waves to the ship. Despite the rocking, Max stood up and started shouting to Nadia that he was coming to get her. There were no police around, there was no one to stop him, and in half an hour at most he would be back ashore with Nadia.

The fisherman kept trying to get Max to sit down, saying he was making it difficult to steer. He finally took Max by the arm and sat him down, and just at that moment, there was a violent explosion aboard the *Struma*.

For a moment, the world was ripped apart. Debris flew through the air, and Max could feel the force of the blast. There was a terrible gurgling sound as the ship's stern disappeared under the sea, and then suddenly there was a terrible silence. For a moment Max and the fisherman just stared at the place where the ship had been, and at the wreckage and the human bodies bobbing about on the waves. Then the fisherman gunned the engine, turned the boat around, and started racing toward the shore. Max rushed back and forth in the tiny motorboat.

"Stop!" he shouted. "Go back, go back!"

The fisherman didn't pay any attention, so he tackled him and tried to grab the tiller. They struggled, and the fisherman fell overboard. Then as Max was trying to turn the boat around, a large wave hit it broadside, and the next thing Max knew, he was flailing in the freezing sea and the waves washed him toward the shore.

When Max came to, he wasn't sure at first where he was. There were men gathered around him, and all of them were gesticulating. One of them was completely wet, and was trying to attack him. The others seemed to be holding him back. Suddenly, he heard the sound of the waves and of the men shouting. Then, when he looked out to sea, he saw the wreckage and the bodies.

More people had arrived, as well as several official-looking vehicles and men in various uniforms.

Max shouted something unintelligible, jumped up, and began running toward the sea. Almost immediately a man tackled him. He recognized the man—it was Remzi, the taxi driver who'd been with him for over two months now. Why was his friend hurting him, why wouldn't he let him go?

Eventually the police arrived, handcuffed Maximilian, and took him to Istanbul. He kept asking them if anyone had survived. Eventually one of them told him that only one person had been rescued. One person out of all 769 passengers and the additional crewmembers. Of course he prayed that Nadia had been the only survivor. But no, it had been a young man called David.

As soon as Max heard this he began to shout and scream.

"Murderers, murderers, murderers!"

They threw him into a cell in the basement of the police station. It was damp and smelled of mold. A bright light was left on and, because the cell had no windows, he didn't know if it was day or night.

He alternately banged his head against the wall and lay curled up on the floor, and he refused to eat. Whenever he closed his eyes he could see the bodies floating on the waves. Where had Nadia been when the explosion occurred? Had she been waiting on deck, had she seen him coming to save her? Or had she been in the hold? What was the last thing she'd thought? Had she died instantly? Had she had time to be afraid? Had she survived for hours, flailing in the freezing water?

Whenever a guard came to check on him he shouted, "I'm going to spend my life telling people about this. I'm going to make sure the whole world knows about this murder." It was 24 February 1942.

Within days, rumors began to circulate about who had sunk the *Struma*. Some said that the Turks had torpedoed it, and others that the

Germans had blown it up by attaching a mine or concealing explosives aboard. Years later an investigator for the Frankfurt prosecutor's office discovered that it had been torpedoed by the Soviet submarine SC-213, which was under orders to sink all unidentified shipping in the Black Sea. The submarine commander, Lieutenant Denezhko, radioed the *Struma* several times asking for identification. But the *Struma* had no radio, and when he received no reply, Denezhko gave orders to fire the torpedo.

They released Professor Wagner from prison and took him home, telling him that he was under house arrest until they had completed their inquiries. A few days later they informed him he was to be deported. They asked him where he wanted to go, and he told them the United States.

He was given no time to pack his things, and among the possessions he had to leave behind was the score of *Serenade für Nadia*. He was allowed to make one final telephone call, so he called the university and asked them to give his belongings to the Arditi family.

When he left Istanbul he never imagined he would return fifty-nine years later. When he arrived in the United States he did not maintain any ties to Turkey or anyone he'd known there. For some months he remained in a state of shock and depression; then he slowly began to recover. Then, unexpectedly he received a letter that turned his life upside down again. It was a letter from Nadia.

My darling,

Please don't be upset when this unfortunate woman, I mean, Medea, gives you this letter. Whatever she tells you, don't believe her. This young woman is in a very sensitive state because of her pregnancy and illness. The situation on the ship has affected her more than any of us.

I'm not writing this to reassure you. Believe that I am well. I know that I will manage to escape.

Two days ago I looked up at the sky and closed my eyes. I begged God to send me a sign. When I opened my eyes I was afraid I would see an empty sky, but that is not what happened. God heard me. Right over my head I saw a flock of birds flying in a perfect V formation. Yes, they were right over my head. I believed this was the sign I had asked for.

God, who is both your master and mine, and master of all people, sent me a victory sign from heaven. I was filled with gratitude and joy. I know that this is not just a feeling. I know without a doubt

that I will be rescued and reunited with you. Then I
can hear you play the Serenade *I've missed so much.*

It gives me such joy to know that we're so close,
that we're in the same city, that we're breathing the
same air.

We will be united soon, we will tell each other
everything.

But in the meantime, please don't be upset. I'm
well, I'm in good health, we are warm and we have
enough to eat.

I long for the day when we're together again.

Your wife,
Nadia

Nadia had given the letter to Medea knowing
that Max would go see her, but at that moment
Medea had forgotten about the letter. When she recovered and was allowed to travel on to Palestine,
she sent the letter to the university, and from there
it began its long, circuitous journey to the United
States, by way of Egypt, South Africa, and Argentina.

After he read the letter, Maximilian returned
for some time to a state of listless despair. The only
thing that finally began to draw him out was the
effort he made to remember all the notes of *Serenade für Nadia.*

CHAPTER 15

You have read the heartrending story of Maximilian and Nadia as a separate section of my book in a form that is very often encountered in Eastern literature. To place sections that can be read as part of the book or as independent stories was extremely popular with Feridüddin-i Attar, in *One Thousand and One Nights*, and in the *Mesnevi*. Of course, I do not aspire to be a professional writer or claim to represent Eastern literature. But in this humble narration, there can be no harm in my exploring avenues in keeping with the tradition to which I feel close. I shall now continue my story from where I left off.

The following day I woke with a surprising amount of energy. I wasn't at all tired despite having slept very little. After sending Kerem off to school, I sent an email to the Foreign Ministry. I told them that an academic attached to Istanbul University was writing a book about the "regrettable" *Struma* disaster of 1942, and asked if permission would be granted to look into the ministry's files on the subject.

I did not expect a favorable answer but I wanted to try my luck.

They might not see any harm in the files being opened after all these years.

After that I quickly got ready and left the house. Once again, it was a day of freezing rain mixed intermittently with snow. I took a bus to Beyazit, and then followed my usual route to the university. This time, however, my purpose and destination were different. I had a photocopy of Maximilian Wagner's deportation order, which included the address he'd lived at then.

Several coffee shops in Beyazıt Square had revived the water-pipe fad of the Ottoman period. They were full of students and tourists. I'd never smoked a water pipe and decided to try it one day. I wondered what effect the smoke had when you inhaled through water.

As I passed the food stalls lining the square, the smell of toasted sausage sandwiches made me stop. I'd left home without eating anything. I sat at one of the small, white Formica tables and ordered a toasted sausage sandwich and a yogurt drink. I also showed the waiter the address and asked where Nasip Street was. The waiter didn't know the street but perhaps the elderly owner of the shop next door might.

After I finished my sandwich, I went to the corner shop and asked the elderly man behind the counter. He thought for a while, frowned and then said, "I remember vaguely but...I don't know. They've changed the names of a lot of streets around here. You might try asking at the police station."

They'd never heard of Nasip Street at the police station either. The name had definitely been changed. But they had some old maps, and after a while they found it. The name was now Akdoğan Street. On my way there I wondered about this whole business of changing names, not just of streets but of villages, towns, and entire districts as well. It must, I thought, be an attempt to erase one version of history and replace it with another. The result was layers of conflicting versions of history imposed by each elite that came to power.

I wondered what Erich Auerbach would have said about a country wanting to change its past? Had he mentioned this "excessive desire for change" in the letters he wrote to Walter Benjamin? In other words, without realizing it, we were constantly shedding skins. Get rid of the Byzantines, get rid of the Ottomans, get rid of the Arab culture....And now the new trend, "Get rid of Kemalism!" Hide the truth about the Tatar Legions, the *Struma*, what was done to the Armenians.

But somehow the past broke through the surface here and there. All the towns in Turkey named Ereğli were once called Herakleon. All place names containing "bolu"—Inebolu, Tirebolu, Safranbolu, and Galibolu—actually contained references to *polis*, the Greek word for city.

Akdoğan was a short, unevenly paved street lined with a mixture of old wooden houses, all of them in sorry shape with all of their paint long since flaked off, and hastily and cheaply built concrete houses. Number 17 was one of the new buildings, its facade covered with gaudy multicolored tiles. I decided this couldn't be the right house, so I went to the corner grocery store to ask if anyone knew the Arditis. The owner of the store had a white beard and wore a skullcap, and the walls were covered in Arabic prayers.

"We only moved here from Kayseri five years ago, so I don't know anyone who used to live here. But I still have some Jewish customers, they might know."

Then he called to his daughter.

"Kübra, Kübra... Take this young lady to Madame's house."

A slim girl with a fine face and a firmly tied, patterned headscarf emerged from behind the counter. As she put on her coat, the elderly man asked me, "Can I offer you some refreshment, something to drink perhaps?"

I thanked him but I didn't want anything. Then the elderly man gave me a small card printed with a prayer in Arabic.

He said, "Carry this with you at all times. It is the *Ayete'l-Kürsi*, a verse from the second Sura of the Quran, in short, the word of God. It will protect you from all kinds of accidents and trouble, and from the evil eye."

I was touched by his kindness and genuine goodwill.

Kübra led me to one of the old houses about halfway down the street and rapped the old-fashioned knocker on the ancient door. An old woman leaned out and peered down from a second-story window.

"Is that you Kübra? I'm coming, child," she said.

She spoke Turkish with a very pronounced accent. When the door opened, a thin, elderly lady greeted us, obviously Sephardic from her accent and everything else about her. She peered at us over the wire spectacles that were attached to a chain around her neck.

"Yes, what can I do for you?"

Kübra explained the situation, said that she had things to do, and left. But before she went, she asked, "Is there anything you want, auntie?"

Madame answered her saying, "No, my child. Thank you, my lovely girl."

Then as she invited me inside, she explained, "They're a very good family. My sciatica gets bad and I can't go out, so I telephone the shop and Kübra brings me what I want straightaway. Oh, and they never forget to bring sweets and Turkish delight on religious holidays."

Madame ushered me into a small sitting room. The house had its own special smell that evoked memories of the old world. Dozens of framed photographs stood on worn carved and inlaid coffee tables.

"Would you like some coffee?"

"Please don't go to the trouble."

"I haven't had my morning coffee yet. We'll have one together."

Soon she came in carrying a tray with little bone china cups of aromatic, frothy Turkish coffee. Beside each cup was a glass of water and a piece of rose-petal Turkish delight. You couldn't find anything like this in the modern cafés. I wondered yet again why people abandon these delightful traditions and drink instant coffee.

Billions of different people, living in different parts of the world, had to like the same type of food and drink, buy the same style of clothes, and for this, live the same style of life, so that the large international firms could sell their products all over the world. Perhaps what was even more frightening was that this system wiped out local cultures. And then I laughed to myself. Since last week I had become an expert on nostalgia.

I soon learned that "Madame's" name was Raşel Ovadya. She was from one of the families of Sephardic Jews who had been living in Istanbul for five hundred years. They had fled the Inquisition during the reign of Ferdinand and Isabella aboard Ottoman ships sailing from the port of Cádiz in 1492. Christopher Columbus's three ships had set sail from the same port on the same night.

Madame Ovadya spoke Turkish with a Ladino accent. She described the people in the photographs and talked about how handsome her late husband had been.

It was clear that she was lonely and happy to have some-one to talk to.

"Madame Ovadya, my name is Maya Duran. I work at Istanbul University. I came to ask you something. I wondered if you knew the Arditi family who used to live on this street?"

She stared into space and looked thoughtfully at the ceiling to try to fish out the name Arditi from among all the jumbled up memories that she had accumulated over the years.

"Arditi, Arditi…"

"Matilda and Rober Arditi. They used to live at Number 17."

Suddenly her face lit up.

"Of course," she said. "How could I forget. Matilda. When I was a young girl she used to give me handker-chiefs with embroidered edges. They were a very good family, excellent!"

"Do you know where they are now?"

"They're older than me. I'm afraid Rober died. As for Matilda, I think she was in a nursing home. She must be over ninety."

"I wonder if she's still alive?"

"I don't know."

"Do you know which nursing home she was in?"

"Oh, my dear girl, I don't know that either. Istanbul has changed so much, so much. If only you knew what it was like here in the old days."

I could see that she was going to begin talking about old times again and said, "Please Madame, it's very important that I find Mrs. Matilda. Could you possibly think a little harder?"

"Why are you looking for this family?"

"It would take a long time to explain but I'm doing some research on the university. I have some questions for her."

"Let me answer your questions. I'm very knowledgeable. At one time I studied at Dame de Sion."

"Thank you, but this is something concerning that family," I said. "If I could ask…"

"In that case let me think," she said. "I have a feeling our Izi mentioned Mrs. Matilda. Let me ask her."

She went over to the old-fashioned, black Ericsson telephone that stood on the corner table. She removed the lace doily that covered it and then, lifting the receiver, slowly began to dial the number.

She spoke with Izi in a language I couldn't understand, and which was sprinkled with French, Spanish, and Turkish words.

"All right, dear, au revoir," she said and hung up.

Then she addressed me, "We've traced Matilda. She's living in the Artigiana nursing home in Harbiye. Wait, I'll bring you some of my milk pudding that I made yesterday."

"Please, don't trouble," I said. "I'm in rather a hurry. You've done me a great favor, Madame Raşel. Goodbye."

I then left the elderly lady with her memories and her incurable loneliness, and went out. As she said goodbye there was a look of indescribable sadness on her face.

I walked toward the square, and when I saw the university's massive ornamental gate, I felt a sense of freedom. Being absent even for a week had made me feel much lighter and happier. I got into a bus that was heading toward Harbiye. I didn't know where the Artigiana was, but after asking around a little I was able to find it.

According to what I read later, Artigiana was founded in 1838 by Sultan Abdülmecid with an endowment of 20,000 piastres. It was established as a home for elderly people from different religious backgrounds who were utterly alone. Everyone was given a room. If they wished they could bring their own possessions. They were free to go out during the day and come back in the evening.

When I told the people on duty at the entrance that I was looking for Matilda Arditi, they directed me to the second floor. The names of the residents were written on the well-worn doors. Kuyumcuyan, Stavropoulos, Mavromatya, Serrero.

Who knows what memories were sheltered in this old building. What dramas, what pleasures, what passions were remembered. After walking for a while, I saw the name Arditi across a door on the left and, after knocking, I went in. The very old lady in bed sat up when she saw me.

"Yes, can I help you?" she asked.

"I'm looking for Matilda Arditi," I said.

"Why are you looking for her?"

"To have a little talk."

The elderly lady said, "In that case, please come in."

She pointed to the green chair by the window and I sat down.

"Are you Matilda Arditi?"

"Yes, yes. Though sometimes I don't even remember who I am anymore."

"Madame," I said. "Please accept these."

I held out the bunch of purple flowers that I had bought from the flower peddler on the corner.

"Oh," she said. "How kind of you. I can't remember the last time I got flowers. At least a century."

"Oh, please, don't say that, Madame Arditi. You're not that old."

"I feel as if I've been alive since the beginning of time. What did you say your name was?"

"Maya."

"Ah, Maya! I love the name Maya. We had a neighbor in Izmir who had a daughter named Maya. We were the same age and we were best friends. I don't know if she's still alive."

"Madame Arditi, I want to ask you something?"

"Please go ahead!"

"Do you remember Maximilian?" She hesitated, tried to think, to remember. Then her face lit up.

"Yes!" she exclaimed. "Maximilian. Certainly. Of course I remember him."

"You were neighbors on Nasip Street."

"Yes, Nasip Street, of course."

Then she hesitated, and seemed confused.

"That's the Nasip Street in Geneva, isn't it?"

"No, Madam Arditi. The one in Istanbul."

She hesitated a little. Still confident she said, "Yes. Of course, the one in Istanbul."

"Do you remember Max?"

"Max? Oh, Maximilian...Of course I remember him."

"Could you tell me a little about him?"

"Ah!" She winked flirtatiously. She beckoned me over. I drew my chair toward her. Chuckling she said, "He was so courteous, such a gentleman, such a rich man. He was rather a womanizer of course; but, my lamb, one can expect that! Women didn't leave him alone. The Istanbul of my youth was wonderful. Max and I would go hand in hand to Le Bon to eat cakes. I used to love their éclairs. We went everywhere! There was the Petrograd, such a lovely café."

She paused as though she'd remembered something else. Then with a gesture meaning, "Never mind," as though she had decided not to say anything after all, she continued.

"We went everywhere. I used to shop in the Karlman Arcade; I used to buy my shoes from Paçikakis. Then there was the Lion store and the Mayer store. We used to go to the theatre in the Petits-Champs to listen to music."

She stopped and mused as though she had forgotten something.

"Dear Max never bought anything for himself. I would go and buy him his socks, pants, and vests from Mayer's. There was a man named Fritz there, a German Jew. And there was Lazaro Franco. It's not long since he closed; twenty years, I suppose. They sold curtains there. Furniture I mean...And there was my special hat shop...I used to go to the Russian milliners who knew how to make hats like no one else. The name was Madame Bella. Above the Lale Cinema. And then there was Marieta; she was a milliner too. But mine was expensive, and also very good. There were tailors and milliners everywhere. People paid more attention to their clothes then, and nothing was mass-produced."

When she stopped talking she looked as though she was thinking about something. She gestured for me to wait. She didn't want to be interrupted.

"I adored classical music. Bach for example. I always listened to it in Taksim. There was no opera house before that. There was a restaurant called Novotni, in Tepebaşı. Five or six Russian brothers and sisters ran the place. Sometimes they had piano music that I used to listen to. We loved their food, if we were going to eat out we always went there. Unfortunately, there was nowhere else that had classical music. We also went to concerts. Rubinstein came for example, and so did Yehudi Menuhin. When I entered that hall on Max's arm I felt like a queen. Every Tuesday I used to play cards with my friends. Just little games, you know. But we used to dress up as though we were going to an important party. There were eight of us. We wore different dresses each time. We laid elegant dinner tables. We always tried our best."

I began to wonder if she was talking about the same Max, or if she had confused Max with someone else

"Madame Arditi," I queried. "Are you sure you are talking about Professor Maximilian Wagner?"

"Of course. I could never forget either him or his music."

Yes, it seemed that we were talking about the right person.

"Do you remember the *Serenade*?"

"How could a person forget that piece! It was so beautiful, it moved me deeply every time I heard it."

Then she started humming a melody and swaying as if she were dancing a waltz. As she waved her right arm in time to the rhythm, the sleeve of her tattered flannel frock fell away, revealing a thin, bony arm covered with what looked like brown, spotted leather.

Then she beckoned to me. I got up and went over to her. She held my hand and struggled to her feet. Without letting go of my hand she tried to sway her shrunken, emaciated body to the incoherent tune she was humming. Finally I couldn't take it anymore and sat her down.

"Madame Arditi, you have Max's possessions."

She winked flirtatiously. "Who else would have them?"

She kept implying that she'd had a love affair with Max, but this wasn't consistent with what Max had told me about the state he'd been in as he waited for Nadia. Her memory had unraveled and she was confusing either Max with someone else or her fantasies with what had actually happened. I was ready to give up and leave.

Just at that moment a nurse entered and said, "I see you have a visitor, Rita. It's time for your medicine."

"Rita?" I asked.

"Yes!" said the nurse "Rita. She's been here four years."

"But I thought she was Madame Matilda Arditi."

"You've mixed them up," she said. "Madame Matilda is in that room."

She pointed to a door on the left. So there were two rooms, one within the other. Madame Arditi was in the other room.

Rita, deeply embarrassed at being exposed, hung her head and wouldn't look at me. My heart melted and I went over and took her hand.

"I'm very happy to have met you, Rita," I said. "We've had a pleasant chat. I'll come and visit you again."

She looked at me hopefully. "You're not angry with me?"

"No, why should I be angry? I enjoyed your company."

"May Allah bless you!" she said and made the sign of the cross over her heart.

I thought, this is Istanbul. Someone saying a Muslim prayer and using an Orthodox gesture. The city of interwoven prayers, religions, and cultures.

I kissed her on both cheeks and went into the inner room. Madame Matilda wasn't in as good shape as her roommate. She lay with her eyes half closed as though she were drained of life. She seemed to want to take leave of this world as soon as possible. But her mind was still sharp.

"Mrs. Arditi?" I asked.

She lay on her side with her face buried in the pillow. Without changing her position, she asked in a feeble voice, "What do you want?"

Her voice was so weak that I had difficulty hearing her.

"I'm Maya Duran from Istanbul University, madam. I wanted to ask you something."

"Well, ask me then."

"You used to live on Nasip Street in the late thirties?"

"Yes?"

"You had a neighbor at the time, Professor Maximilian Wagner. Do you remember?"

She turned slowly toward me and gave me an annoyed look.

"Why shouldn't I remember? What do you want to know about him?"

"When the professor was deported he asked that his documents be left with you."

"They were."

"Where are they Mrs. Arditi?"

"Someone from the German consulate came and took them."

"Who was it, do you remember his name?"

"I can still picture him, he had a sharp, mean face, but don't expect me to remember his name. I think it began with an S."

"Scurla?"

"*C'est possible*," she said. "The name rings a bell."

I was amazed at her memory. It was better than mine and I was less than half her age. I left the nursing home thinking about the two old women. Rita had really fooled me because I couldn't tell a Greek accent from a Jewish accent, but I felt genuinely fond of her. I decided that should I reach such an advanced age, I would rather be like Rita than Matilda. In her own addled way, Rita was still enjoying life, but Matilda was waiting for the end like a prisoner on death row.

Then I thought about Max, who would die in six months, taking all his bitter, tormented memories with him. If I could at least find the *Serenade* it would bring him some consolation during his last days.

As I emerged onto the street, large snowflakes were drifting down. They had already begun to accumulate—on the streets, rooftops, branches, and even on people's shoulders. Istanbul was so beautiful when it was blanketed by snow, all the harshness and ugliness was concealed, and it became a fairytale city—the mosques, synagogues, churches, and bridges covered in white—with a light mist drifting in the air, and the color of the Bosporus changed from blue to a magical teal green.

I walked slowly through the snow in pursuit of traces of Max's tragic adventure. My destination was very nearby, but again I had some trouble finding it. Then, after asking around a bit I learned that once again the name of the street I was looking for had been changed. Ölçek Street had, I thought fittingly, been renamed Papa Roncalli Street. It was a narrow street running behind the Notre Dame de Sion School and the St. Esprit church, in a neighborhood that seemed to be inhabited mostly by Kurds from southeastern Turkey and Syriac Christian refugees from Iraq. Partway down the street I came to a large, walled enclosure that occupied an entire block. Inside the enclosure were a large garden and several buildings. I found that many of these buildings were occupied by Caritas, the Catholic charity organization, and included a school for the refugee children. One of the buildings on the upper side of the enclosure had a disc above the door bearing the papal coat of arms. A marble plaque, also bearing the papal coat of arms, announced in Latin that this was the *Nunciatura Apostolica*, and in Turkish that it was Vatican Embassy Istanbul Mission. Max had walked through this door, spoken to Father

Roncalli and had a Roman Catholic baptismal certificate issued for Nadia.

So many of the countless throngs of people in this city had little idea of what had happened here. But then, until recently, neither had I. When I walked down the Grand Rue de Pera, renamed Istıklal Caddesi (Independence Avenue), I was too busy looking in shop windows to even notice the grand old buildings, let alone wonder about the countless stories associated with them.

Continuing on the trail of Max's past, I hailed a taxi and told the driver to go to the Or-Ahayim Hospital on the Golden Horn.

As we passed over the bridge, I noticed that the seagulls seemed more lively and active than usual; they were circling around and diving into the water. Even though I knew they were after the migrating sprat, I somehow felt they shared my sense of joy and liberation. As we drove along the shore we passed the remnants of the Byzantine sea walls on our left, and on our right a Bulgarian church that had been built in Vienna, entirely of cast iron, and then shipped down the Danube to Istanbul.

The Or-Ahayim Hospital was a beautiful old building on the waterfront with a more modern annex next to it. I went through a gate in the iron railings, through the front door, and made my way through the crowds of patients to the information desk. I told them I was from the office of the rector of Istanbul University and asked to see the director of the hospital.

After a while, a portly, middle-aged gentleman arrived and greeted me warmly. When I told him I was there to do some research he graciously showed me around. Most of the corridors were lined with old photographs, and I asked him why so many of the men with Jewish names had the title of pasha. He told me they were Ottoman generals and officials who had played a role in founding the hospital. He also pointed to photographs of personalities such as Admiral Dr. Izak Molho Pasha, Dr. Izidor Gravyer Pasha, and Dr. Eliyas Kohen Pasha, and Atatürk's doctor, Dr. Samuel Abravaya Marmaralı, who had also been a member of parliament. He also explained that the hospital had been built on a plot of land donated by Abdülhamid II in 1898. I asked him about the elderly ladies in pink I'd seen rushing about here and there. He told me they were volunteers, known affectionately as the Pink Angels.

While I was having coffee with the director in his office, I asked him which room Medea Salomovici had been in. He didn't know. He didn't even know who she was. When I mentioned the *Struma*, he confessed that he wasn't very familiar with that story, but that Leyla, one of the Pink Angels, might be able to tell me more.

He had Leyla summoned to the office. She was a cheerful, healthy looking woman in her seventies. When I asked her about Medea she hesitated for a moment and then said,

"No one ever remembers what happened to those people. Or rather, no one wants to remember it and no one ever talks about it. But I've been working as a volunteer here for a long time and I know which room she was in."

As she led me to the room, I felt a strange sense of excitement. I felt as if I were going to see Medea herself, and that I would find the young Maximilian standing by her bedside, beseeching her for news of Nadia. But of course, it was just another hospital room occupied by a frail old woman who seemed to be struggling to breathe. I just looked around briefly, then closed the door, and left without disturbing her.

I felt somehow let down, felt I should never have come. What was the point of going to visit all the places Max mentioned in his story? I wanted to get out of there as soon as possible, but Leyla wouldn't let me go until she'd given me a jar of the rose-petal jam that the Pink Angels made.

It was early evening by the time I left the hospital, and it was still snowing quite heavily. Rush hour was in full swing and I had trouble finding a taxi, but I finally got one and struggled home along the slippery, crowded streets. After feeding Kerem and cleaning up the kitchen, I went inside to read the rest of the information I had on the *Struma*.

It was a depressing story to read, and although I'd heard Max's story, the information Kerem had gathered was a bit haphazard and random, and it was difficult to find the connecting threads.

There were pictures of the ship, which made it easier for me to visualize the story, the statements of residents of the coast near Şile who remembered the bodies washing up on the shore, the story of David Stoliar, the sole survivor, who'd clung to the wreckage with a Bulgarian crewman who died before the rescue, and who'd told him he'd seen the torpedo speeding toward the ship.

There were also some articles about the aftermath: the ensuing tensions between the Jewish Agency and Sir Harold MacMichael, the High Commissioner for Palestine; the protests throughout Palestine; the posters that appeared of MacMichael and the words "WANTED, murderer, Sir Harold MacMichael, High Commissioner for the British Government in Palestine, for the crime of causing the death by drowning of 800 immigrants on the ship, the *Struma*!"

Walter Edward Guinness, Lord Moyne, Britain's most senior official in the Middle East, who had put pressure on Turkey not to let people on the *Struma* ashore, was seen as the main culprit. Lord Moyne was assassinated 6 November 1944. The assassins, seventeen-year-old Eliahu Hakim and twenty-two-year-old Eliahu Bet Zouri, were hanged on 22 March 1945 in Cairo Prison. When they were questioned in court as to their motive they said, "We were avenging the *Struma*!"

MacMichael survived an assassination attempt in August 1944.

It was only years later that the cause of the explosion that sank the ship was discovered. In the early 1960s, the public prosecutor of Frankfurt appointed Dr. Jürgen Rohwer, a military historian, to investigate the sinking of the *Struma*. He learned that the German Danube U-boat flotilla was not present in Black Sea at that time. Warships based in Varna were later deployed to escort and protect Italian tank supply ships, but they were not yet present in February 1942. The *Struma* had not been sunk by a German ship or submarine.

In the course of his investigation, Dr. Rohwer spoke to the head of the military history department of the Soviet Navy and learned that the Soviet submarine SC-213 had been in the southern Black Sea at the time the *Struma* sank, and that this submarine had sunk an unidentified ship 14 miles north-northeast of the Bosporus on 24 February 1942.

I also learned that the then prime minister of Turkey, Dr. Refik Saydam, had touched on the subject in his speech at the Turkish Grand National Assembly, 20 April 1942: *"We did everything we could in this respect, we are not in the least responsible, either materially or morally. Turkey cannot be the destination of undesirable refugees. This is the course we follow. This is why we could not detain them in Istanbul. It is extremely regrettable that they fell victim to an accident."*

There was no doubt in my mind that this was mass murder. The governments of Britain, Romania, Germany, Turkey, and the Soviet Union had conspired in the deaths of at least 769 innocent refugee people, and then had avoided responsibility, and tried to pretend it had never happened.

Maximilian used to say, "No government is innocent!"

They had deported him so he would not be able to investigate this crime. His unexpected return to Turkey so many years later had to do with the *Struma*, and that was why they'd put security agents on his tail. That was why the British and the Russians wanted to know what he was doing in Istanbul.

Yet what did Maximilian, a lecturer at a university, and Nadia, a harmless student, have to do with all this? They would have lived a good, peaceful life together. They would have worked to advance their academic careers, raise their children, and be happy.

As I was thinking about this, I suddenly thought about the score of the *Serenade*. I was determined; I was going to find it. For me, searching for the *Serenade* would be to take a stand against the kind of mentality that had led to the deaths of these people.

It seemed very likely that the score of the *Serenade* was being kept in Nazi archives in Germany, together with the file and other documents taken from Istanbul University.

I got up and collected the papers that had scattered as I threw them down. There were a few things to clear away in the kitchen as well. As I went along the corridor, I saw that Kerem was at his computer. I felt a pang of guilt as I wondered whether I was neglecting him. I went over and put my hand on his shoulder. He pretended not to notice.

"Could you help me?" I asked.

He turned his head, looked up at me, and raised his eyebrows.

"Can you find out where the Nazi archives are stored? I really need to know and you're so much better at this internet stuff than I am."

He laughed, and seemed pleased that I'd asked him for help. I already knew part of the answer and could have found what I needed on my own easily enough, but I felt that his involvement was good for both of us and for our relationship.

He got to work right away, and called me about half an hour later to show me what he'd found. The International Tracing Service had been set up in Bad Arolsen, Germany, in 1955 to help the victims of Nazi persecutions and their families, and its archives contained 50 million reference cards on 17.5 million people. Its archive holds 26,000 meters of various types of records and 106,870 microfilms. To date the center had responded to 11.8 million requests for information.

I was sure that I could find Scurla's report on Max there, and I was excited that I might be able to find the score for the *Serenade.* Bad Arolsen was a spa town about 45 kilometers west of Kassel. I was eager to go right away, and indeed, if possible, I was prepared to set out the next day.

Unfortunately, however, the next day my world was turned completely upside down.

CHAPTER 16

I was still in bed when the telephone rang. I'd been making the most of my sick leave and had been sleeping late every day. I knew somehow that whatever it was, it wasn't going to be good. The telephone makes the same sound every time it rings, but sometimes it seems to have a different quality. You know somehow that it's going to bring good news, or bad news. That morning the sound of the telephone ringing had an irritable, strident quality. I hesitated, then reached for the receiver.

The first thing I heard was Ahmet's voice shrieking at me.

"What the hell were you thinking!? You've brought shame on the whole family. How are you ever going to look Kerem in the eye again? How are you going to face your parents?"

"Hey, slow down a minute, I just woke up and I have no idea what you're talking about."

"Don't you feel any shame at all?"

"Look Ahmet, why don't you just tell me what your problem is?"

"Shame on you, shame on you!"

"What the hell are you talking about? Why are you shouting at me like this?"

"Haven't you seen the papers?"

"No, why?"

"Well, you'd better, you shameless slut."

"Oh, go to hell!"

I hung up on him.

I was annoyed at being woken up this way, but I was also curious. Ahmet usually didn't have the courage to shout and carry on like that—he preferred the passive-aggressive approach. What had got him so worked up?

I got up. Kerem had gone to school. When I glanced at the kitchen table, I saw that he'd eaten the breakfast I'd put out for him the night before. So at least I wasn't going to go through the whole rigmarole of making sure he caught the school bus.

I rushed to the front door. The janitor left a newspaper on the doorstep every morning and Kerem never touched it. I opened the door, grabbed the paper, and began to skim through it. The usual political news, a picture of a pretty woman at the top right corner of the first page, celebrity news on the second page, on the third page, news of murder...And then I saw it on the fifth page. It was a medium-sized article.

SCANDAL AT
ISTANBUL UNIVERSITY

Once again rumors of scandal are rippling through Istanbul University. Maya Duran, (36) a university public relations officer, is alleged to have been involved in an illicit affair with a visiting American professor, Maximilian Wagner (87).

Another member of the university staff and a motel employee found the couple naked in bed together and described what they'd seen as "disgusting." The news has stunned the university community.

Asked about his views on the scandal the rector said, "We are looking into the allegations, and the appropriate steps will be taken if they are substantiated."

The university's Secretary General said, "We can't ignore allegations that would tarnish the university's image."

Professor Wagner has already left the country, and our reporters have been unable to reach Maya Duran for her comments.

I ran to the bathroom and vomited. I vomited until green bile came up.

When the telephone rang again, I answered out of habit. A woman's voice asked for Maya Duran.

"Speaking."

"I'm calling from the..."

I hung up before she could finish her sentence. The telephone began to ring continuously. I put the telephone on silent. The red light kept flashing.

I went to the kitchen, made myself a strong cup of coffee, and sat down to pull myself together and try to figure out what to do. This was a disaster—it was going to change my whole life. I kept telling myself to calm down, that allowing myself to panic wasn't going to help anything, but I just couldn't get a grip on myself. The coffee upset my stomach and I tried to eat a biscuit but I just couldn't manage it.

Then I remembered the pills Filiz had prescribed for me. Something called Lexotanil. I'd been experiencing insomnia and I'd asked her for something to help me sleep. I'd never taken any, but the bottle was still in my bedside drawer. I found them and took a quarter of a pill right away.

Everyone was going to be talking about this—all the staff at the university, the lecturers, and the students. Everyone was going to be making crude jokes about an eighty-seven-year-old man in bed with a thirty-six-year-old woman.

And what about Kerem? He didn't read the papers and his friends didn't know me, but he might come across the news on the internet.

After a while the drug started to kick in. I felt numbness in my limbs and my mind stopped racing. I still felt deeply upset, but I began, slowly, to see things more objectively. I lay facedown on the bed, watched the light on my phone as it kept flashing, and felt my mind slowly go blank.

I don't know how long I lay like that, but when I got up, I felt better. I had a hot bath and forced myself to eat something. For a moment it all came back to me and I started to cry. Then I pulled myself together again and started to make a plan. I wasn't going to let that miserable Süleyman ruin my life. I was smarter than he was, and I was going to put up a fight.

I picked up my phone and called the reporter who had called me that morning.

"Yes, Sibel speaking."

"You called me this morning," I said. When she heard my name, she gave me all her attention.

"I'd like to make a statement."

"May we come and interview you?"

"No. I just want to make a statement."

"What kind of statement?"

"The story you printed is completely untrue."

"We didn't say it was true, Mrs. Duran. We just said that these allegations were being made at the university."

"Now look, I'm a mother. I have a fourteen-year-old son. I have parents. I have a brother who's a colonel. Just imagine how your news makes me seem to them!"

"Calm down, Mrs. Duran."

"How can I calm down, I've been humiliated in front

of the whole country. Please print my statement. At least write that I categorically deny these allegations."

"We'll come and interview you straight away. You can say whatever you want."

I was annoyed enough at her to agree.

"Let me give you my address."

"We know your address, Mrs. Duran. We'll be there as soon as we can."

I had to do this to clear my name. I made myself presentable and tidied up the sitting room. In the meantime, I saw on the phone that my mother had called five times, so I pressed the call button.

"Mother."

"Oh, Maya! I've been so worried. Where are you, darling?"

"Mother, have you seen the news in the papers?"

"Yes, I have."

"It's a lie, it's all a lie. It's cheap slander!"

"Of course it's a lie, my darling. Do you think I don't know you?"

"A reporter is on her way here, I'm going to put the record straight. Just hang in there 'til tomorrow. Is Dad all right?"

"Yes, thank God, but of course he's upset."

"Tell him not to get upset. I'll set it all straight, I'm going to sue the people who did this."

Just then the doorbell rang.

"They're here, I've got to go. I'll call you back later."

"God bless you, sweetheart."

I opened the door. A young, dark-haired woman and a young man with a huge camera slung round his neck came in. I was annoyed that she'd brought the photographer, but there was nothing I could do. I tried to look as resolute and sure of myself as possible.

As I sat talking to the young woman, the young man was circling round us, changing lenses, and taking our picture.

"I just want to say that this gossip is completely fabricated. It's just a malicious attempt to hurt me."

"OK. Who's trying to hurt you?"

"The rector's driver, Süleyman."

"Why?"

"He wanted me to talk to the rector for him about getting his cousin a job and I didn't think this was appropriate. He also tried to steal the visiting professor's violin. I caught him and got the violin back to the professor. He wanted to get back at me."

"Wait a minute. Did the professor play the violin?"

"Yes."

"Did he play his violin for you?"

"Of course not."

"Well, did he at least play well? I mean professionally? A scientist playing the violin seems rather odd to me."

"I don't know, I didn't get much of a chance to hear him play, he probably did play well, but that's not the issue."

"I've seen photos of Professor Wagner. He's a very good-looking man."

"So what? What does that have to do with me?"

"He is a good-looking man though isn't he?"

"He might be... So?"

"Well, did you go to Şile with him?"

"Yes."

"Why did you want to go to Şile on a winter's day?"

"I didn't want to go, he did. It had to do with something in his past. We took him in the rector's car, and Süleyman drove."

"But you were alone for a few hours in the Black Sea Motel."

"Yes, the rector's old Mercedes broke down, as it often does. Süleyman went to get a mechanic from Şile. We didn't want to wait outside in the cold."

"Süleyman came later."

"Yes."

"I'm sorry to ask you this, but is it true that he saw you both stark naked in bed?"

Well, this I couldn't explain. If I said I'd undressed him and held him to my half-naked body to stop him from freezing, that I only did it to save his life, no one would believe me.

To keep the reporter wondering why I'd paused, I acted as if the question had annoyed me—as if I'd paused to control my anger.

"No! What bed?"

"In other words, you're saying that nothing like this happened."

"It didn't!"

"OK. That's all we need"

I stopped her at the door, took her hand, and looked her in the eye.

"Now look," I said. "We are both women. We know how women are viewed in this country, especially divorcées like me. I have a fourteen-year-old son. I'm asking you as a woman to put this right. I swear that all this is slander."

The reporter gave me a sympathetic look. She was the type of woman who always seemed to be in a hurry, but at that moment she slowed down. "Don't worry," she said. "I understand. I'll do my best."

After they'd gone, I felt a bit more relaxed. Everything would be straightened out by tomorrow.

I called my mother and told her that the newspaper was going to print my side of the story. Then, making an effort to control my anger, I called Ahmet.

"You're the one who should be ashamed, attacking me like that because of some slander you read in the paper. Buy the paper tomorrow and read it."

I hung up before he could answer.

After that I called Tarık and then Filiz. I told them both what had happened. Then it was time for the last and most difficult phone call. I called the rector's office. I asked Neylan to put me through to the rector. She made me wait, and then said that the rector was busy and couldn't speak to me.

I'd said the same thing many times to people he had wanted to get rid of. He wasn't going to speak to me.

I called the secretary general on his cell phone and he answered.

"Someone is spreading malicious gossip about me and I want to come in and set things straight."

"Aren't you ill, Mrs. Duran?" he asked scornfully.

"Yes, I am. Under other circumstances, I wouldn't leave my bed but I have to clear my name. Besides, the newspaper is going to tell the real story tomorrow."

"Do you know that we've opened an administrative inquiry into the matter?"

"I know, I read your statement. That's why I want to come and explain, to tell you what really happened."

"Do that, but first, let me warn you that it won't be easy. There's a lot of evidence against you."

"What you call evidence amounts to nothing more than Süleyman's lies."

"It's not only his evidence."

"What other evidence could there be?"

"The boy who worked at the Black Sea Motel. The waiters at the Pera Palas, the people on duty at the reception desk and room service, even Ilyas!"

I was taken aback. Things looked bad for me. They'd connect the Black Sea Motel with the dinners at the Pera Palas Hotel and the night I spent in Max's room. Then nothing I said would change anyone's mind. Still, I had no choice but to try my best anyway.

"When should I come in?

"Tomorrow morning. The rector is furious and he wants this dealt with as soon as possible."

We hung up.

I understood. They'd already decided to fire me, and the inquiry was just a formality.

I began to scramble desperately, like a trapped animal, to think of a way out of this mess and to rationalize the situation I was in

It didn't matter that much if I got fired. I could find another job, perhaps even a better job. I'd been unhappy there for some time anyway. Besides, Tarık said I'd made quite a bit of money on the stock market. As long as the newspaper presented my side of the story convincingly and cleared my name, there was no problem. A significant change in my life could do me good. I could move to a different city, perhaps even a different country. I kept telling myself the same thing over and over again in different ways, and as I did so I felt a growing urge to leave this life far behind.

The doorbell rang. It was Kerem, and as soon as I saw him, I realized I'd been deluding myself. I wasn't free to just pick up and go wherever I wanted. I was tied here. I was trapped.

I could tell right away from Kerem's attitude that he had no idea about what was going on. I didn't turn on the television after dinner just in case some news program or talk show might mention the story. Everyone loved a juicy bit of gossip.

Kerem never visited news sites on the web, but just in case I asked him to look into getting online access to the archives in Bad Arolsen and see if he could find anything on Scurla and Wagner. He was eager to try and got right to it.

What an odd relationship there was between the written word and people's lives. Like flying, writing is something invented and not part of the natural order. Hence we're often as frightened of the written word as we are of flying. Claude Lévi-Strauss went as far as to associate the regression of humankind with the invention of the written word.

The most innocent of human actions could take on a sinister air when put down in words, especially when they became news. In the evening you could leave home, meet a friend in Beyoğlu, eat dinner at Rejans, and return home. Nothing could be more natural. But when a newspaper article or a police report described the same events, they could seem incriminating.

"The subject left the house at 19:14, got into a taxi, license number 34 AF 6781, and went to Taksim. The subject proceeded along Istıklal Avenue and met another individual in front of the French consulate. They proceeded along the avenue to a restaurant called Rejans, founded by Russian émigrés. Two hours later they parted in front of the restaurant. The subject then proceeded to Taksim where he entered a taxi, license number 34 ZD 2645, and arrived home at 23:27."

The written word could imply guilt and destroy a person's reputation. A film of the same incident would show how commonplace it was, would show the facial expressions and the friendly banter and reflect the harmlessness of the meeting. But the written word could be charged with insinuation and imply significance where there was none.

Of course it was a double-edged sword, and the written word could have a positive influence as well as a destructive one, could clear up misunderstanding, and could elucidate. It depended on who was writing what and why. After all, both Hitler and Tolstoy wrote books. Even the word of God is transmitted through writing. But then, didn't God exist before the invention of writing?

I went to bed and curled up under the quilt. I felt deeply hurt and deeply frightened. I felt as I had as a little girl when I was terrified at night by a moving shadow or a creaking floorboard, and I'd rush to my grandmother's room for comfort and reassurance.

But now I had to face the monsters all alone, without my grandmother to stroke my hair and make me feel safe.

CHAPTER 17

I woke before dawn after an uneasy, fitful sleep. The first thing I did was rush to the door to see if the paper had arrived. It hadn't.

I went back to bed but sleep was out of the question. I was too worked up. Then I remembered the pills. Why hadn't I thought of them last night? Filiz had told me to take a quarter of a pill, but I took half. I didn't think even that would be able to calm me down.

I went and checked for the newspaper three more times. Then I heard the janitor's footsteps as he went slowly from door to door. I waited inside, and heard him pause outside my door and then move on. I waited until I heard him head upstairs, and then opened the door and grabbed the paper.

There was nothing about me on the front page, but I was stunned to see a large picture of me on the second page. I was looking at the camera with a coy smile, and the caption read, "He was a very good-looking man."

And beneath this, "The woman at the heart of the university scandal."

There was also a photo of Max.

I was quoted as having said, "He was a good-looking man. He played the violin beautifully."

I was furious. I immediately grabbed the phone and called Sibel, the reporter who'd interviewed me. They told me she wasn't in yet. I called every ten minutes. The fourth time she answered herself. I shouted at the top of my voice.

"How can you do this to me? Is this what I told you? I'm going to talk to my lawyer and get a court order for a retraction."

I was so angry that I couldn't control the pitch of my voice or what I said.

The quotes and the pictures were so skillfully manipulative that they painted a picture of a slutty university clerk having a fling with an elderly, romantic, violin-playing professor. They also made a point of stressing that I was divorced.

After a while I heard the reporter say, "I'm sorry. You're right—I was very upset too. I really think you should fight this."

"Then why did you write such a skewed article?"

"Believe me, I'm not responsible. I just wrote down what you said and handed it in, that's all. My headline was, 'It's all slander!'"

"Well, what happened then?"

In a low voice she said, "This is what the editor wanted. I'm just a lowly reporter. I don't get to decide what they print."

"But why are they going after me? Don't they have any regard for the truth?"

"You're right. Please believe that I'm truly sorry. I think you really should take them to court." She said this very quietly and I believed she meant it.

"I'm sorry I screamed at you."

"It's OK. I understand."

As I hung up I was startled by Kerem's voice.

"What's the matter? Who were you shouting at?"

"It's nothing," I said. "There are some problems at work and...Come on, I'll get breakfast ready."

After sending Kerem off, I called Tarık. I told him what had happened, what the editor had done, and said I needed a lawyer.

He told me to be calm and not to panic. He would find a lawyer, and he also had friends at the newspaper. He would ask them to retract the article and print an apology.

"Just hang in there. There'll be a bigger scandal next week and another the week after, and in a month no one will remember."

"But my relatives, my neighbors, and my colleagues will remember. Besides, I can't just take this lying down. They have no right to do this to me."

"This is nothing, much worse things happen in this country every day. Killers are set free; rapists are imprisoned for a year or two and then released. Reporters are put in prison on trumped-up charges. Writers are imprisoned for treason for books they haven't even published. People are put on trial for belonging to organizations that don't exist. The prime minister closes all the public theatres in the country because his daughter didn't like a play she saw. I could go on and on."

He wasn't belittling my situation. He was just trying to put it in perspective, but this didn't make me feel any better.

"You wouldn't talk like that if you were in my shoes."

"You're right, but that doesn't make what I'm saying any less true."

After a long silence he said, "We could hold a press conference if you want. I could say, 'she's my fiancée, I believe her, she wouldn't do that kind of thing.' We could hold hands and smile sweetly for the cameras."

"No thanks, I can't see myself doing that. And it would probably just make things worse."

"What are you doing today?"

"I'm going to the university," I said. "They've started an administrative inquiry."

"Call me later and I'll arrange a meeting with a lawyer. We can sue the university, too, if we have to."

I hadn't expected him to be so kind and supportive. It's only when you're in trouble that you find out who your true friends are. But things weren't as clear-cut as Tarık thought. Witnesses could testify that I was half naked in bed with Max, that we'd had meals together, that we'd had drinks sent up to his room, and that I'd spent the night with him there. I knew that I was innocent, but how would I be able to prove it?

I got dressed, choosing a very plain and sober outfit, and went to the university. The sedative had calmed me down a little. I was ready for the veiled looks, the smiles, and the whispering.

I went straight to the secretary general's room. This time he didn't look at my breasts. He did his best to be very stern.

"Sit down, Mrs. Duran. You've put our university in a very difficult position."

"No, I don't accept that. What the newspaper printed was a lie. I've done nothing wrong."

The secretary general took me to the rector's office. I walked past the people in the outer office with my head high.

The rector was very distant. There were a few other faculty members in his office.

The secretary general said, "Mrs. Duran denies everything. She says it's all slander."

The rector asked the private secretary to call Süleyman and he entered the office cringing with embarrassment. He waited with his hands clasped in front of him. He didn't look at me at all.

The rector said, "Mrs. Duran says you're lying. Tell us what you saw."

"I swear, I swear to God, may I be struck down if…"

"Stop swearing and tell us what you saw."

"That day we set out for Şile before sunrise. That man started playing the violin at the edge of the sea. I thought he'd gone mad. Then we brought him to the hotel so that he wouldn't freeze. The car had broken down. I went to Şile to look for a mechanic. When I returned about three hours later I saw the two of them naked in bed."

The rector turned to me. "What do you say to this?"

"It's true, sir."

They'd been expecting a flat denial and were completely taken aback.

"What do you mean?"

"Everything he says is true."

They looked at each other in surprise.

"In that case, you admit your misconduct!"

"No, I am not guilty."

"Explain yourself."

"The summary of the incident is correct but the interpretation is wrong."

"Did you get into bed with Professor Wagner or not?"

"I did but not in the way you mean."

"Well, in what way then?"

"The day that he wanted us to go to Şile to relive an old memory was the coldest day of the year. Please recall 24 February. Imagine how much colder it was on the Black Sea coast. The professor had been standing on the shore for a long time and risked certain death. We dragged him into the car, but it had broken down. The heater wasn't working either. So we dragged the professor to a motel on the hill. There was no heating there either. When I put him on the bed and covered him up, he was purple. His hands were rigid. I thought he was going to die."

The moment I stopped I realized this was not the time to pause so I continued.

"I got into bed to warm him with my body heat. It worked; it saved his life. Süleyman abandoned us there and he might still have died, but I managed to get someone to take him to the hospital. You can check with the hospital, their reports will show that he'd been exposed to extreme cold. I did what I could to keep our guest from dying of exposure. That's all I'm guilty of."

They all looked at each other again; the rector began to doodle on the paper in front of him. They were taken aback and didn't know what to say.

"There is one more thing, sir," I said.

"What is it?" the rector asked,

"Süleyman, I mean, your driver, wanted me to ask you to employ his cousin. When I refused to do so he was angry and wanted revenge. He's also guilty of another offense."

"What offense would that be?"

"The professor left his antique violin in the Mercedes. When I asked him about it, he said it wasn't there. Ilyas can confirm this. We went to the mechanic's shop and found the violin deliberately concealed in the trunk. We were able to get it back to Professor Wagner. Here's Riza the mechanic's card, he can confirm the story."

I left the card on the rector's desk.

I felt as if I'd set everything straight, as if I'd been vindicated. Meanwhile Süleyman looked terrified.

"You've taken the word of a dishonest man and of a sensationalist newspaper over that of a loyal employee with a long record of honorable service. I'm a respectable citizen and a mother, my mother is a retired teacher, and my father is retired bank employee. I can't believe you would treat me like this."

The rector had clearly changed his mind. He was just about to get up and apologize to me. But then, just when I thought the whole nightmare was over, the secretary general chimed in.

"May I ask you a question, Mrs. Duran?'

"Of course."

"When the professor was released from the hospital he was healthy, wasn't he?"

"Yes."

"And the central heating in the Pera Palas was working."

I knew where he was going with this.

"It was."

"In other words, the professor was not freezing as he was in Şile."

"No, he wasn't."

"Well, in that case why did you choose to spend the night in his room, in his bed? Were you trying to save his life again?"

"No."

"Did you order a bottle of Martell brandy to warm the professor up even more?"

"I can explain everything. The professor lived through some very traumatic experiences when he was in Istanbul. He wanted to talk about them; he needed someone to hear his story. I was just listening."

This time the secretary general openly looked at my breasts and laughed, "That was very generous of you."

Everyone else except the rector laughed as well. The rector seemed sympathetic to me and believed I was telling the truth, but there was nothing he could say.

I knew then that I'd lost, that they weren't going to take anything I said seriously.

The rector said, "I'm very sorry Mrs. Duran, but after all of this I don't see how we can work together. I appreciate the work you've done during your time here. Would you prefer to resign or to be dismissed for moral turpitude?"

There seemed no reason to pause and consider this, so I gave my answer right away.

"I'll submit my letter of resignation at once."

The rector glanced quickly at the others.

"This meeting is adjourned."

I went straight to my office, sat down at my computer, and wrote, *I hereby resign my position at the university because of victimization based on slander and the lack of support from the university administration.* I printed the letter, signed it, and left it on my desk. I packed up all my things, a few books, a picture of Kerem, and the various odds and ends that had accumulated over the years, and left the building without saying goodbye to anyone.

There were a few people, like Nermin in the archives, whom I'd have liked to say goodbye to, but I didn't have the strength. It was all I could do to keep myself from crying. But once I got into a taxi, I couldn't hold back anymore and burst into tears.

The poor driver didn't know what to do.

"Don't worry, it'll pass. Death is the only thing we can't find a remedy for."

By the time we were passing Sirkeci Station I'd calmed down a bit and stopped crying.

The driver turned to me and said, "I can stop and get you some tea if you like."

"Thank you, that's very kind of you but it's not necessary."

As we crossed the Galata Bridge toward Karaköy, I watched the dozens of ferries coming and going, with flocks of seagulls following them. There were dozens of boats moored to the quay selling grilled fish, and again the driver turned to me, "I could stop and get you a fish sandwich, that might make you feel better. Don't worry, I'll turn the meter off."

"Thank you again, that's very thoughtful of you, but I'd really just like to get home as quickly as possible."

In our culture, food is the remedy for everything, and offering food is sometimes the only way people know how to express sympathy and offer condolence. When my grandmother died in Antakya, the neighbors wouldn't allow us to cook at home, and they took turns bringing us food. Food was eaten "for the souls of the departed," as if it would do them any good.

When we reached my house, the driver didn't want to accept any money.

"I can't accept money from someone who's grieving. Please allow me to just show you this one kindness."

He had no idea why I was so upset, and he didn't want to know. All that mattered to him was that I was in a state of grief. I did my best to pay the fare, but he refused to accept it.

I called Tarık right away, and he came and got me in his Jaguar. I could imagine the neighbors thinking, *she's moved straight from that elderly professor to this rich young man.*

He took me to one of the fanciest and most expensive restaurants in town. I told him that I didn't want to go there, that I wasn't in the mood for that kind of thing, but he insisted. The headwaiter knew him and addressed him by name, and led us to one of the best tables. When the enormous menus arrived I told Tarık to order for me, and he ordered very well. He told me that I had to eat and keep my strength up. His attitude was no different from the taxi driver's, except that the driver's horizons only extended to a fish sandwich from a rowboat, while Tarık could afford this place.

The restaurant was usually full—people often waited a week for a reservation—but today it was relatively empty. The economic crisis had hit the kind of people who could come here, and those who still had the money didn't want to be seen as guilty of conspicuous consumption.

The food, the surroundings, and Tarık's conversation did take my mind off things a bit, but the pain was still there, and from time to time, it rose to the surface.

At one point I asked Tarık if he'd found me a good lawyer.

"Have you calmed down a little?" he asked.

"What do you mean, 'have you calmed down?' I've just been fired, the newspaper humiliated me in front of the entire nation, and I don't know what I'm going to say to my son. How can I calm down?"

"You need to listen to me calmly," he said. "I didn't speak to a lawyer."

"What?"

"Because a lawyer isn't what you need."

"A least I could expose the newspaper for lying, I could get them to print a retraction and sue them for defamation of character."

The waiter asked us if everything was to our satisfaction, and we thanked him and said it was. We were drinking water because I didn't want to mix the Lexatonil with alcohol.

"Look. Let's say we consulted a lawyer. And he prepared an affidavit. It would go to court and they might decide in your favor. At this point the newspaper could choose to print a retraction."

"What do you mean they could choose?"

"They're allowed to delay for a hundred days. Even if they did print a retraction, it wouldn't make a difference. They would pay a small fine, and months from now everyone would be reminded of the story and it would be in the news again."

"What about suing for damages caused by defamation of character?"

"The way the legal system works here, the case could drag on for at least five years. Then they could appeal. If the appeals court dismisses the case the whole thing would start again from the beginning."

"Is it really that hopeless?"

"Unfortunately, yes. The courts have such a backlog of cases that the system barely functions anymore. I advise you to give it up. It'll just wear you out, and every time you appear in court you'll be in the news again."

"How can anyone in this country ever get justice?"

"They can't. There are cases that have dragged on so long that criminals get off because of the statute of limitations. I know of cases that have dragged on for thirty years."

"Thirty years?"

"Yes, thirty years."

I was so discouraged by what he'd said that I could barely eat.

"So what am I going to do?"

"First you can stop playing with your fork and finish your dinner. Then you'll go home and have a good sleep."

"Then what?"

"Tomorrow there'll be an article in the paper defending you and telling your side of the story."

"You spoke to your friend?"

"Yes. Just take it easy, and we'll think about what to do later. Would you like some panna cotta?"

"No."

"Tiramisu?"

"No," I said and laughed.

"Why are you laughing?"

"Everyone's trying to get me to eat today. Am I still making money?"

"Of course."

"Good, I'm going to need it because I won't be getting a paycheck anymore."

"Don't worry. There are plenty of jobs you can get."

When I got home I sat on the couch for a while and thought things over. Tarık's support had done me a world of good. He might be a show-off with his expensive car and clothes and watches; he was a playboy, not really my type, and we didn't share the same values, but he had a good heart and was a good friend and I was very grateful to him.

I wasn't going to say anything to Kerem unless he'd already heard. I'd talk to him after this next article was published, if in fact it was. I didn't really believe it would be, but Tarık seemed quite confident it would.

I drift off to sleep on the couch, and in my dreams there's an earthquake. The couch is shaking so badly I almost fall off. This, I thought, is the big one. The whole city will be destroyed and everyone will be killed: the people at the university and the people at the newspaper. After this, nothing is going to matter anymore.

Someone taps my shoulder.

"Madam, please fasten your seat belt."

It's Renata, the flight attendant who helped me earlier. "We're experiencing some turbulence."

Drowsily I fasten my belt. The huge plane keeps shaking. Even the lockers above our heads creak. I'd fallen asleep. In the meantime the blinds have been opened. It is bright inside the plane. The passengers have a breakfast tray in front of them and they're holding on to their orange juice, coffee, or tea to keep it from spilling. The flight attendants have stopped serving. The couple who were snuggling under the blanket have woken up from a deep, happy sleep. Their faces are sparkling, and they gaze into each other's eyes.

"Oh that beautiful sleep of youth." Who said this? Max, of course.

He sent me an email. He told me he'd had a comfortable journey, that he'd never forget the week he'd spent with me in Istanbul, and asked how I was. I answered briefly that I was fine, and didn't mention the trouble he'd got me into.

CHAPTER 18

I used the drug to help me sleep again, and when I woke the next morning all my joints were aching, probably from all the tension I'd been feeling. I also felt a sense of gloom and doom, a sense that something was wrong. Then, slowly, I remembered all that had happened and the pain and despair rose to the surface.

I forced myself out of bed and hobbled to the door to get the newspaper, and then turned the pages hopefully. There was nothing on the second page, or the third, fourth, fifth, or sixth, ... I kept turning the pages. I was just about to give up hope when I saw a small article on page twelve.

UNIVERSITY SCANDAL WOMAN
INSISTS SHE'S INNOCENT

There was a new development yesterday in the scandal that rocked Istanbul University two days ago. Maya Duran, the public relations officer who was accused of conducting an illicit affair with visiting professor Maximilian Wagner, has stated that the allegations are false.

Duran said that "there was nothing improper or unprofessional about my relationship with Professor Wagner, and all suggestions to the contrary are malicious slander and patently absurd. Professor Wagner, who is of an advanced age and has held a position at one of the world's leading universities for many years, is highly respected both for his work and for his exemplary character, and my record as a loyal, honest, and diligent employee of Istanbul University speaks for itself. I am a good Turkish mother and an upstanding Turkish citizen, and am outraged by these spiteful allegations."

I was flabbergasted. I was certainly pleased that they'd published the article, but I'd never actually said what they quoted me as saying. They'd given my invented statement a patriotic slant to appeal to their readers. They also hadn't mentioned that I'd been fired from the university. What a powerful tool the press was; it could destroy you or make you a hero.

Then I noticed a picture just below the article, and was struck by how much it resembled Ahmet. I looked more closely, and was stunned to realize that it was in fact Ahmet, my ex-husband.

I was surprised I hadn't recognized him at once. There he was, sitting with the same reporter who'd interviewed me, the same close-set eyes, the same haircut, though his hair was starting to thin out. I'd known him so well once, but at the same time I felt I was looking at a picture of a stranger. Perhaps it was the expression on his face that made him seem different, an expression I didn't remember ever having seen.

The camera had caught him while he was talking. His mouth was partly open and he had a slight frown, and there was something in his eyes that made him seem strong and determined. Beneath the picture were a caption and a brief statement.

SUPPORT FROM MAYA DURAN'S FORMER HUSBAND

Ahmet Baltaci dismisses the allegations against Maya Duran, from whom he was divorced eight years ago.

"I know Maya very well, and have been in regular contact with her since our divorce. No one who knows her would believe these allegations. She's a good mother and possesses a strong and honest character. She's also a woman of strong principles and has always behaved with the utmost responsibility. Of course we've had our differences, but I don't hesitate for a moment to say that these allegations are absurd.

"Maya Duran is a free woman, and her choice of partner is of no concern either to me or to the public. However, it's inconceivable that she would have an illicit affair with someone of such advanced age whom she'd met only a few days earlier in an official capacity. I simply don't believe it. I mean, I know it's not true."

I couldn't believe this was Ahmet. Had the editors altered his statement as they had mine? It just didn't sound like Ahmet. I'd never heard him speak with such confidence and determination.

I put down the paper and picked up the phone, I looked for the number I'd called the other day and found it.

"Hello, may I speak to Sibel please?"

"Yes, speaking."

"Hello, I'm Maya. Maya Du..."

"Oh, hello, Maya! Have you read it?"

She sounded proud, and seemed to think I'd called to thank her.

"Yes, and there's something I wanted to ask you. How did you get hold of my ex-husband?"

"The same way I got hold of you. I called him. The first time I called there seemed to be something going on in the background, there was a lot of noise, but I couldn't make out what it was. He just said something I couldn't quite catch and refused to be interviewed."

"But of course you didn't give up."

"No, it wasn't like that. To tell you the truth, I considered interviewing him because I felt I owed you and thought he might say something to support you. But when he refused, I just let it go. But then he called me an hour or so later from a different number and said he was ready to talk to me."

"How strange!"

"Why are you surprised?"

"It's just not what I would have expected of him."

"To tell the truth, I got the impression he was doing something out of character. I can't put my finger on it, maybe it was the way he managed to be calm and angry at the same time."

"Do you think he was angry about the news or about something else?"

"I really couldn't say."

"OK, I won't keep you. I'd just like to know if he actually said what you wrote or did one of the editors alter his statement."

"What they printed was exactly what he said, word for word. To tell the truth, I didn't think they would use it, but they did."

"Thank you very much. You've been a great help."

"Not at all, I'm just trying to do my job."

After I hung up, I read Ahmet's statement again. What had made him change so dramatically and so abruptly?

I picked up the phone, hesitated for some time, and then finally called. It rang for a long time, and I was about to give up when a woman answered.

"Oh, I'm sorry, I was calling Ahmet."

"I'm his mother, Maya is that you?"

It was only then that I recognized my ex mother-in-law's voice. I hoped I hadn't seemed disrespectful. The best thing was to be straightforward.

"How are you?"

"I'm fine, thank you. How are you?"

"Thanks, I'm fine too."

There was a short and somewhat strained silence. Then she said, "Ahmet's not here. He came to see us yesterday and forgot his phone."

"It doesn't seem like him not to come back and get his phone."

"'Well, he had a bit of a disagreement with his father and…It'll be all right, he'll come and get it when he's cooled down."

I just couldn't imagine Ahmet arguing with his father. He was usually afraid to look his father in the face, and couldn't talk to him without stuttering.

"We were sitting together when Ahmet's phone rang. It was a newspaper reporter who wanted to interview him. Ahmet panicked. He always gets nervous talking on the phone when his father's within earshot. He said that he didn't want to talk and hung up. But his father started to mutter about, well, about...you know...er...and wouldn't let the matter drop."

"I understand, the things the newspaper said about me the other day."

"Yes. Anyway, well, after that Ahmet just left and forgot his phone."

"And he hasn't come back to get it?"

"He phoned about an hour later. He asked for me to read him the last number for the last call he'd received. He hasn't called since."

What I guessed was that Ahmet's father had started putting me down, and Ahmet finally decided to stand up to him. Then he'd called the reporter and agreed to an interview. At last he'd decided to become his own man.

This must have put his mother in a difficult position. She was used to managing her husband and protecting her children from him. She wouldn't know how to deal with her son defying his father.

I'd never been particularly close to her, and her attitude toward me had always been neutral. Indeed, her whole attitude to life could be described as neutral and passive.

I suddenly felt the urge to get moving, but didn't quite know how to end this conversation without seeming rude. Finally I just told her I had to go and said goodbye.

It was still quite early and my body was still aching, but I began to move quickly. I got dressed and went out to buy ten copies of the newspaper before it was sold out. I thought I should have them just in case. I bought them from different shops so that all the shops near my building would still have copies.

Then I went home and had a hot bath to ease my aching joints.

I'd love to have a hot bath right now, too, but you can't do that in a plane at 26,000 feet. On a plane, your seat is the only space you can claim, and it's hardly a private space. Long flights make you appreciate the value of personal space.

I realize that throughout this narrative I keep talking about having baths. But it's a fact that nothing relaxes me more than lying in a hot tub. It's not just about personal hygiene, it's a kind of therapy, and the more stressful the situation the more good it does me.

Wilhelm Reich would interpret this as a desire to return to the womb, like curling up under a quilt in the fetal position. I think it's only a natural thing to want to do when life gets too much for you.

Well, I can't take a bath now, but even just thinking about it helps.

When I came out of the bathroom, I saw that I'd had several calls. My mother, Filiz, and Tarık. I was sure they'd all read the newspaper, but I'd talk to them later.

I got out the family photo album and started looking through the hundreds of photos spanning the family's history: the older ones in black and white and the more recent in color.

The older black-and-white pictures had all been taken at studios. Everyone was carefully posed, and the lighting was arranged to show people at their best: a young woman in an elegant chair, and a man in a suit and tie standing next to her; larger family groups, with the older generation seated, their grandchildren on their laps, and their adult children standing behind them. No one smiled for the camera as they do now, everyone's hair was carefully combed, and all were wearing their best clothes. The formality and manners of a lost age—an atmosphere that I found somehow innocent and tender.

The backs of most of these photographs were dated and bore the words, *I've come to kiss your hand*, written in sloping, cursive handwriting.

I looked carefully at the pictures of my maternal grandmother. Then I took her passport photo out of the album. After that I took out my paternal grandmother's passport photo and placed the two pictures side by side. Then I took out my own passport photo and placed it next to them. Then I put the three pictures in the plastic-covered pocket in my black leather purse. My paternal grandmother, my maternal grandmother, and I were now together. There was a vacant space beside us that I hoped would soon be filled. That's where I wanted to put Nadia's picture.

Then I would be united with these three women whose suffering I felt deep in my soul. History had silenced these women and had almost silenced me as well, but now I would speak for them as well as for myself. I was Maya and Ayşe, and Mari, and Nadia, whose picture I had yet to see. I was Muslim, Jewish, and Catholic. I was a human being. I felt a strong sense of excitement as I envisioned the difficult but radiant path before me.

The first thing I had to do was call Ahmet. But he'd left his phone at his father's house. I looked around and finally found his home number. I tried twice but no one answered. Then, after hesitating a while I called his cell phone again. This time Ahmet answered.

"Hello, Ahmet, how are you?"

"Fine. You?"

He spoke in a low voice that was more timid than usual.

Suddenly I lost my temper. I was hoping to have a nice conversation, and then ask him for the help I needed to put my plan into action. But I made an effort to be patient.

"That was very nice of you. Thank you."

"Yes."

I knew that his father was within earshot.

"Where are you?"

"At my parents' house."

He'd gone to get his phone thinking his father wouldn't be home. But he was, and now he was under the old tyrant's thumb again. His rebellion hadn't lasted long.

"Listen, I need to speak to you."

"When?"

"Come to the S café at eleven."

"But I've got wo…"

"Don't talk to me about your work!" I shouted.

He was probably just saying this for his father's benefit.

"Just be there at eleven."

I knew he'd come. I knew him all too well. He'd returned to his usual state of fear and doubt. I could have invited him to come to my apartment but I didn't want to.

Then I phoned Tarık.

"Did you like it?" he asked.

"Yes, I really would have preferred them to use my own words but…"

"You're never satisfied, are you?"

I realized he was expecting me to thank him.

"All right," I said. "Thank you, I'm grateful for your help, are you happy now?"

"No," he said, "I didn't mean to say that. Your ex really came through for you. Good for him."

"Anyway…thank you. I really mean it. You've been a tremendous support these past few days. By the way, I'm going to need some of that money you said I've made."

"Sure. Whenever you want."

"Can I withdraw some euros from the bank?"

"Of course. But I don't advise it. Foreign currency is very expensive right now. You're earning Turkish lira. I was planning to convert it to foreign currency when the time was right, but it isn't yet."

"All I need right now is five hundred euros."

"Why do you need it?"

"There's something I have to do. Can I withdraw it from the bank this afternoon?"

"All right, but wait until after two o'clock."

After that I talked to my mother and Filiz. My mother was very pleased, and I was sure that she had also bought several copies of the paper to show her neighbors to prove I wasn't really a shameless hussy. My parents were a bit cold about Ahmet's statement but gave him credit for it all the same.

"I can't tell you how relieved your father is. He hasn't been able to sleep for days. He's been pacing up and down the living room all night. He never believed it was true, but it still upset him."

I didn't tell her I'd been fired. Filiz, though, had already heard, "I'm terribly sorry."

"Don't be, I think it's for the best."

"Why?"

"It'll give me a chance to make a new start. I was never terribly happy there anyway."

"You're going to get a new job?"

"I'm going to get a new life!"

"I don't understand."

"A more creative, more colorful life. More meaning-ful! This is why I'm so excited, do you understand?"

"No."

"Let's get together and I'll tell you what I'm planning."

As I made my way through the cold toward the shop-ping mall, I felt increasingly strong and determined. So much had changed within me since my crying fit in the taxi.

Ahmet was already there when I got to the S café. When he greeted me with his usual phony politeness I was disappointed. I'd hoped he really had decided to be-come his own man.

"Were you sincere about what you said in the paper?"

He answered with a nod, but I didn't know quite what it meant. When I looked at him, I felt a sudden resurgence of all my residual anger at him.

"Why did you call me and shout at me when you saw that first article."

"I guess I just reacted without thinking."

"Never mind," I said. "Now listen to me carefully."

"What would you like to drink?"

"I don't want anything to drink. Just listen to me for five minutes and then I'll leave."

He was thrown off by my determined manner, and I was pleased by the look of suspicion I saw in his eyes.

"I've been fired," I said.

"What! When?"

"Yesterday."

"Because of this incident?"

"Yes, because of this slander."

"I'm very sorry."

"Don't be sorry for me, be sorry for yourself."

"Why?"

"Because now I have no job and no salary. I can't maintain a home, pay Kerem's school expenses, and feed and clothe him. You're his father."

"You mean you want me to pay child support?"

"No."

He suddenly looked frightened.

"It's not about child support. This is what you're going to do. You're going to take Kerem, clothe him, send him to school, help him study for his exams, take care of him when he's sick, try to help him get over his psychological problems. I'll have him for the weekend whenever I choose, take him out, and buy him presents."

"But I'm a man, how can I take care of a child?"

"You'll do the same thing I've been doing all these years. You don't have a choice. I'm moving out of my apartment and leaving Istanbul."

I could see the panic on his face. He tried to interrupt but I wouldn't let him get a word in.

"If you don't want your son left out on the street you'll come get him tomorrow."

Then I just got up and walked away, and it felt good. I was beginning to feel happy about what had happened, and about being fired. A new Maya was emerging and she was standing up for herself. I went upstairs, sat in another café, and had a large coffee and a delicious sandwich.

Later I went to the travel agency on the ground floor and asked about flights to Kassel. The agent looked at his screen and said, "There are no direct flights to Kassel. You can fly to either Frankfurt or Hannover and then continue by train."

The next day I bought an economy-class round-trip ticket to Frankfurt and paid with my credit card. I was able to get a good deal because it was low season.

When the travel agent asked if I had a visa for Germany, I told him I had a green passport. This so-called diplomatic passport, which I'd got because of my job at the university, allowed me to travel without a visa to most countries in Europe.

In the afternoon I went to the bank and withdrew 500 euros. It wasn't a lot, but I wouldn't be in Germany long and I could use my credit card if I had to.

That evening I gave Kerem a somewhat cleaned-up version of what had happened to me. I showed him the last newspaper article that had appeared but not the first two.

Then I said, "Sometimes unexpected things can happen to people. This last week I've seen what a clever, what a brave and astute young man you are."

"What does *astute* mean?" he asked.

"In other words," I said, "In other words...it's something like being clever. Knowing what to do and where."

He nodded.

"You're very mature for your age and I know you'll understand what I'm going to say. I've lost my job at the university because of the lies someone told about me."

"You mean they fired you?"

"Yes, you could say that. I think the real reason has to do with those security agents. They are using the other business as an excuse."

"So the man really was a spy, eh?"

"No, I don't think he was, but that's what they think. Now that I'm unemployed, I can't keep this apartment or support you. That's why I want you to stay with your father for a while. We don't have any other choice."

"For how long?"

"Until I work things out. There are only a few months left in the school year. We'll stay with your grandparents in Bodrum for the summer and we'll be back living together in the fall. In the meantime I'll see you as often as I can. What do you say?"

He shrugged his shoulders. "What can I say?"

I felt a stab of remorse, even though I knew that everything I was doing was to make his future better. I was going to be taking a huge step forward and I needed to be free, at least for a while.

I'd worked for years and had managed to get by on my salary. I'd tried to save a little, and paid for what I bought in installments. You get used to living at a certain standard, and your whole life is spent struggling to maintain that standard. You've already eaten into your future salary with your credit card and installment plans. Once you got caught in that trap, it became almost impossible to change your life.

I hadn't chosen the events of the past few days, but they'd brought about a revolution in my life. I was going to take a step toward the kind of freedom every salary-slave secretly dreams of, to become self-employed. The money Tarık had made for me was certainly going to make things easier. It no longer mattered that I didn't have a regular paycheck. It would be enough to make a little here and there. Of course at some point, I was going to have to deal with health insurance and some kind of pension plan.

Perhaps if this had happened a few years from now I would have taken a different attitude. I might have been more frightened, more worried about security. But now I felt I'd found freedom.

The more I thought about it, the more grateful I felt to Max. He had no idea, of course, what he'd done for me. He was the reason I'd been slandered in the newspaper and then fired. It was because of him that I now had this opportunity to grow and change, and escape a life of dreary and meaningless servitude.

Before I went to bed, I spent some time on the internet. I looked up the weather in Germany. The whole country was freezing, and it was snowing in Bad Arolsen.

Then I went to the www.its-arolsen.org page and read the conditions for access to the archives. The records were open to relatives of victims and to governments, but researchers could also examine them. They only asked a nominal fee for photocopies and copies of compact discs. I had to fill out an application form, but I could do this online. I filled it out, using my position at the university. After all, I was still officially on the books as an employee until the end of the month.

I checked the hotels in Bad Arolsen. It was a spa town so there were quite a few hotels, and they weren't very expensive at this time of year. I made a reservation for two nights at the LandKomfort Hotel. It would cost me 47 euros a night, and from the pictures, it looked clean and comfortable. Then I started packing my heaviest winter clothes.

The next day I got up early and prepared breakfast for Kerem. I left 100 lira for him on the table. Then, after watering all the plants I went into Kerem's room. He was asleep, so I leaned down and kissed him.

I texted Ahmet to remind him to pick Kerem up from school, then put on my thickest coat and my winter boots, picked up my suitcase, and set out to start my new life.

CHAPTER 19

The airport in Frankfurt was so busy and crowded I felt overwhelmed. People rushing here and there, from one plane to another, dashing from one line to another, constant announcements, planes landing and taking off every minute, thousands of people wrapped up in their own lives and adventures, hardly aware of the people around them, everyone playing the leading role in their own movie.

I went to an airport bookstore and bought a guide to Bad Arolsen. I asked whether they had any books by Erich Auerbach, but they didn't have them in German, let alone English.

On the train I looked out across the frozen landscape and thought about all that had happened here over the years, times of terrible war and times of peace and prosperity, Roman legions and invading Goths; princes, poets, and scholars; the Nazis and the armies that defeated them;

a devastated nation rebuilding itself; the iron curtain and reunification.

Then I dozed off for a while, and when I woke I looked at the pictures in the book on Bad Arolsen. It looked like a beautiful town with its baroque houses, parks, and chateaus. The Grand Avenue, I read, was lined with exactly 880 oak trees. The picture had been taken in summer, of course, and the trees would be bare now.

The Augustinian convent of Aroldessen had been founded here in 1113. It had been the seat of the Principality of Waldeck and Pyrmont from the seventeenth to the twentieth century and had been the capital of the independent Waldeck State until 1929. I must confess that I'd never even heard of the Waldeck State. The International Tracing Services, or ITS, had been established here in 1946, and was run jointly by the International Red Cross and the German government.

It was almost dark by the time I stepped onto the platform at Bad Arolsen, and it was very, very cold. I got into one of the white Mercedes taxis waiting in front of the station and we made our way along icy streets to my hotel. Snow sparkled in the streetlights.

After settling into my room I went down to the hotel restaurant, had the fried trout the region was famous for and a large glass of beer, and then went back to my room to check my emails. There was a message from the Turkish Foreign Ministry to the effect that they had no records pertaining to the matter about which I'd inquired.

Then, suddenly, I felt very tired, so after a hot shower I got between the clean, sweet-smelling sheets and fell right asleep, without having to take a pill.

In the morning I left the hotel alert and full of energy. When the taxi dropped me off in front of the ITS, I felt a surge of excitement. As soon as I stepped out of the taxi, I was struck by the deep silence, almost like the silence in a cemetery. And then it struck me that it was, in a sense, a kind of digital cemetery containing the memories, personal details, and pictures of millions of war victims.

I crossed the garden, entered the building, and told the stout, middle-aged man at the information desk that I had submitted an application the day before. He asked for my identification, found my application on the computer, and made a photocopy of my passport.

For some reason I blurted out, "We had German Jewish scholars at our university during the war."

The man smiled indulgently and said, "I know. Have you read our rules?"

"I have."

"Very well. Your registration is complete. Please follow me."

I'd imagined I'd be led through miles of shelves stacked with files, but instead I was led into a large hall that contained nothing but tables, chairs, and computers.

I saw two children, a boy and a girl in dark clothes, at a table near the window. It seemed odd to see children in a place like this, and the children themselves seemed odd, seemed somehow very old. The man left me there, and I had no idea what I was supposed to do. The boy said something in German, in a deep voice that sounded adult.

I gestured that I didn't understand, and he whispered in English, "Please sit down. They'll attend to you in a moment."

I realized that he and the woman were little people. Their heads barely reached above the table. I smiled and thanked him. A little later a tall, slim woman with brown hair came over to me and shook my hand. She introduced herself as Angelika Traub, asked me what I wanted to look up, and guided me to one of the computers.

"I want to look up Herbert Scurla."

"Was he a victim?" she asked.

"No, he was a Nazi official. I'm looking for information in his reports on the professors who went to Istanbul University in the 1930s. I'm particularly interested in any mention of Professor Maximilian Wagner."

"That's not a Jewish name either."

"No, but he was a victim."

There were thousands of entries under Scurla, and most of the documents she pulled up were stamped with the emblem of the double-headed eagle. We narrowed the search down to Istanbul University, and eventually found the report on the Jewish professors in Istanbul that Scurla had presented to Hitler. We entered Maximilian Wagner's name, and my heart jumped when I saw that they had the documents Scurla had taken from Matilda Arditi.

Angelika went out to fetch the files, and I waited impatiently, cracking my knuckles and barely able to stay in my seat. The two little people gave me a look of sympathy and understanding. Then Angelika returned with the files, placed them on the table, and left me alone with them.

I lifted the cover of Max's file slowly, as if I were lifting the lid of a tomb, and the musty smell of old papers rose up. I sifted through manuscripts and notes in German, and then I found a number of photographs: a young Max, and beside him a beautiful dark-haired woman. Nadia!

She had high cheekbones and deep soulful eyes, and looked straight at the camera with a frank and honest expression. There were pictures of her alone as well, in different settings, and in all of them her sensitivity and the strength of her character were reflected clearly. These were the pictures that had been removed from Nasip Street in 1942, and I could hardly believe that I'd found them.

I went over to the little people. "Do you know if I can get copies of these?"

The man said, "Of course. You're not allowed to take anything out of this room, but the people on duty will help you."

"Are you relatives of victims?" I asked.

We couldn't have a conversation because we had to whisper. The woman suggested we go out to the cafeteria and talk there.

"I'd like that," I said. "Let me just get the copies I need first."

I returned to my seat and glanced through the rest of what was there. Then suddenly I saw it. I picked it up, unable to quite believe it was real. A yellowed sheet of music titled *Serenade für Nadia, Maximilian Wagner*.

My eyes began to fill with tears, and it took me a few moments to compose myself. Then I pulled myself together and asked if I could have copies made. The man on duty told me to wait in the room.

Frau Traub came within a few moments, and I showed her the music and the pictures I wanted copied. She took the whole file with her and returned in about five minutes with the copies.

"You can pay the cashier," she said handing me a receipt. I thanked her. "Excuse me but there's one more thing," I said.

She looked at me.

"The Tatar Legions!"

"What is that?" she asked.

"A number of Crimean Turks fought on the German side and retreated with them. They were settled in Northern Italy and Austria, but when the British captured them, they were handed over to the Red Army. Some of them killed themselves and the rest were shot by the Russians."

"This is the first I've heard of it," she said. "Are you looking for someone in particular?"

"Yes, my maternal grandmother. Her name was Ayşe, but her people didn't use surnames then so I don't know how to search for her."

"I'll help," she said. "But there's something you have to do to first."

"What?"

"You have to make some additions to the form."

"Why?"

"Before, you were acting as a researcher. Now, you're acting as a relative of a victim. You have to state this on the form."

I returned to the information desk, explained the situation, wrote what I had to write on the form, and returned to the room.

The two little people got up and introduced themselves, shaking my hand very politely. They came up only to my waist. They were Romanian. I'd thought they were husband and wife, but they were brother and sister.

They were delighted when they heard I came from Istanbul. We went to the cafeteria and Mr. Ovitz asked what I would like to drink and insisted on getting it himself. His sister and I sat at a wooden table. Ovitz brought coffee and cakes on a tray that seemed so large in his hands that I feared he'd drop it.

As we drank our coffee, I told them that my research was related to Romania, and how happy I was to have found the photos of Nadia. They knew the story of the *Struma.*

They told me that they were writing a book about their ancestors and that they'd been coming here every day for weeks.

When I asked whether their families were victims, the man said, "Yes, you could say that. People assume all the victims were killed in the camps, but our grandfather and his family were among the few people who survived."

The family, seven of whom were little people and two of whom were of normal height, was sent from Romania to Auschwitz. Here they were stripped and led to the gas chambers with the others in their group. The gas had just been turned on when Dr. Mengele had it shut off and the little people brought out, then made them drink milk and vomit to alleviate the effects of the gas they'd already breathed in.

I could picture the panic that gripped them when the gassing began, families clasping one another, naked and vulnerable as they faced death, the gassing being halted and the Nazis coming in and removing naked little people, and then the doors being locked again and the gas being turned on...

Dr. Mengele had used them as subjects in the research he was doing on hereditary diseases. He put them in different sections. Every day he took blood and bone marrow samples, exposed them to radiation, poured hot and cold water into their ears, blinded them with chemical drops, and filled the girls' wombs with liquid chemicals.

One day he had had them stripped naked and showed them to his colleagues, and on another occasion he had had them filmed, making them sing songs and do comical things, and then had Hitler watch it to amuse him.

The little people were rescued when the Red Army took the camp.

He told the story in a normal tone of voice, without dramatizing it, but it moved and horrified me, and it disturbed me deeply to think that people could do this to each other. Yet this building contained evidence of millions of equally horrific stories.

When we went back to the hall, Angelika Traub told me she'd found documents related to the Tatar Legions, but they were in German and Russian. I asked if there were any pictures and she said there was a group photo of the refugees in the camp in Austria. I asked for copies of the pictures and the Russian and German documents. Then I said goodbye to the little brother and sister and left the ITS building.

At the hotel I borrowed a magnifying glass and looked carefully at the picture of the inmates of the Drau camp. I examined each face, but could find no one in that wretched, miserable crowd who resembled my grandmother.

Much later I was to remember my thoughts on my return journey as I looked again and again at Nadia's pictures and the score of the *Serenade*, of which I could read not a single note. It was while reading an essay on Pascal by Auerbach, titled "The Triumph of Evil." He quoted Pascal's statement that it was right to pursue what was just, but it was inevitable that the strong would lead. Justice without power is ineffectual and power without justice is tyranny. There would always be those who would undermine and overthrow justice that lacked power. We had to integrate justice and power by making the just powerful and the powerful just.

Justice is difficult to define, but we recognize power at once. We could not empower justice because power has negated justice and asserted itself to be just. Since we have been unable make what is right powerful, we have made power right.

The essay goes on to discuss those who value the state for its own sake, who praise its dynamic vitality like Machiavelli or who are concerned, like Hobbes, with the benefits the ideal state might bring. For Pascal, however, the state had no inner dynamics and the preference for one form of statehood over another was meaningless because all forms were equally repressive. Though I would not have been able to express it like this then, the essay summed up my thoughts at that time.

Before the plane began to descend, I took out my brown purse and looked inside. Four women were now looking at me from the plastic-covered pocket.

Maya, Ayşe, Mari, and Nadia.

CHAPTER 20

The flight attendant made several announcements while the plane was descending to Istanbul. One of them concerned transit passengers coming to Istanbul from abroad who were to continue on domestic flights. She announced that if these passengers were continuing to an airport that had customs facilities, they should complete their customs procedures there; but if they were continuing to an airport without customs, they should go through passport control in Istanbul.

This was an announcement that did not concern me at all, it was directed to the tourists on their way to holiday resorts.

But as the plane was descending and I saw how gray, dreary, and depressing Istanbul looked I thought, "Why not?" There was no one waiting for me at home, and I no longer had a job to go to. I was free, and if I wanted, I could catch the next plane to Bodrum. I could use a break, and my parents would be very happy to see me.

I asked the flight attendant and she advised me to go through immigration control in Istanbul and then go to the domestic terminal to catch a plane to Bodrum. My suitcase had been checked in only as far as Istanbul.

I did exactly as she told me. I got out at the international terminal, waited in line, passed through passport control, and collected my suitcase. As I emerged and saw the crowds waiting just beyond the barrier, it occurred to me that it was exactly ten days since I'd stood there waiting for Max.

I went to the domestic terminal and checked flights to Bodrum. There was a flight in an hour and fifty minutes. I was delighted, and after buying my ticket and checking in my suitcase, I went to a shop and bought presents for my parents. I wasn't going to tell them I was coming; I thought it would be better to surprise them.

I bought a newspaper and a magazine and sat in a café. The papers were full of the same old depressing news: the economic crisis, and politicians blaming each other for the situation.

I called Kerem but he didn't answer. I wondered what he was doing, and if he was all right. I tried not to think about him, but the more I tried the more guilty I felt and the more I missed him. But it wasn't going to be for long and it would all be for the better. I thought about calling Ahmet but decided not to.

I wondered if I was being unfair to Ahmet, but when I remembered how unhappy I'd been with him I decided

I wasn't. Then again, if I could change, if I could start a new life and become a new person, then perhaps he could too. I couldn't expect him to transform overnight. He'd stood up to his father once, he could do it again, and perhaps, step-by-step, emerge from the cloud of intimidation and manipulation that had poisoned his life. If I could control my anger and be kind and supportive to him, perhaps I could help him.

On the plane, as I looked out the window at the Aegean coast in the light of the setting sun, my spirits began to lift.

It always makes me happy to go to the Aegean coast, the world of olives, basil, and wine. The atmosphere enchants me the moment I step off the plane: the warmth of the air, the smell of the sea, and the scent of the wild thyme from the mountains.

I waited with the German and English tourists in the baggage claim area, and then bargained with a taxi driver while they filed onto their tour buses. I opened the window as we drove along the coast and breathed in the clean air. We reached the crest of the hill and suddenly the town of Bodrum was spread out before us, the medieval castle on the water illuminated by spotlights, and the moonlight reflected on the bay.

My parents lived in a mid-priced compound. My father had joined a co-op and paid installments for years out of his modest salary. Then, finally, they became the owners of a badly designed and cheaply built apartment.

The walls were damp, the wiring and the plumbing were faulty, the windows were badly fit, and the doors were cracked, but the view from the balcony made it all seem worth it. Over time, as they repaired and remodeled and put in air-conditioning, theirs and the surrounding buildings became covered with purple, pink, red, and yellow bougainvillea, and in the end, they had a small but comfortable apartment in a compound that had taken on a delightful Aegean atmosphere.

In summer the compound was full and the beach was crowded with families. There were people coming and going all the time, and in the evening everyone sat on their balconies to eat and drink and enjoy the view. In winter, though, there were only a handful of retired couples like my parents.

As the taxi entered the compound, I realized how much I had missed this place. Memories of the summers of my youth came flooding back. The smell of food that drifted from the houses at dusk, the nights of guitar music around fires on the beach, swimming in the glittering phosphorescence of the dark sea, early loves and the thrill of kissing in secluded corners. Ah, how good and easy life seemed then.

My mother gave a shriek of delight when she saw me, and my father came shuffling out when he heard her. They both embraced me and fawned over me, and I felt a deep happiness at being greeted with such genuine delight by people who I knew loved me unconditionally—a rare pleasure in such a hostile world.

We spent the evening talking and eating fragrant tangerines that had just been picked. I told them as much as I could about what had happened, but they weren't demanding any explanations or chiding me for disgracing them in the eyes of their neighbors.

Many Turkish parents would have created a drama and condemned their daughter regardless of whether or not she was guilty. In some families, particularly in Eastern Turkey, disgraced daughters were condemned to death by family councils. If I'd come from a family like this, they would have given me a rope to hang myself with, thrown me in front of a tractor to make it look like an accident, or taken me to a remote field where I would be shot and buried.

The next morning, after a breakfast of local Seville oranges and local jams, cheeses, and olives, we got into my father's sturdy old Opel and went to the Yalıkavak market. The weather was almost spring-like, and such a contrast to the numbing cold I'd experienced in Germany just yesterday. Aloe and broom were blooming along the side of the road and the hills were green, though they'd be burnt brown by the sun by the beginning of summer.

Going to the weekly local markets in different villages was a favorite pastime for people who lived on the Bodrum Peninsula. On Tuesdays it was Bodrum Center, on Wednesdays it was Gündoğan, and on Thursdays it was Yalıkavak. There were seemingly endless stalls selling fruit, vegetables, cheese, olives, jam, yoghurt, and cream. There were also stalls selling beautifully worked, hand-woven cloth from Buldan and Milas. American interior designers often brought this cloth to New York to sell it for fifty times what they'd bought it for here.

Recently a lot of Europeans, mostly British, had bought houses in the area, and sometimes as many as half the people shopping in the markets were foreigners.

We'd finished our shopping and were drinking tea under the wisteria vines at my father's favorite café when my phone rang. It was someone from the university saying that a package had arrived for me from America and asking what they should do with it. I asked them to send it on to my mother's address. Then I walked a few steps away and called Ahmet.

"How's Kerem doing?"

"He's doing fine, but this isn't easy for me."

"I'm not asking about you, I'm asking about my son."

"He's fine."

"Is he going to school?"

"Yes, I'm bringing him there and picking him up because we haven't worked out the school bus yet."

I was glad he had to go through even part of what I'd had to go through for so long. I was also enjoying my newly discovered power to intimidate him.

"I'll phone this evening and speak to Kerem."

I drank in the midday sun for a while and then went into the fabric market. I still had some clothes at home from the previous summer, but I bought four T-shirts, jeans, and a couple of pairs of shorts from the stalls that sold counterfeit brand-name clothes. In Europe I couldn't even have bought a vest for what I paid.

Then, when I rejoined my parents at the café, my mother said, "What a wonderful coincidence, the whole family is getting together. It couldn't have been better had we planned it."

"What's happening?"

"Your brother and his family are coming tomorrow. They're staying for the weekend."

"Where are they going to stay, with you?"

"They never stay with us, they always stay at the army resort."

There was a five-star military resort with its own hotel, restaurant, and beach on one of Bodrum's most beautiful bays.

I wasn't crazy about them coming, but there was nothing I could do.

I fell asleep that afternoon caressed by the breeze that drifted in through the window, gently stirring the curtains. There was no sound but that of the waves washing onto the beach, and if my mother hadn't come to wake me, I might have slept through till morning. But my mother didn't want me to miss the five o'clock tea she'd prepared, a generous spread with hot bread, cheese, and jam.

"But I'll put on weight!" I exclaimed.

"No you won't," she said. "Tomorrow you'll start going for walks and nothing will happen. You're young, you'll burn it off."

I wanted to talk to my mother about her mother, but I wanted to talk to her alone. I was reluctant to bring up the subject in front of my father because he'd made it clear he didn't want to talk about his mother and her past. As in so many families, an unspoken agreement had been reached to keep the tragedies of the past from the younger generations. With us, the family history would begin anew. We were like children who were forbidden to play in the back garden because it was full of scorpions and snakes and dangerous wells.

I found the chance to talk to my mother after my father went to bed. We were sitting on the balcony, wearing light jackets because the evening was cool. The moon was nearly full, and its light was reflected in a silvery path across the bay.

"Mother, what was my grandmother's name?"

"Ayşe, of course!"

"No, what was her real name?"

She paused and remained silent for a while.

"I know all about the Tatar Legions, what happened to my grandmother, the sealed railway cars, Kizilçakçak Lake. Why didn't you tell me before?"

"Where did you hear about this?"

"My brother told me."

"He shouldn't have."

"Why?"

"There's no point in reopening old wounds."

"But maybe my grandparents would want us to know their stories."

"No, they wouldn't," she said, but she sounded more ashamed than adamant.

"How do you know?"

"If they'd wanted you to know they would have told you. They didn't even tell us."

"You never talked about it?"

"We talked about it once. My mother sat me down one day and told me everything. She got me to write down the names of our ancestors, her mother and father who were shot, and her two brothers who jumped into the River Drau."

She paused, as if she were waiting for me to ask something. Then she continued.

"My grandfather's name was Seyit, and my grand-mother's, Ayşe. The Russians shot them. Her brothers' names were Ömer and Kurban. They committed suicide by jumping into the River Drau. After she had got me to write these names, she said, 'Have someone read the *Mevlit* for the souls of the departed, give alms to the poor. They were all very good people.' She herself was illiterate. That's why I wrote everything down."

"They were all Turks and Muslim, weren't they?"

"Yes."

"How could this happen? How could the Turkish government send these people to their deaths?"

"That's something we can't know. They must have had their reasons."

"Wasn't my grandmother angry about this?"

"No, she accepted her fate. But she did weep when she told me to write down her parents' and brothers' names. She recited the opening verses of the Quran for each of them."

"Didn't your father ever say anything about what happened?"

"He never talked about those things. He didn't talk much about anything. But my mother told me he used to have nightmares."

"But it was terribly heroic of him to jump into the lake and rescue her."

"Yes."

She smiled.

"People will do anything for love. He loved her deeply to the moment of his death. You could see it in the way he looked at her as he held her hand in his last moments."

"Did he call her by her real name?"

"Yes."

"Well, what was it?"

"Can't you guess?"

"No."

"You know that my mother gave you your name, don't you?"

"So her real name was Maya?"

"She wanted her real name to live on in you."

Maya. The name that had been kept secret for a lifetime. Ever since I was a child, I'd wondered why I'd been given such an unusual name. I did like my name. It had a musical ring, but it was very uncommon.

Three women who'd had to take new names.

Maya had become Ayşe, Mari had become Semahat, and Nadia had become Deborah.

These three women hadn't been allowed to use the names they'd been given at birth.

Nadia was the least fortunate of them. Maya and Mari had at least married men who loved them, had lived to see their children and grandchildren grow up, and in the end had finally been able to tell their stories.

My maternal grandmother was the most fortunate. She'd lost her family and had to live under an assumed name, but she hadn't had to change her religion or ethnic identity.

Nadia's story had been buried with her in the dark waters of the Black Sea, but I would raise it and tell the whole world. I felt that this was my sacred duty.

My mother and I sat in silence on the balcony, watching the shimmering lights of the Greek island of Kos. But even this beautiful scene gave me cause to feel deep sadness. There, just across the way, was land held by another state, a state with which our state had been in conflict for generations. There had been half a dozen wars between these states and their predecessor states, millions had been killed, villages, towns, and cities had been burned, millions on both sides had been uprooted and forced to migrate to unfamiliar lands, all in the name of the artificial constructs of sovereignty and nationality.

Stefan Zweig had hoped that the invention of the airplane would bring an end to wars because their very nature transcended borders. But he lived to see the airplane used as an instrument of destruction that obliterated the cities of Europe.

CHAPTER 21

Even though it was a holiday resort, the military facilities in Bodrum were just as spotless and regimented as the command headquarters in Istanbul. My parents and Necdet and his wife, Oya, were sitting in the restaurant by the seaside.

"I had a meeting in Bodrum," my brother said, "and I decided to bring Oya so we could have a little break together. What wonderful weather."

"It's not always like this," my father said, "but this year for some reason we haven't had a winter, it's been like spring."

White-coated waiters were bringing the meticulously prepared seafood. Prawns had been arranged on top of a lettuce leaf elaborately dressed with mayonnaise. The plate was so decorative that I was almost afraid to touch it.

As we ate, we looked out across the shimmering water at Bodrum Castle and made the usual small talk. Then, as we were drinking coffee, my brother suggested that he and I go for a walk together.

When I was growing up, I saw my brother as an authority figure. He was considerably older than me, and he looked and behaved like my father. We never laughed and played together, never shared a secret world as some siblings do. He was always distant and somewhat severe. I never doubted that he loved me, but he never showed his affection and expected me to treat him as a respected elder.

When I reached adulthood, I slowly stopped accepting his authority without question. I would argue with him and challenge his opinions. I tried to establish a relationship in which our different strengths balanced each other and we could be equals. But he was never able to accept this, and over time our relationship became increasingly strained. Now, we no longer had any common ground at all. We had almost nothing left to say to each other.

As we walked along the shore we both felt ill at ease, like two strangers who didn't know how to begin a conversation.

"Do our parents know?" he asked.

"Do they know what?"

"About what happened at the university?"

"Yes."

"What did they say?"

"They trust me and knew that what had been said about me couldn't be true."

"They weren't angry at all?"

"Why would they be angry? It's not my fault if people tell lies about me."

"Well, do they know you were fired?"

"I haven't told them yet. I said I'd taken an unpaid leave, but I'm planning to tell them tomorrow."

"Oh, Maya!"

"What's the matter?"

"I warned you. I told you to stay out of it."

"Yes, you did."

"But you wouldn't listen to me, you had to dig yourself in deeper. What happened to you, the article in the paper and you getting fired, didn't just happen out of the blue."

"You mean these things happened because I was looking into the *Struma*."

"You'd better believe it. There's more to the story than meets the eye, and governments will go to great lengths to protect themselves."

"But the governments of Britain, Russia, Turkey, Germany, and Romania all share responsibility for what happened to the *Struma*."

"Yes, and none of them want to accept responsibility."

"The Germans are the only ones who've acknowledged responsibility, but the others are equally guilty."

"Look, Maya, you're my sister and I'll do everything I can to protect you. But I beg you not to take this any further. You can't fight the state."

"The state is an artificial construct that only keeps its authority because no one challenges it."

"You sound like an anarchist. Nothing would function without government. Even the most primitive societies have some form of government."

"But I have the right to express my ideas."

"These are undeveloped ideas, utopian ideals like those of Bakunin and Kropotkin. Look at how well this camp is run, how smoothly everything works. The only reason is respect for authority. Take that away and it would fall apart."

"I don't object to order, I just object to it being arbitrarily imposed by whoever manages to seize power. I believe in true democracy, in cooperation and reconciliation."

"Did you learn all of this from that communist Jew?"

"Which communist Jew?"

"Wagner!"

I laughed.

"Why are you laughing?"

"Wagner is neither a communist nor a Jew. So much for the quality of the intelligence your agency gathers."

"Of course I know he's not a Jew, but all those professors were either communists or Jews.

"He was married to a Jew, was that his crime?"

"You have no idea of the threat that Israel poses to our country, its connections with the Kurdish groups in Northern Iraq. You have no idea of what Zionism really represents."

"Look, neither Max nor his wife were Zionists, not that I think it matters whether they were or not. They just had to get out of Germany because the government arbitrarily decided to start killing Jews. Was our maternal grandmother Jewish?"

"No, what has that to do with it?"

"Well, was she a communist?"

"No!"

"She was a Muslim Turkish girl, wasn't she? Her family was Muslim and Turkish too."

"Yes, I'm the one who told you the story."

"Well, didn't our government knowingly send her people to their deaths?"

He didn't have an answer for that.

My parents and Oya were sitting at the table, happily eating their fruit, and glancing over at us once in a while.

"You don't have to explain anything to me, but I wish you could have told our grandmother's family why they had to die. Our grandfather Ali was a soldier like you. He wasn't an officer, he was a simple private but he showed more courage and honor than I would ever expect from you."

"This argument isn't going to lead anywhere. I just wanted to tell you to be careful. If I hadn't protected you, you'd be in a much worse situation than you are. But there could come a point when I won't be able to help you."

On our way home my mother said, "It was nice to see you and your brother having such a nice chat."

"We've missed each other, it was good to see him again."

"Hopefully we'll be celebrating his promotion to general soon."

"That would be nice."

My phone rang. It was the delivery service telling me that my package had arrived. Their office was only five minutes away, and we wound our way there through Bodrum's narrow streets between high, whitewashed garden walls.

I tore open the package as soon as I was back in the car. It was a book.

MIMESIS:

THE REPRESENTATION OF REALITY
IN WESTERN LITERATURE

The title page was inscribed,

With love from Max

At that moment I realized how very much I missed him.

CHAPTER 22

That evening my parents took me to a fish restaurant in Gümüşlük. My brother was going to an official dinner with his wife. My mother was disappointed that the whole family couldn't be together for one more meal, but I was relieved. It was clear to me now that my brother and I would never see eye to eye.

The sun was just beginning to set when we arrived in Gümüşluk, and the restaurants on the waterfront were opening for the evening. They'd arranged rows of sea bass, red sea bream, and sole on the counters in front and placed heaters among the tables to ward off the chill that would come off the water once it got dark.

The sunset on this bay was particularly beautiful, and I felt the urge to get into one of the boats moored to the quay and sail out to sea. The nearest island was Kos, and after that was Kalimnos, then Leros and Patmos, where John wrote the Book of Revelations.

We'd traveled to all these islands one summer, eating sea urchins at Takis's restaurant on Milos, swimming on the beautiful beaches of Leros and visiting the cave on Patmos where John is said to have received his revelation. Yet even these beautiful islands had their share of ugly history, particularly during World War II, and the Greek Civil War, when intellectuals such as the poet Ritsos and the composer Theodorakis were imprisoned and tortured there.

Perhaps Arthur Koestler was right to say that man ceased to evolve. No mother gives birth to a child with the thought that it will be killed in wartime. We all hope to grow old and die a natural death, but hundreds of millions die unnatural deaths at the hands of other people. Not long ago 50 million were killed in what has been considered the most civilized continent, in the lands of Goethe, Schiller, Beethoven, Dante, and Cervantes.

"Where has your mind wandered off to?" asked my mother. "Or are you worried about Kerem?"

"Yes, I wonder what he's doing. I should call him."

I got up, moved a few steps away from the table, called Ahmet, and asked for Kerem. It took him a little while to come to the phone.

"I'm with your grandparents in Bodrum. You'll be here in three months, we can go out in a boat together. I've missed you so much. Is your father taking good care of you? How are you doing in school?"

He mumbled brief replies to each of my annoying questions, but just as we were about to hang up, he said, "The kids at school are talking about you."

I felt a jolt like an electric shock.

"What are they saying?"

"They ask me if my parents are getting divorced."

"Well, what do you say?"

"I say my parents are already divorced. Then they ask me if you're sleeping with a man who's old enough to be your grandfather."

"And?"

"I say of course you aren't, the man's a spy and you're keeping track of him."

"Good for you."

He sounded in such good spirits that I felt suddenly relaxed and happy. I could stay here for a while and begin my translation of *Mimesis*. I returned to the table just as the fish was arriving. It was so delicious that for a time we didn't speak.

Then, when we'd finished, I said, "There's something I have to tell you. I've been fired from my job at the university."

They were dumbfounded.

"It was because of the slander they printed in the newspaper."

My father said, "Don't worry, I know you can find another job."

My mother said, "Take your time. Relax here for a while and regroup. Kerem seems to be doing fine with his father."

"Yes, in fact I was thinking of staying on here for a while. I'm going to translate a book."

"Wonderful," said my father. "Something more meaningful. Come on, let's drink to it."

We raised our ice-cold rakı glasses in a toast to the translation of *Mimesis*.

I felt lucky to have such supportive parents. When I'd told them I was leaving Ahmet they'd supported my decision without question.

I knew they were very curious about this Professor Maximilian Wagner who'd stirred up so much trouble, but of course they were too discreet to ask. So I told them Max's story in detail, about his love for Nadia, their marriage, how they'd been torn from each other, and what had happened to the *Struma*. Then I told them that the professor was dying of pancreatic cancer and had returned to Istanbul to bid farewell to her in the place she'd died.

The next day I began the translation of *Mimesis*.

I'm nearing the end of my story. All I have left is some copying and pasting and a few minor corrections. I want to finish before they ask me to turn off my laptop when we begin our descent.

There's a lot of activity in the cabin. People have had a good night's sleep and a good breakfast and are moving around. The map on the screen shows that we've crossed the ocean and are flying over North America.

I have to fill out an immigration form. The same information I wrote on the forms at the U.S. consulate in Istanbul when I was applying for my visa.

The pilot has informed us of the weather conditions in Boston and that the local time is 2:00 p.m.

I was only able to work on the translation for two days before I had to rush back to Istanbul. Here's what happened:

I was sitting on the balcony in Bodrum working on my translation. The book was open in front of me, I was using a beautiful speckled green stone I'd found on the beach as a paperweight, and I was writing the translation directly onto my laptop.

Later I took a break and looked up some articles on Bodrum. Alexander the Great had captured the city and appointed one of its previous monarchs, Queen Ada, to rule in his name. Bodrum was also famous for King Mausolos's tomb, one of the Seven Wonders of the Ancient World and the source of the word *mausoleum*. In the city's famous castle was an underwater archaeology museum. When I took my morning walk, I walked on the same ground Herodotus had walked on.

I was planning to visit the museum the following day. I'd read that the oldest recovered shipwreck and most of its cargo were on display there. It was a 50-foot Lycian boat of cedar wood that had sunk 3,300 years ago, and was later named the "Uluburun shipwreck" after the location from which it had been recovered.

It had sunk in the fourteenth century BC and sat at the bottom of the sea until 1999. The ship had been carrying cobalt blue, turquoise, and lavender class ingots; the ebony logs so valued by the Ancient Egyptians; elephant tusks and carved ivory; hippopotamus teeth; a kind of tortoise shell thought to be used in the making of musical instruments; pottery; metals; and a large number of ostrich eggs. It had also been carrying ceramic oil lamps from Cyprus; Canaanite jewelry; silver bracelets and anklets; a gold goblet; agate, gold, ceramic, and glass beads; two cosmetic boxes shaped like ducks whose hinged wings served as lids; and a trumpet made of hippopotamus tooth.

The next morning I walked out to the castle along a causeway paved with stones that had been worn down over thousands of years. The lighting in the museum created a murky, underwater atmosphere. A young, dark-haired man was guiding a group of tourists through the museum, and I tagged along after them.

Then, as I was looking at the Uluburun shipwreck, I wondered what state the wreck of the *Struma* was in. If this ship had survived 3,300 years, that one must still be fairly intact after fifty-nine years, though of course a torpedo hadn't sunk the Uluburun ship. But I wondered if I might be able to start a campaign to recover the *Struma*. Perhaps this could be one of my new goals.

When the tour was over and we emerged from the museum, I asked the guide if he'd ever heard of the *Struma*.

"Certainly," he said. "The *Struma* is quite well known."

"If this ancient ship was recovered, couldn't that ship be recovered too?"

"Certainly!"

"Well, why haven't they made at least an exploratory dive?"

"They have, didn't you hear about it? It was in the newspapers. Some friends of mine from the AUE found it last year."

"I didn't hear about it. What is the AUE?"

"The Association of Underwater Exploration."

"Could you give me their number?"

"Of course," he said. "Why not?"

As I left the museum with phone number of Levent, the leader of the *Struma* dive, my heart was beating fast. I was one step closer to the story.

As soon as I returned to my parents' home, I called Levent. He wanted to know who I was, and this time I didn't pretend I was still with the university. I told him

I was researching on my own. I asked him for as much information as he could give me about the dives and the state of the ship, and told him that I was particularly interested in any pictures or video footage of the wreck. He agreed to meet me in Istanbul in a couple of days.

CHAPTER 23

The plane stayed in a holding pattern over Istanbul for over half an hour, and as I looked down at the city it seemed like a monstrous stain, shrouded in smog, spreading for miles in every direction. I regretted leaving the tranquility and clear air of Bodrum, and wouldn't have done so if I hadn't felt it to be urgent. For my parents, my sudden decision to leave had been an unpleasant surprise, but they didn't question it, and besides, I would be back myself in a few days, and Kerem would join us in a few months.

It took me longer to get home through the traffic from the airport than it did to fly from Bodrum to Istanbul, and as I unlocked the door and walked into my apartment I felt suddenly as if I'd never left, as if I'd never been to Bad Arolsen or ITS, and as if Bodrum had been just a dream. Dostoyevsky once said that returning to St. Petersburg from Europe was like putting on old slippers, and I felt the same way.

I watered the plants, all of which had survived, unpacked my bag, and then called Ahmet and asked him to drop Kerem off so he could spend the night, and when he came he was so thrilled to be home that he helped me in the kitchen instead of going straight to his computer. As we had dinner together, he talked about every detail of his life, and I was happy to see him so cheerful.

Among the things he told me was that Ahmet's girlfriend, Lale, visited often, and that they were talking about marrying. It didn't bother me to hear this. I felt no jealousy whatsoever and indeed felt pleased, though I did pity Lale because she didn't know what she was getting herself into.

The next morning I woke Kerem, made him breakfast, and sent him off to school just as I used to, and what had not so long ago seemed just a part of my daily drudgery now seemed like a pleasure.

Then I went to my meeting with Levent and three of his colleagues from the AUE. They were curious about why I was interested, so I told them briefly about Max and Nadia. Then I asked how they were able to get permission to make the dive. They looked at each other and laughed, and then told me it had taken years of writing proposals and fighting bureaucracy.

The next problem was to locate the wreck. Their first clue was from fishermen whose nets were getting caught on what they referred to as the "Jewish Ship." They spent three years making sonar soundings and later made three dives to wrecks that displayed similarities to the *Struma*. Their job was complicated by poor visibility, strong currents, and often extremely low temperatures. They were able to eliminate two of the wrecks and concentrated on one that was the same length and width as the Struma.

"There are people who claim that the wreck we found was not the *Struma*, but I'm absolutely sure it is. Unfortunately the hands-off approach we committed to out of respect made bringing up any positive proof impossible. My certainty was based not just on what I saw, the unmistakable resemblance, but also on what I felt. I've seen other shipwrecks, but I've never felt what I felt there, the sense that I was seeing a mass grave."

I asked whether they could give me a copy of the video footage of the dive, and they were able to give me a DVD.

The next day I left Kerem with his father and returned to Bodrum.

I spent the next two months working on the translation, exploring my memories, and enjoying the opportunity to spend time with my parents. I slept a lot, took walks along the shore, and gained almost five pounds eating my mother's food.

Then, one day, when I was checking my email, I saw a message from someone I didn't know, someone named Nancy Anderson. She'd been Professor Maximilian Wagner's assistant, and was writing to inform me that his illness had progressed more rapidly than expected and that he was now in the hospital in critical condition.

For a time I just sat there, stunned, with no idea of what to do or how to respond. Then the obvious struck me. I had to go see Max. I wrote back to Nancy, thanking her for informing me and saying I would come to see the professor as soon as possible.

Then I called Tarık. I was now unemployed, which would make it difficult for me to get a U.S visa. He told me it would be no problem. He would list me as an employee of his firm.

"I'll need some more money too. Dollars this time."

"That's fine. You can withdraw as much as you want from the bank anytime. Now, have I earned at least a dinner with you?"

I laughed. "Yes you have, as soon as I get back from America."

We've been informed again that we have to turn off all electronic devices, bring our seats to an upright position, and close and lock our tray tables. As she passes, Renata tells me nicely that I really have to turn off my laptop. I smile and say I need just one more minute.

"You really have to turn it off."

"Just one more sentence."

And I keep typing as fast as I can.

Soon I'll get off the plane, pick up my suitcase, get into a taxi, and go straight to Mass General Hospital.

With the score of *Serenade* and the DVD of the sunken ship.

How will Max respond when he sees me? When he sees the sheet music, and the DVD, the images of the *Struma* lying underwater?

"Log off!"

I've made some typographical errors...but the flight attendant won't leave//* me alon...

EPILOGUE

Below me is a large black-pepper tree that, with its red berries and feathery leaves, gives off a bittersweet fragrance when the wind blows through it. And everywhere there's bougainvillea, spilling in cascades over balconies and down walls in a riot of bright colors. The afternoon sun shimmers on the sea, and there's a hint of pine and thyme in the breeze that drifts down from the mountains. From inside comes the sound of a novice on a violin, a scraping, screeching sound that's almost a torture to hear.

I'm very happy.

When does a girl stop growing up? At puberty? At eighteen? When she marries? When she gets her first white hair? Or does she never feel she's grown up no matter how old she gets? Is she still filled with girlish dreams when she takes her last breath?

But she goes through changes. Life constantly changes her, and the principal agent of these changes is always a man. Even Ahmet helped me to become mature, and though Tarık had less impact he helped, too, but I owe the deepest changes in me to an elderly man. A man I knew only briefly, with whom I shared neither passion nor sex, or even a common culture or language.

A new Maya has emerged, a Maya who's learning to come to peace with herself and to be more compassionate and considerate. I've begun to understand Ahmet and the nature of his problems, and also to see the ways my own faults contributed to the breakup of our marriage.

I can see now that my harsh attitude toward people was based on insecurity, and on trying to control people and situations rather than controlling myself. I can also see how controlling, manipulative, and overprotective I've been as a mother, and how I kept Kerem from being himself.

I light a cigarette and inhale with deep pleasure. And as I write this, I glance at my finished oeuvre.

MIMESIS:
THE REPRESENTATION OF REALITY
IN WESTERN LITERATURE

Translated by: Maya Duran

I dedicate this translation to my esteemed teacher Professor Dr. Maximilian Wagner who not only led me to this outstanding book, but also helped me to gain enough depth to distinguish between right and wrong, and to his dear wife, Nadia Deborah Wagner.

After months of work, I've finished both the translation and the story of how Max, Nadia, Mari, and Maya entered my life and changed it. I didn't set out with the desire to write a book or to be a writer. I simply felt I had to tell the story, to confess, to pour it out. I feel no need to edit or rewrite, to polish or perfect, or even to correct minor errors.

I've considered several titles, including "Max and Nadia," "The Tale of Three Women," "Private Lives," "The Graveyard by the Sea."

My themes are the same themes that writers have addressed since writing began and that storytellers in the Homeric tradition told of before then: love, hate, revenge, ambition, jealousy, destiny....

The same themes you see in Shakespeare and in soap operas. The only difference is in how the story is told. This is something I haven't concerned myself with. I just described what happened.

Some feel that the manner of telling is more important than what is told. A thousand years ago, in the introduction to his *Shahnameh,* Ferdowsi said that everything there was to say had already been said, and the only thing left was to say it in a more beautiful manner.

But I've told this story because I felt it needed to be told and not in an attempt to create something beautiful.

I'm thinking about quoting a verse from Paul Valéry's, "The Graveyard by the Sea" at the beginning of the book, but I haven't decided yet.

When I began this book, only two of the main characters in the story were still alive. Now Max is gone, and I'm the only one left.

After I went through immigration and picked up my bag, I got into a taxi and went straight to Massachusetts General Hospital. I didn't want to waste time checking into my hotel because I didn't know how bad Max's condition was.

I'd heard that American hospitals are very strict about visiting hours, but I had no problem getting in to see Max. I just gave his name at the information desk and they directed me to his room on the fourth floor.

Max was pale and seemed thinner, but he still looked like himself, and as soon as I saw him, I realized how much I'd missed him. When he saw me his eyes shone with joy, and despite how weak he was, he tried to sit up in bed. I went over and kissed him on the cheek.

"Nancy told me you were coming. I didn't want you to go to so much trouble, but I was happy to hear you'd come. I wanted very much to see you one last time."

"One last time?"

"Yes, one last time. There's nothing left to hide. I'm dying, my suffering is coming to an end. But you already knew that in Istanbul."

"No, you didn't tell me anything."

Max laughed.

"I'm not that naïve, Maya. Do you think I didn't notice the change in your attitude after I got out of the hospital?"

"Max, I know it means opening old wounds, but I brought you some things, some mementos."

"What sort of mementos?"

"From Nadia!"

He suddenly went pale and I felt a bit alarmed.

I sat at the foot of his bed, opened my bag, and took out the yellowed score of *Serenade für Nadia*.

He looked at it in disbelief, as if I'd performed a miracle. He began humming the melody, then stopped, and turned to me.

"How on earth did you find this?"

I told him about my talk with Matilda Arditi, about Scurla, the archives at Bad Arolsen, and the documents I'd found. I took the photos out of my bag and showed them to him.

A nurse came and told me that I should let the professor rest, and that I could come back tomorrow. Max immediately protested.

"No, please let her stay. It's very important to me. She's brought some things from my past that I have to see."

He said it with such conviction that the nurse allowed me to stay and left us alone. While he pored over the pictures, I went over to the window. It was dark out, and the room was reflected in the glass. I could see Max even though I had my back to him, though I don't know if he was aware of this. At one point he pressed Nadia's picture to his chest and muttered something in German. Later, when I turned to face him, he thanked me.

"I brought something else for you too."

"What is it?"

"This might be upsetting, but I felt you should see it, that somehow it would be like visiting Nadia's grave."

I turned on my laptop and loaded the DVD. Then the wreck of the *Struma* appeared on the screen. Max stared intently, barely breathing.

The divers' lights pierced the darkness of the Black Sea, illuminating the skeleton of the *Struma*, its hull covered with barnacles and seaweed swaying from the rusting iron. The camera moved in closer, following the deck and then moving through an open door to the interior. This was where Nadia had spent the last months of her life. She'd walked down this corridor. This was where she'd slept, where she'd eaten, where she'd written her letters.

It was like diving into a tomb, an underwater tomb. There was some wreckage scattered on the seabed, and when the divers went down to take a closer look, they raised a cloud of sand. Max and I watched in awed silence. Sixty years later, he was seeing the ship he'd watched so desperately from the shore, that he'd scanned with his binoculars day after day in the hope of seeing Nadia. It was on that deck that he'd caught his last glimpse of her.

When the DVD ended, we sat in silence for some time, not knowing what to do or say. Then I turned off my laptop, put it in its case, and placed it next to my suitcase. Max didn't even seem to know I was there. He just sat and stared at the wall. I waited for a time, then gathered my things quietly and tiptoed out of the room.

On the way to my hotel I suddenly felt bad, and began to wonder if I'd done the right thing. Had I come all this way just to reopen old wounds? Had I been tactless, had I caused him unnecessary pain, had I robbed him of the chance to die in peace?

As soon as I got to my room, I unpacked, took a hot bath, and then ordered clam chowder from room service. Then I went to bed but found I couldn't sleep. I was too uneasy, too restless. Too many things kept turning in my mind. I finally took a pill, and sank into a deep, dreamless sleep.

I called the hospital after breakfast to ask if Max wanted to see me. The duty nurse told me that Max was scheduled for chemotherapy and probably wouldn't be in a condition to see anyone. She took my number and said she would call tomorrow.

I had a whole empty, pointless day ahead of me, and I didn't know what to do with myself. In the end I took a taxi to Harvard Square and spent most of the day wandering around the university, unable to escape the feelings that kept gnawing at me. In the evening I ate alone at the hotel, then tried to distract myself by watching television, but couldn't find anything to focus on. I took a pill again and waited for that sweet numbness to start spreading through me.

The next morning the nurse, Barbara, phoned to say that Max was asking to see me. I rushed straight over, and as soon as I saw him I knew he wasn't upset with me. Indeed, he looked at me with great warmth and affection. He took my hands and told me how very much he appreciated that I'd gone to so much trouble, that I'd brought him a connection to his past that was profoundly meaningful to him.

"There's one more thing I'd like to ask of you. I've thought about this a lot, about whether I have the right to burden you with such a responsibility. If it's something you feel you can't take on, I'll understand completely."

I saw that he was struggling, that he couldn't bring himself to say what he wanted to say.

"You know that I'll do anything for you, Max. Please tell me. Don't hesitate."

When he told me, I was completely taken aback. I knew I couldn't say no, but it was going to be very difficult.

A doctor came in to examine him and I was asked to leave, so I went down to the cafeteria and had a latte and thought about what I was going to do.

They wouldn't let me see Max that afternoon. I asked Barbara how he was and she was noncommittal, but I could tell from her expression that it wasn't good. He didn't have much time left.

For the next two days, I wasn't allowed to see him, and when I called Barbara on the third day she told me that he had passed away during the night.

Even though I'd been expecting this since I arrived, it came as a blow. Somehow, I suppose, I'd been expecting a miracle, or at least to be able to spend a bit more time with him. It took some time for the reality of it to sink in. I spent the rest of the day lying on my bed, staring at the ceiling, remembering and trying to sort out my feelings.

The next day Nancy called and asked if we could meet. I invited her to my hotel, and she arrived in the evening after work with a large package.

Her voice had given me the impression she was quite young, and I was surprised to meet a woman in her fifties. We went to the bar and had a drink, talked about Max and about the funeral arrangements, and toasted his memory. Then she gave me the package.

"He wanted you to have this."

I took the package and started to open it, but she put her hand on my arm to stop me. But as soon as she'd gone I rushed up to my room and tore it open. It was Max's violin. The one he'd played by the seaside that morning in Şile.

Inside the case there was a letter addressed to Kerem. It wasn't sealed, so I read it.

Dear Kerem,

This violin was given to me by my father eighty years ago, and I would very much like you to have it. We met only briefly, but this was long enough for me to see that you are an intelligent young man with

*great depth. It pleases me to believe that you will
learn to play this instrument, and that it will bring as
much beauty into your life as it did to mine.*

The greatest spy, Max.

Kerem is now taking lessons from a Dutch woman, a retired music teacher who lives in Bodrum. He's very enthusiastic about it; he loves the violin and is determined to learn to play well. But unfortunately until then, his practice sessions are almost torture to have to listen to.

Before Max's funeral at the crematorium, there was a memorial service for him at the university. A number of colleagues spoke of his friendship, his character, and his work. Then I was invited to say a few words.

"I have nothing of substance to add to what Professor Maximilian's friends and colleagues have said. If you will excuse my broken English, I should like to talk briefly about his years in Istanbul. A few months ago he returned for the first time to the city where he'd lived from 1939 to 1941, and it was during this visit that I had the good fortune to become acquainted with him. Through him I also had the opportunity to learn about the work of other scholars who had escaped from Nazi Germany and worked at Istanbul University.

"In the talk he gave at our university and in our private conversations, Professor Wagner touched on a very important matter. With his *The Clash of Prejudices* he built upon the ideas presented in Professor Huntington's 'The Clash of Civilizations'? and Edward Said's 'The Clash of Ignorance.' During the Second World War he personally experienced the destruction, the disaster that arose from prejudice."

I paused for a moment. The room was completely silent.

"I would also like to mention another person whom, had Max been with us, he would have wished us to remember—his dear wife, Nadia Deborah Wagner. The love between these two remarkable people proved stronger than the hateful prejudices that tried to destroy it.

"May their memory light our path."

Later, about fifty of us gathered at the crematorium. There, a young woman stood and played Max's *Serenade* on the violin. I turned on my digital recorder, closed my eyes, and pictured Max playing before the crashing waves on that cold, stormy day. It was the first time I'd heard the piece all the way through, and it was truly a magnificent piece of music. I could understand why it had moved Nadia so deeply.

As I listened to the beautiful "Serenade for Nadia," I spoke silently to Max: "Now I know, Max," I said. "I know that the letter you sent to the rector changed Nadia's destiny. I know you've always condemned yourself. And that burning question never left you alone. In your mind, you always saw Nadia's begging face, urging you not to send that letter. I didn't dare to ask you about it then, but now I know. I understand. I'm sure Nadia has already forgiven you. Rest in peace."

Then each of us got up in turn and stood in silence by the coffin. When it was my turn I placed a bouquet of carnations on the coffin, bowed my head and whispered, "Farewell Max. I will carry out your last request."

When we had finished paying our respects the stone under the coffin moved and the mahogany coffin began to descend to the crematorium below. I left as Max descended toward the flames.

There was nothing left for me to do in Boston. My flight to Frankfurt wasn't until midnight, so I had plenty of time. I went to the hotel and packed, and in the evening Nancy and I had dinner together in the hotel restaurant. We talked about Max.

"There are so many things I'm grateful to you for, Nancy," I said, "but there's one thing in particular that I'll never forget."

A slight smile appeared on her lips and there was a look of bewilderment in her eyes as she gave a questioning glance.

"It was because of you that I first heard the serenade that Max wrote for Nadia," I said.

"Thank you," she said, "but I did nothing except give the score to a music student and ask that it be played at the ceremony. You were the one who found the music. Ah, Max. What an unexpected gift it was for him."

———

Later Nancy drove me to Logan Airport and came with me as far as the check-in counter. After I'd checked in my suitcase she gave me a package and some papers, shook my hand, and left. Then, with the package in one hand and the violin in the other, I went to customs.

I explained the situation and was taken into a back office where a customs officer asked me if the package was metal.

"No, it's mahogany."

"Can you open it?"

I took off the paper wrapping, opened the cardboard box, and took out the mahogany urn. The front of the urn was very tastefully decorated with the figures of two white doves.

"Whose ashes does it contain?"

"The ashes of Professor Maximilian Wagner from Harvard University."

"Where are you taking them?"

"To Istanbul. It was his last request."

"Are you a relative?"

"No."

"May I see your passport?"

"Certainly."

The officer perused it for a while and said, "I presume you're Muslim."

"Yes."

"In your religion isn't it a sin to cremate the dead?"

"Perhaps, I don't know, but it might be. There's no crematorium in Istanbul."

Clearly the circumstances seemed very odd to the officer; a Muslim woman carrying the ashes of a Roman Catholic professor with a German name to Istanbul. "Do you have the death certificate?"

"Yes, here it is."

I handed him the brown paper envelope Nancy had given me.

"OK, the international cremation certificate?"

"They're all in the envelope."

After he had looked at these he checked the violin.

"OK," he said. "Everything seems to be in order. I apologize if I've upset you with my questions."

"No," I said. "But why were you so curious?"

The officer said, "Because I'm a Muslim too." He followed it up with *"Alhamdulillah!* Thank God!"

I carefully packed the urn away and went to the waiting area.

I didn't turn on my laptop once during the journey; I didn't write anything. I held on to Max's ashes the whole time, except when I was eating. Somehow, holding that box seemed to be a way of holding on to him, of keeping him in the world of the living.

In the transit lounge in Frankfurt, it struck me as appropriate that Max, who hadn't been back to Germany since 1939, should pass briefly through his home country before arriving at his final resting place.

He hadn't wanted his ashes to be scattered in Germany, on his parents' grave, on the Rhine, or at their old house in Munich—whoever owned it now. His life had ended on the shore of the Black Sea, and that was where he wanted his remains to rest.

No one asked about the package at Turkish customs, and as soon as I got my suitcase, I took a taxi home. I put the mahogany urn and the violin in the middle of the table, took a bath and a pill, and went to sleep.

The next day I hired a driver to take me out to Şile. I directed him down the side road and asked him to stop when we reached the ridge. It was a beautiful day, and couldn't have been more different from the last time I was there. The sun was out and the sea was as smooth as glass.

I carried the urn to the beach without even glancing over at the Black Sea Motel. When I reached the edge of the sea I took out my digital recorder, pressed play, and put it on the sand. Max's *Serenade* began to play. Then I opened the lid of the urn, said a last farewell, and scattered the ashes onto the Black Sea. The ashes became darker the moment they touched the water, and I could see the gentle waves pulling them out away from the shore. Max was on his way to join Nadia. With the *Serenade* still playing behind me, I tossed the urn into the sea and watched it bob on the slow waves.

Then I lay on my back on the beach and watched the high, thin clouds drift past. I remembered Nadia's letter, in which she spoke of looking up to the sky for a sign, and seeing a flock of birds flying in formation. I, too, looked for a sign, but saw none.

The music ended and there was no sound but the gentle washing of the waves. I closed my eyes, and at just that moment the *Serenade* began to play again from the beginning.

I must have drifted off to sleep for a moment, because when I opened my eyes there was a man standing over me. I recognized him at once—the strange-looking boy from the Black Sea Motel.

"Well done!" he said to me.

"What have I done well?"

"You've fulfilled your duty."

"Which is?"

"You've laid the professor to rest. You've buried him beside Nadia."

"How do you know all this?"

"Actually I know much more than that, but I don't know how much of the truth you can handle."

"Who are you?" I asked.

"You wouldn't believe me if I told you."

"Tell me anyway."

"No, you won't believe me."

"Why?"

"Because your heart isn't ready for it yet."

"I will believe you, I promise I'll believe you. Tell me, who are you?"

He thought for a while, hesitated and then he asked, "But you won't laugh will you?"

"Promise," I said. "I won't laugh, I won't not believe you. Tell me, who are you?"

He looked around and then he leaned toward my ear.

"I'm Azrael, the Angel of Death," he whispered.

I felt like laughing.

"Look, didn't I tell you!" exclaimed the boy.

"What's the matter?"

"You laughed."

"I didn't."

"But you felt like laughing."

"How could you know that?"

"I told you, didn't I, I'm Azrael. I know everything, but I can give my secret only to those whose hearts are ready. I can see that your heart isn't. Otherwise I was going to tell you some more interesting things."

He turned and began walking toward the Black Sea Motel. I followed him. I was walking faster than he was, in fact I was running, but somehow I couldn't keep up with him. The distance between us was increasing.

Finally I gave up and dropped to my knees on the sand.

He stopped and came back to me.

"Do you know, you're a very odd woman," he said. "In fact you're the oddest woman in the world."

"Why?"

"Because no one asks Azrael not to go away.'"

"But you didn't come for me."

"You're right, I didn't, and your time isn't up yet. Why did you call me? What do you want?"

"Please, please tell me," I said. "Please tell me everything."

"Your heart isn't ready yet."

"It's ready now, tell me, and please tell me." I began to cry.

"You see, those tears of yours are more convincing than your words. Everyone feigns reluctance at first but believes in the end. Do they, in fact, have any other choice?"

"Tell me!"

"Very well. Max was supposed to die on February 24. He was supposed to die at the Black Sea Motel. That's why I was there."

I didn't know what to say. He looked deep into my eyes and the continued.

"You know Nadia also died 24 February. Max could no longer bear the loneliness of living without his wife. My job would have been very easy."

"Well then?"

"But you upset my plans. You brought him back to life. Just as he was about to die, his body remembered love and he didn't want to go."

"Are you telling me the story about the vizier who died in Samarkand? The one who had an appointment with Azrael?"

"No, I don't tell stories, the stories are all in your mind."

"Wait a minute. You're part of the story. That means you're in my mind too."

"Now you understand. Now your heart is ready to tell the story."

He laughed aloud as he walked away.

The digital recorder on the sand beside me began to play the *Serenade* from the beginning again.

I woke up in terror, got up, brushed the sand off me, and picked up the recorder.

I hoped the driver was still waiting for me, and that I wouldn't have to go to the Black Sea Motel and ask Azrael to call me a taxi.

I looked for the urn, but it must already have been carried out to sea.

"Farewell Max, farewell Nadia," I said.

That was when I decided to tell their story. Only those whose stories are told can exist.

ZÜLFÜ LIVANELI is Turkey's bestselling author, a celebrated composer and film director, and a political activist. Widely considered one of the most important Turkish cultural figures of our time, he is known for his novels that interweave diverse social and historical backgrounds, figures, and incidents, including the critically acclaimed *Bliss* (winner of the Barnes & Noble Discover Great New Writers Award), *Leyla's House*, *My Brother's Story*, and *The Eunuch of Constantinople*, which have been translated into thirty-seven languages, won numerous international literary prizes, and been turned into movies, stage plays, and operas.

BRENDAN FREELY was born in Princeton in 1959 and studied psychology at Yale University. His translations include *Two Girls* by Perihan Mağden, *The Gaze* by Elif Shafak, and *Like a Sword Wound* by Ahmet Altan.

▐ OTHER PRESS

You might also enjoy these titles from our list:

LABYRINTH by Burhan Sönmez

From a prize-winning Turkish novelist, a heady, political tale of one man's search for identity.

"Provocative... profound... [*Labyrinth*] reads like a fever dream." —*New York Times*

"Subtle... stirring... A thoughtful novel that asks many unanswerable questions worth pondering, *Labyrinth* is a mind-twister." —NPR

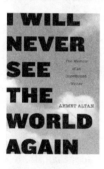

I WILL NEVER SEE THE WORLD AGAIN: THE MEMOIR OF AN IMPRISONED WRITER by Ahmet Altan

In this extraordinary memoir written from his prison cell, Altan reflects upon his sentence, and the hope and solace a writer's mind can provide, even in the darkest of places.

"Urgent... brilliant... a timeless testament to the art and power of writing amid Orwellian repression." —*Washington Post*

MADONNA IN A FUR COAT by Sabahattin Ali

First published in 1943, this unforgettable tale of love and alienation has been topping best-seller lists in Turkey since 2013.

"The surprise bestseller... Read, loved, and wept over by men and women of all ages."
—*The Guardian*

"A rare point of common cultural experience for a deeply polarized country." —*New York Times*

Additionally recommended:

THE GLASS ROOM by Simon Mawer

In 1920s Brno, modernist architect Rainer von Abt builds the Landauer family a home to embody their exuberant faith in the future. But as the years pass their honesty and idealism quickly evaporate beneath the storm clouds of World War II.

"A gorgeous novel." —*Washington Post*

"A stirring historical novel." —*The New Yorker*

NEVER ANYONE BUT YOU
by Rupert Thomson

NAMED A BEST BOOK OF THE YEAR BY *THE GUARDIAN, THE OBSERVER*, AND *SYDNEY MORNING HERALD*

A literary tour de force that traces the real-life love affair of two extraordinary women.

"There's so much sheer moxie, prismatic identity, pleasure, and danger in these lives … the scenes are tense, particular, and embodied … wonderfully peculiar." —*New York Times Book Review*

"Gorgeous and heartrending." —*The Observer*

AMONG THE LIVING by Jonathan Rabb

A moving novel about a Holocaust survivor's journey back to a new normal in 1940s Savannah, during the last gasp of the Jim Crow era.

"Jonathan Rabb is one of my favorite writers, a highly gifted heart-wise storyteller if ever there was one. What a powerful, moving book." —David McCullough, Pulitzer Prize and National Book Award–winning author